Friendship and teenage rebellion have never looked better than in JC Hopkins' vivid prose. I WAS A TEENAGE COMMUNIST is an endearing, funny and touching coming-of-age story set in 1980s Orange County. You want to root for the young revolutionaries, and see them fight for their lives and ideals. The novel brings you right back to the part of yourself that hungers for justice, the spirited and some may say naive part that exists in all of us.

Linh Luu - Vietnamese/American novelist

Within the sphere of an ending marriage and a high school revolution in Southern California, a brief and endearing narrative unfolds of relationships between teenagers stuck in the bardo of puberty. Through the lens of their mistakes, God, communism and love, not only do the high schoolers partake in a crash course of self-discovery but so do the people around them.

Laurie Oakley-Coleman - American author

In "I was a Teenage Communist" JC Hopkins gives us the most likable and diverse set of teen misfits since Bill met Ted, the Breakfast Club skipped lunch and the Brat Pack broke up.

Bibee Hansen- American author and poet

I Was A Teenage Communist

A Novel

JC Hopkins

EPONYMOUS
BOOKS

Copyright © 2024 by JC Hopkins

For public appearances contact:

www.eponymousbooks.com

ISBN NO: 979-8-990863217

Dedicated to my children Tigerlily, Thelonius, and Hart and to all the youth who dare to dream of a more egalitarian civilization.

For my wife – Linh

Karl Marx and Fredrich Engels
Came to the checkout at the 7-11
Marx was skint- but he had sense
Engels let him the necessary pence

"Magnificent Seven" - The Clash

We will root out the communists, Marxists, and the radical-left thugs that live like vermin within the confines of our country.

-Trump

I Was a Teenage Communist

x

Chapter One

Sunshine lived at the end of a cul-de-sac in one of the nice houses on Vista Del Sol: a four-bedroom, two-and-a-half-bath, two-car garage, brown stucco palace. A crew of gardeners came once a week to keep the hedges shorn tightly, the grass manicured and hewn to the edge of black granite pathways, and with long-reach pruning shears, the climbing roses with their spiny green tendrils covered in blood-red bulbs were cut to cling tightly to the arched cedar trellis that served as the proscenium to the home. The pool cleaners, dressed in baby blue coveralls with "Orange County Pool Maintenance Inc" written in white Helvetica lettering on the back, arrived bi-weekly to maintain the pH and chlorine levels, remove any debris from the pool, do preventive maintenance on pumps, filters, chlorinators, and clean and disinfect the pool deck area. The pool was rarely used. It had been years since the whole family had been there at the same time. All three of them.

Sunshine carried the key to the front door on a silver beaded necklace she had nicked from her mom's jewelry box. She leaned down, gripped the dangling key, stuck it in the lock, and let herself in. She dropped her backpack on the sofa and went directly to the kitchen. She turned on the little television that sat on the counter. A stentorian voice spoke over various images of masked terrorists, atomic bomb explosion, and other anxiety-inducing images, and then the DOW logo. "This program was made possible by a grant from the Dow Chemical Company," the voice reiterated. A gray-haired talking head came on.

"Good evening. I'm Frank Reynolds. The United States moved forward today with plans to support its friends in the Arab world, mainly Egypt and Sudan, and to caution its enemy, Colonel Quaddaffi of Libya…"

As Frank Reynolds continued, Sunshine reached into the liquor cabinet and gathered a bottle of gin and one of vermouth, placing them on the kitchen counter. From the shelf above the liquor cabinet, she pulled down a shiny stainless steel cocktail shaker and a jigger. She poured the exact amounts she had seen her father use into the jigger and then into the shaker: six parts gin to one part vermouth. She shook it vigorously. Taking a chilled martini glass from the refrigerator, she placed it on the counter. She removed the cap from the shaker, and poured the pellucid liquid into the glass. Opening a jar of olives from the counter, she plopped one into the glass, took a sip, smiled, and absently watched the news.

Walking away as the newscaster began to talk about the civil war in Nicaragua and Reagan's support of the Contras, Sunshine went through a sliding door onto the patio in the backyard and sat down on an aqua blue nylon-strung chaise lounge. She sipped her martini and looked out onto the dense, verdurous lawn. She thought about how in science class they studied photosynthesis, wavelengths, and cellular compounds called organelles, and how because chlorophyll, grass absorbs light at two wavelengths, red and blue, reflecting green. So, the grass appears green but is actually red and blue. And if the grass is kept in darkness, it will turn white and die. She thought that nothing was as it appears, including herself. She put on her Walkman headphones. The song "White Riot" by the Clash played. She sang along. "White riot, I want a riot, white riot, a riot of my own." She didn't really want a riot, and she wasn't exactly white, Japanese-Jewish, but she was definitely bored with the U.S.A. She looked at the tranquility of her private suburban sanctuary and thought, I don't hate this. In fact, I love it. And I love a martini every day after school and kind of love that my parents are never home. I also wonder what it would be like if they were. Home. But this way is good too. And then she began to cry. It wasn't so much succumbing to tears that emanated from her eyes as it was just relinquishing control for a few moments. Losing control while something cleared for her.

Chapter Two

When they found Davy crucified at the fifty-yard line, they weren't completely surprised; after all, he had sort of been asking for it. Nevertheless, it was a shocking sight all the same. The idea for the first cross came to him months earlier, the night before Halloween, though he wasn't thinking of it in terms of Halloween. He knew it would cause a stir, and yet he had the kind of fearlessness that came with youth. Using one of his father's Sears Craftsman chisels and a ball-peen hammer, he carved out an indent at the middle of a five-foot-long two-by-four. Once that was done to his satisfaction, he set another two-by-four in the indent, this one seven feet in length. A few nails hammered, and the cross was complete. He leaned it against the closed garage door and was impressed by the simple beauty of it. He went into the house and then into the bathroom to shower and get ready for school. After blow-drying his sandy blonde hair with his mother's Clairol Super Zap, he stood admiring himself in the space of the fogged-up mirror which he had cleared with the palm of his hand. It was a handsome and proud face he thought; thanks to the high cheekbones he inherited from his Native American grandmother. None of his friends had yet to achieve anything resembling facial hair, and already he had a decent peach fuzz goatee. Which is why he was given the nickname, 'Savior'.

In his pre-teen years, Davy was consumed by the confusions of shyness, self-consciousness, fear of being ridiculed for his ungainliness, and an intermittent stutter. Now there was a sense of pride in his posture and an ever-earnest forthrightness and righteousness that stood him somewhere between childhood and maturity. The stutter was gone. In his bedroom,

Davy picked up the latest record by an English group called The Clash from a pile of new wave and punk rock records scattered in front of the combination 8-track player, radio, and turntable; a record called Sandinista!

*The Sandinistas are a Nicaraguan revolutionary organization who after years of struggle overthrew the tyrannical regime of Anastasia Somoza. Trained by the U.S. military, Somoza's brutal National Guard used torture and political persecution to make the country ripe for United Fruit and other U.S. corporations to exploit. ** (from Revolutionary Press Issue 1)

Davy pulled out the second vinyl disc from the band's ambitious triple record album and put on his favorite track, a song called 'Washington's Bullets'. He cranked it up loud, singing along to Joe Strummer's raspy bag-of-nails Cockney-affected voice while he put on his white Adidas tracksuit and the leather sandals that his father brought back from a business trip to Tijuana.

The year was 1981, and the place was Orange County, California: suburbia, the sprawl, a residential block like any block in the megalopolis, this one called Moody Street. There stood the Jones' tract house, which Davy's father bought with help from the GI Bill after his service in the Korean War. It was just a simple one-story ranch house; small yard in front and decent-sized backyard, wall-to-wall shag carpeting, linoleum floors in the kitchen, which was outfitted with a dishwasher, a garbage disposal, and a double-doored refrigerator filled with processed meats, pasteurized milk, liters of soda, Miracle Whip, Cheez Whiz, cubes of margarine, assorted condiments, and more processed foods. In the freezer, cartons of ice cream, meat, and frozen vegetables.

The garage door of 2023 Moody Street opened, and emerging from the darkness was Davy 'Savior' Jones, resplendent in white, with a large wooden cross over his shoulder. Trudging down the sidewalk passing ghosts, vampires, witches, and monsters, Davy heard the rabble's voices, curses, and aghast sounds of shock and dismay. When he got to campus, which was only a few blocks from his house, it was getting crowded with students adorned in various costumes. He bumped into a girl dressed as a punk rocker. It was not a costume; she was an authentic punk rocker.

It was Sunshine. She was new to the school. She could have remained and begun high school in the private school she had been going to since middle school, but her parents were informed by the administration that they preferred that she went elsewhere. Sunshine concurred. Her parents were dismayed and reluctant to send her to a public school, yet Sunshine insisted. She was sick of the entitled brats at Flintridge Academy. And she hated the stupid uniforms. Her mother was a second-generation Japanese American civil rights lawyer turned real estate attorney. Her father was a former member of the SDS turned investment banker, who much to his parents' satisfaction and as a kind of consolation, joined his father's firm on the very day of Richard Nixon's resignation. Sunshine wore crimson lipstick, heavy black mascara, and dyed pink hair put in ponytails. She dressed in a Catholic schoolgirl's skirt, fishnet stockings, combat boots, and a leather jacket covered in safety pins; the placard on the back, made of white cloth, had the words Anarchy in the U.K. written with a black marker. "Excuse me," Davy said to Sunshine after bumping into her. "Fuck off, Jesus," Sunshine said brusquely. Davy trudged on.

A few jocks from the football team were waiting for Davy by his locker. Each wearing a gray 'Cypress Centurions' hoodie. "What the hell is this?" One of the jocks shouted, truly indignant at the sight of his sweet savior's cross being desecrated. He had recently been born again. Davy leaned the cross on the bank of lockers, opened his, pulled out his Geometry and History of Western Europe textbooks, and closed the locker. A jock, this one named Duane; tall, thick, golden, with pallid gray eyes and dusty brown hair moved in close to Davy and said, "I am not sure what you are trying to prove, but it offends me. It really offends me. I want to hurt you. Understand?" Davy looked him in the eyes and tilted his head ever so slightly. He turned, put his cross over his shoulder, and walked away from the jocks. "Just where the hell are you going?" another jock shouted. "To class, my children, just to class." They followed him, but then the period bell sounded, and they dispersed.

Chapter Three

Terrific bouts of anxiety plagued Geraldo, which he kept hidden from the world. They had been happening since he was ten years old. He knew of only one way to ameliorate them: to think about the black hole of death. Somehow, the idea of an endless void comforted him. He sat at the back of the class, barely listening to his A.P. History teacher, Mr. Calder, a lanky man with curly prematurely graying hair and an ingratiating affectation not unlike Alan Alda's "Hawkeye" character from the television show M.A.S.H. Rumors swirled that during the summer trips to Europe, which Mr. Calder organized for his senior class, he had inappropriate relations with his favored female students.

The kids in the class seemed vacant to Geraldo. He envied his older brother Charles and his classmates. Charles' friends were smart, even brilliant; all had graduated at the top of their classes and had gone on to prestigious universities in the East. Charles opted to stay closer to home, attending UC San Diego. It was the three years that separated the brothers that made the difference. Charles was the class of '79, the end of the seventies, a decade that still carried over a sense of radicalism and anti-establishment fervor from the sixties. The seventies had great music and great bands too: Bowie, Queen, Led Zeppelin, and in '77 punk rock and new wave took the stage. For Geraldo, the class of '82, the empty music of his zeitgeist symbolized his idea of vacant youth. Bands like Styx, Supertramp, and Journey made him sick. Literally sick to his stomach. Edgy genius guitars had been replaced by the carnival sounds of synthesizers. He felt he had been born too late, missing the great years. He felt he had been born in the wrong place—why fucking Orange County,

California, and not New York City or San Francisco or any cool city? Yet, he was a good boy, got decent grades, and never got into trouble.

Mr. Calder was on the subject of imperialism. Soviet imperialism, to be exact. "After the end of World War Two, the Soviet Union occupied Eastern Europe, installing puppet governments in Poland, Czechoslovakia, Romania, Hungary, and East Germany." Geraldo raised his hand. "Yes, Geraldo. You have a question?"

"What about U.S. imperialism?"

"I don't think you can actually compare the two."

"You can't? Why can't you?"

"Because the Soviets were the aggressors. And their occupation of the Eastern Bloc was much more repressive than any U.S. involvement in other countries' domestic affairs."

"I don't see how you can say that. What about Haiti and Baby Doc, or Duarte in El Salvador, or Allende in Chile, or Somoza in Nicaragua, all installed by the U.S. and all brutal fascists."

"I don't think any possible involvement of the U.S. in these smaller countries compares to the ethnic cleansing the Soviets perpetuated in East Europe."

"What about Vietnam? Ethnic cleansing by way of napalm and Agent Orange. Or Laos. Or Cambodia. Because of Nixon's illegal bombing of Cambodia, he enabled Pol Pot to come to power and commit the greatest genocide since the Holocaust."

"Yes, but Geraldo…" The period bell rang, much to Mr. Calder's relief. "That's all for today's class. Remember to read the chapter on the Marshall Plan and write a one-page summary. Due Monday. Have a fun Halloween and be safe."

As he was walking out of class, somebody shoved him and his books fell from his hands. He heard a garish chuckle and saw the bulging back of a gray hoodie. He knelt to retrieve his books; another leaned down to help. They stood in tandem; the boy handed Geraldo one of his fallen books. A beat-up paperback of Catcher in the Rye. "Thanks," he said, taking the book from the boy. The boy wore an overcoat like Geraldo's. He had seen him in class and differentiated him from the others. This kid did not seem vacant. In fact, he had a thoughtful face. Yes, there was something different about this boy. Geraldo had thought so before but now, up close, it was quite apparent. He had intelligent eyes and, it appeared, just a little eyeliner around them. They talked as they walked to the next period's class.

"I liked what you said in class. I was thinking the same thing, only I'm a little shy when it comes to that kind of thing. Mr. Calder is a pretentious ass."

He wasn't sure if he had heard the word "pretentious" before, and not from a classmate. Geraldo said, "Well, just the facts, you know."

Tommy laughed in a burst. "They want to brainwash us. That's pretty much what school is for. That and television. The twin engines of ignorance."

"True. So true."

"What are you doing after school? Want to come over to my house? My brother Barry and I live with our mom in those condos next to the Safeway. Apartment 123. That's easy, right? My father is dead. Killed in Laos. He was in the C.I.A. It's a long story. He knew things."

"Oh. I don't think I can. I have band practice."

"You're in a band? That's cool."

"Not really a band."

"Either way. My brother was a big fan of your brother. He was a sophomore when your brother was a senior."

"Oh."

"He told me all about him. About his running for class president and winning but the school not letting him become president because he said he was a commie. And how he took the only black girl in the school to the prom. So cool."

"Yeah. He has always been a little crazy."

"I don't think that's crazy. My father is black. Was black. I guess he still is. What's left of him. Are you a commie too?"

"Me? No. I don't think so. I don't know enough about it."

"Well, it seems you know a lot. More than most."

Chapter Four

The essay for English Literature was titled "The Hell That is School." Apparently, Mrs. Blum did not approve. She had Sunshine come to the front of the class to explain to her how she ever thought it was appropriate to use such foul language in her class. Sunshine tried to explain that the title and the essay were a direct allusion to Dante's Inferno. How school, like Dante's Hell, was a place where students and teachers had rejected the ideas of humanism to yield to the glorification of violence (the obsession with the football team) and greed (the stupid economics class), therefore perverting their intellect to unmitigated fraud and malice towards their fellow human. Mrs. Blum said, "Well, I didn't understand a word of it."

"That's because you are a simpleton," Sunshine said quietly.

"What did you say?!"

"I said that you are a sim-ple-ton. Do you understand that?"

Chapter Five

Davy left geometry class, picked up his cross, put it over his shoulder, and headed towards the plaza for lunch. The cross had caused a stinging sensation on the back of his right shoulder. Davy liked it. He liked the feel of it, the burning discomfort. Stopping at a water fountain, he leaned the cross against the wall and bent over to take a sip. He could hear and sense being surrounded by a negative force. Standing, he wiped his mouth with the back of his hand and turned around. He was enclosed by jocks. One of the jocks touched his cross like one of the primates touching the monolith in "2001: A Space Odyssey." Duane slapped Davy hard across the face. Davy held back the tears. He felt his face encased in anger. The anger subsided. He remembered who he was today. He turned his head so that his other cheek faced Duane. He pointed to it. The jock became self-aware. Does that kid really want me to slap him again? he thought.

The rest of the jocks took Davy's cross as if it were an opposing player and threw it to the ground. It succinctly broke in two. They looked at Davy, their faces contorted in anger. Davy looked back at them, curious, somewhat shocked by their violence. Then his expression turned to a slight smile. The jocks walked away grumbling. Sunshine had been standing not too far off and witnessing the whole altercation was begrudgingly filled with a tremendous amount of respect for Davy. She walked by him and muttered, "Stupid idiot." Davy thought. Me or them?

Geraldo approached Davy. Looked down at the cross on the ground, "Broke your cross."

"Yeah."

"What can you do?"

"Nothing."

"Lucky, they didn't break you."

"They wanted to. I've never seen anyone want something as much as those animals wanted to hurt me."

"Yeah. Not surprising. Do you want to jam after school?"

"I don't know. I'm just not into it."

"Not into playing music?"

"I'm not into the Beatles and that's all you want to play."

"I like the Beatles."

"No. You love the Beatles. You worship the Beatles. But guess what. It's not the sixties anymore. It's 1981. John Lennon is dead. Murdered, probably by the C.I.A."

"I know," Geraldo said, filled with immeasurable sadness.

"And Ronald Reagan is president, and we might die any minute from Nuclear War. Have you ever seen pictures from Hiroshima, Nagasaki? Not a pretty sight."

Davy reached into the pocket of his sweats jacket and pulled out a cassette tape. He handed it to Geraldo. "Here, listen to this." Geraldo took it, looked down at the cassette, and saw the names of the bands Davy had scrawled on the cover of the cassette jacket: X-Ray Spex, The Sex Pistols, The Buzzcocks, Elvis Costello, The Clash, Generation X. Davy reached out and touched the overcoat that Geraldo was wearing.

"What are you, Columbo?" Geraldo looked down at his coat, then back up at Davy, and shook his head.

Chapter Six

The trees were turning autumnal, as much as they can in Southern California. It was the last day of school before Thanksgiving break. Geraldo had his headphones on, connected to a plastic yellow Walkman in the pocket of his overcoat, listening to the cassette Davy had given him as he walked to school. He cut through the back parking lot of the mini mall. He stopped by the trash bin in the back of the Cypress Cinema. He looked inside and pulled out a piece of 35-millimeter film. He held it up so that the sun illuminated the images in the frames. It looked to be from the movie "History of the World Part One," the French Revolution segment, and images of Harvey Korman as Count De Money. Geraldo had seen the movie the preceding weekend, with his mom. They were going to movies together, just the two of them now that his brother Charles was in college and his father often busy on weekends doing things for the Kiwanis Organization. He liked the movie though he didn't find it as funny as the other Mel Brooks' movie he had seen, "Blazing Saddles." He put the piece of celluloid in his pocket.

Geraldo's mother, Carmen, had the kind of beauty that was natural and simple in that it required no participation on her part. She had beige skin that glowed like the sands of the deserts of Sonora Mexico where her people were from. Her dark brown hair, full lips, ruddy cheeks, and open demeanor were very appealing. Her Papa said that she was the spitting image of her mother who had died of tuberculosis when she was very young. She had grown up hearing compliments in regards to her beauty, it imbued her with a permanent sense of calm even though inside she was often shuddering, not just from the profound questions of life, yes those, but also the importance of staying relevant, relevant to the times, relevant in her own mind as far as being part of the fabric of society; and lately as a mother and as a wife. One son was out of the nest, the other mostly nonverbal, clouded in the insular bubble of teendom and exploding hormones. They had always been close, but now Geraldo was often preoccupied, and when she tried to converse with him, he had a great deal of difficulty articulating even the most basic events from his day. Most inquiries were met with a one or two-syllable utterance. As far as her marriage was concerned, a sense of fatalism was impossible to shake.

"Pump It Up" by Elvis Costello and the Attractions was pumping through his headphones as he got to the school. Geraldo was surprised at how much he liked the music on the tape that Davy had given him. Such passion and fervor in the songs and he could hear the Beatles' influence in the beats and the harmonies. The music somehow captured the anxiety and frustration that was constantly percolating through his veins. Made him want to smash things. He was so lost in the music that when he got to the school, he barely registered the fire trucks lined up in front as plumes of blue-gray smoke billowed from the science building. The sound of fire alarms from the school and sirens from the fire trucks blared loudly, cutting through the din of the music coming through the orange Styrofoam that pillowed the little dynamic speakers of the headphones. He removed them and watched the firefighters jump from the hook and ladders and drag bulging yellow hoses into the school. Geraldo put his headphones back on and went through the commotion to his locker. He sang along, "Pump it up!"

Chapter Seven

He hated algebra more than anything except disco, Ronald Reagan, and the Los Angeles Dodgers. His team was the luckless Angels, and it peeved him that so many of the kids from the neighborhood were fans of the Dodgers, even though the team in closer proximity to where they lived was the Angels. But the Angels sucked, and the Dodgers were always at the top of their division. He wasn't really paying much attention to baseball these days. The teacher, Mr. Rosenbaum, a stout and pockmarked fellow who smelled of liniment oil, rattled on with formulas and scrawled illegibly on the chalkboard. Geraldo wanted to wear his headphones and listen to the new-wave music. He wondered if he could get away with it. He was in the back of the class; Rosenbaum wouldn't notice. He wouldn't fail him no matter what, as long as he did his homework. Even if he got it wrong. The worst would be that Rosenbaum gave him a D minus. Again.

Very slowly and slyly, he opened his backpack and pulled out the headphones and Walkman. He set them in his lap. He lowered his head, slipped on the headphones, and then pressed the large black button on the top of the Walkman. The Pretenders, a song called "Precious," played. The beat was driving, the guitars slashed, and the singer Chrissie Hynde, her voice was not harsh or strained like some of the other singers on the tape; it was almost like she was crooning, though she sang things like "shitting bricks" or "do it on the pavement," things he had never heard a girl say. He couldn't help it; his head started bobbing up and down. And when she sang, "I'm too precious. Fuck off!" He exclaimed, "Yeah!" Someone tapped him hard on the shoulder. He looked up to see Mr. Rosenbaum's large dragon nostrils fluctuating angrily against the fluorescent lights.

Chapter Eight

The American flag hung sadly from a short metal pole. It was tattered and mangled, making Geraldo very uncomfortable, even more uncomfortable than he already was with Vice Principal Mr. Magg staring him down. Mr. Magg was a squat yet muscular man with a head shaped like an iron, a face like a punch-drunk boxer, and a voice like a cement mixer. "So, tell me, Geraldo. Do you carry a card?"

What would carrying a card have to do with listening to his Walkman in class? "A card?"

"Yes, Geraldo."

"I have a library card. I don't carry it though."

"Don't be smart. You know damn well what I mean. Are you a card-carrying communist?"

Geraldo raised his eyebrows and shook his head.

"Yeah right. Just like your brother. That kid was the worst. A real pinko. You punks have no respect. Let me ask you another question. Why did you try to burn down the school?"

At first, this accusation took Geraldo wholly by surprise. On second thought, it made sense. Somebody set fire to the school and who would be one of the prime suspects other than the younger sibling of a well-known rabble-rouser. "You've got the wrong guy, copper."

"What! You little smartass. If you did it, I will nail you."

Mr. Magg sipped coffee from a mug with a campaign picture of Nixon, Agnew - 1972. He grimaced exaggeratedly and put the mug back down on his desk. He looked long and hard at Geraldo.

"You see that flag? That flag came from a little place called Lamb Chop Hill. People think Vietnam was wrong. But what was wrong was a lack of commitment. A lack of good old-fashioned American balls. Listen, you little pinko punk. Listen about balls. The platoon, my platoon, was getting hit hard, but we'd been hit harder. The goddamn commanding officer blamed inadequate air coverage. And maybe he was right. We were ordered to retreat. But my best pal, Private George Crater, told me he would not leave without the flag we had planted when we took the hill. Well, let me tell you, you ungrateful little prince know-it-all; I pried that goddamn flag from his cold dead hands. He was a hero, and that flag symbolizes what this country stands for. Liberty, freedom, and sacrifice. Words that you know little of."

Geraldo walked out of Mr. Magg's office and saw Sunshine and another kid sitting on the chairs in front of the reception desk. The other kid wore a trench coat and a blue cap with a small red star above the brim. He was smiling. He was smiling at Geraldo. Sunshine was not smiling. In fact, she looked downright pissed off. Mr. Magg shouted, "Alright Barry, get your ass in here!" Barry stood up and said, "It's a good day to die," and followed Mr. Magg into his office. Geraldo watched them go in and then looked at Sunshine. He smiled awkwardly. Sunshine smiled back, batted eyelashes. She lifted her left hand and touched her forefinger to her lips while she placed her right hand on her inner thigh. "Hmm. You don't look like an arsonist."

"I don't?"

She shook her head.

"Then, what do I look like?"

"You look like a nice boy. Except for that coat you're wearing. Are you a nice boy?"

"Um. I guess so."

"Do you like boys or girls?"

"What do you mean?"

"I mean to kiss."

"Girls," Geraldo said shyly.

"Would you like to kiss me?"

"I don't know. I guess so."

"Just goes to show."

"Just goes to show what?"

"You just never know. You run along now, nice boy. I don't want to corrupt you here in the vice principal's waiting room."

Chapter Nine

That was strange, Geraldo thought while taking a leak in the boy's bathroom. That girl was like an actress, like a kid from a John Hughes movie. It was like someone had scripted her lines. Geraldo said he wanted to kiss her but wasn't sure. She scared him in a good way. He finished, zipped, and went to the sink to wash his hands, then looked at himself in the mirror. I am a nice boy, he thought. Look at that face. Such innocence. I still look like Opie. I am innocent, I guess. There was that thing that happened with Joey Goodman a few years ago. Playing in my room. He lay on my bed, pulled down his pants, and asked me to give him a blow job. Since he was older than me, I went to do what he said. His penis was small, wrinkly, and folded, and there was a short crown of black curly hair above his dick. I leaned over it and blew on it. Joey laughed. We heard my brother coming, and he pulled up his pants. That was weird.

It was quiet in the bathroom. Usually, there were lots of kids and a lot of noise. Now, during class time, empty, it was peaceful there. Geraldo liked the coolness of the white tile and the smell of bleach. He looked at the mirror, and it gave him back a boy, serious, big hazel eyes, radiant, trembling, waiting for something, waiting for something to happen. He hardly dares breathe for fear of breaking the moment, the peace of the moment. It was almost unbearable. He closed his eyes. Stopped his breath. He held it until he couldn't any longer. He exhaled and then opened his eyes. Duane was standing close behind him.

Duane was smiling like Jack Nicholson was smiling on the little piece of celluloid that Geraldo had found in the bin behind the movie theater. Geraldo hadn't seen The Shining; his mom wouldn't let him, but he knew about it from his brother Charles, who had seen it a few times. Charles would mimic the Nicholson character, "Here's Johnny!" Duane didn't say that, but he laid his hand heavily on Geraldo's shoulder. "You know, you're a fucking freak. You and your sicko friends and your stupid trench coats."

"Please take your hand off of my shoulder."

"Were you going to do something about it?"

"Please."

"So polite." Duane spun Geraldo around and pushed him up against the sink. He pulled his arm back to slap Geraldo, but somebody caught his arm. It was Barry Griswold. Duane broke loose from Barry's grip and punched him in the stomach. Barry doubled over. He started to laugh. A crazy, stifled laugh, like Elisha Cook Jr. in The Big Sleep after he got poisoned. "Fucking freak," Duane said.

Barry straightened up and got close to Duane. They locked eye to eye; androgens were pumping like teen Incredible Hulks. Barry took deep breaths from his diaphragm and then exhaled through his nose, puffing himself up. He started making growling sounds like Cujo.

Duane blinked first and said, "Why don't you commies go to Russia if you hate the U.S. of A so much?"

"First of all, The Soviet Union is not a communist country. The communist state emerges from the last stages of post-industrial capitalism. Stalin's forced industrialization doesn't cut the mustard! The Soviet Union is a despotic oligarchy. It is not a true communist country. Idiot."

"You guys better watch out. If I killed you, no one would care."

Barry smiled largely. Duane spat in his face and then walked out of the bathroom. Barry went to the sink, washed the spit off his face, and dried it with stiff brown paper pulled from the white metal wall dispenser. He turned to Geraldo, who hadn't moved.

"Hey. I'm Barry Griswold. I saw you in Magg's office. I think my brother, Tommy, is in your class. I know your brother. Charles. He inspired me. A real revolutionary. Where is he going to college?"

"U.C.S.D."

"Nice. How was old Mr. Magg? Did he tell you all about Lamb Chop Hill?"

"Yeah."

"Of course. Let me ask you: Are you a revolutionary too?"

Geraldo thought about it. "Everyone thinks I am because of my brother. But I don't know. What does it mean to be a revolutionary?"

"A revolutionary wants to change the way things are; he wants to break an evil system that treats men and women as chattel. Who is willing to sacrifice everything for the cause of the emancipation of humankind?"

"Was John Lennon a revolutionary?"

"Oh, most definitely."

The sound of doors busting open and mobs of kids leaving classrooms in a hustle sounded. Barry and Geraldo walked out of the bathroom, cut through a mob of kids, and went to the plaza. "I like your coat," Barry told Geraldo. "I think it's so cool, like a cold war spy. I like it so much that I copied it."

Geraldo looked at Barry's coat and said, "I started wearing mine in the fifth grade because of Harpo Marx. I became obsessed with Harpo from watching Marx Brothers movies on TV, so I started wearing the overcoat and keeping all sorts of things in my pockets, including bike horns that I would steal off of bikes. And I stopped talking, like Harpo. The school thought I was crazy, and the school psychiatrist wanted to put me on drugs. My dad got mad—not at me, at the school—but I stopped wearing the coat. I started wearing it again this year for some reason. It fits better now."

"And I thought your brother was weird. In a good way."

Barry's brother, Tommy, came up behind them. "Hey comrades!" Tommy shouted. "Who's a weirdo?"

Barry and Geraldo looked at Tommy and laughed. He very much seemed like a weirdo at that moment. In fact, Geraldo was aware of how they looked—all three of them in trench coats. Someone could certainly consider them a trio of weirdos. Maybe they were weirdos. Was that so bad?

"Don't forget," Barry said. "Being a revolutionary weirdo in the suburbs can get you killed."

They walked off campus through the football field. Geraldo showed the Griswold boys how to cut through the rear of the mini mall through an alleyway between the cinema and the supermarket. They stopped at the trash bin in the back of the movie theater.

Geraldo reached in and pulled out a piece of film to show the boys. It was a long one. He held it out to Tommy. Tommy's face turned red. He passed it on to Barry, whose face got very serious. Barry handed it back to Geraldo. It was a man and a woman naked, holding each other and kissing. Geraldo scrolled through the film; it got even more explicit. He abruptly dropped it from his hands and let out a big yelp. The boys all laughed.

As they strolled through the streets, Barry and Tommy engaged in a conversation about the imminent collapse of capitalism, using terms like super-stagflation. Geraldo started to tune them out. He was enjoying the cool breeze and a sense of freedom. There was a feeling of exaltation that always accompanied breaks from school.

For Geraldo, Thanksgiving was one of his favorites: the football games on television and the food his father cooked. It was his father's big day to cook, and he always went all out. Everything from the turkey to the pies. He fancied himself a gourmet, which was hard to dispute. Working in the kitchen, hard bop jazz music blasting, a cigar perennially being smoked—that smell of the turkey and the cigar was what Thanksgiving smelled like to Geraldo. And hard bop was what it sounded like.

Chapter Ten

Geraldo walked into his house. It seemed different somehow. Something was missing. It was as if there was a hole in the air, as if the molecular structure of the living room had been altered. The sun pervaded the room, a glinting light like yellow wedges of Jello. His perception of the place where he had dwelt since the beginning had realigned itself to something outside of what he had known. It came in an instant—this revelation. Geraldo looked at the Modigliani that hung above the gas fireplace, along with the u-shaped sofa with its orange floral print, and at his brother Charles, who stood by the credenza holding a manila envelope. "There's one for you. And one for Mom, too," Charles said.

Charles looked different, too. He looked the same, but was different. His Jew-fro, as his father referred to Charles' hair, was longer and bushier but well-kept. He was skinnier, and somehow, he was taller. Or seemed taller. He wore blue jeans, an ultra-wide belt, a baby blue Oxford button-up shirt tucked in, and penny loafers with no socks. He looked at the envelope as if it were something from outer space, inadvertently dropped by an extraterrestrial. He removed from it a single typewritten page.

Dear Charles,

Please try to understand why I am taking this action at this time. For the last many months, I have explored what I have wanted from life, and time and time again, I found that I felt no real meaning any longer with your Mother. She is a wonderful and loving person, but I am deeply in love with someone else. In order to spare my mental and physical health, I had to go now!

We are so proud of you and the fine progress you are making in college. I deeply hope you will not let this occurrence swerve you from the wonderful path you are on. Keep up the school work at the level you are going and achieve great things.

I will provide financial support for you as long as you are pursuing your university studies, and I will help you in any way I can.

I will call you next week and arrange to get together to talk about all this.

I love you very very much, and I feel joy for the fine young man your mother and I have raised.

Love Dad.

Charles methodically put the paper in the envelope and set it back on the credenza. The words were swirling around in his head. He felt displaced. He revered his father. This did not square with how he saw him as a sort of moral barometer. It was true they did not agree about certain things, like capitalism versus socialism, rock versus jazz, and Kubrick versus Spielberg, but they agreed to disagree with mutual respect. Since Charles had gone away to college and was becoming a man, he saw his father as the model, the archetype to strive for. A man who indulged his intellect in history, philosophy, literature, and cinema; and his fancies for food, music, and recreation. Charles did not consider that he was also indulging in his other fancies. If he was deeply in love with another woman, then he had been cheating on Charles' mom for who knows how long. This made Charles indignant, to the extent that it was too much to take, and so he just shut it off. He shut off all that he was feeling and said to Geraldo, "This is going to be one hell of a Thanksgiving."

Chapter Eleven

Thanksgiving was a complete disaster. The grandparents had been given a heads-up by their son before arriving but were wholly unprepared for what they were about to encounter. Carmen was upstairs, in her bedroom, with a bottle of Chablis. Charles was blasting his collection of punk rock 45's on the record player in the living room. He had chosen not to take them to college, saying he had outgrown them and had bequeathed them to Geraldo, who had no interest in them. When the grandparents arrived, he was playing a 45-rpm record from a punk rock group called the Angry Samoans. The song was called "They Saved Hitler's Cock." Charles shouted along with the singer.

> They saved Hitler's cock
>
> They hid it under a rock
>
> I discovered it last night
>
> I couldn't believe my eyes
>
> If Hitler's cock should start to talk
>
> It would say kill today
>
> If Hitler's cock should choose its mate
>
> It would ask for Sharon Tate

Geraldo answered the doorbell and greeted his grandparents. He helped his grandfather get groceries from his car, a beautiful beige Ford Thunderbird. The car shimmered in the late afternoon sun. It was like an advertisement the way it sat in the driveway near the immaculately trimmed lawn and was in such stark contrast to what was happening to the family that it made Geraldo laugh. Jessie, whom the kids called Nana, got busy in the kitchen with food preparations. As it would take too long to make a whole turkey, they brought a chicken instead. Jessie thought she would use the carcass to make chicken soup. What could be more healing? And this family needed healing, especially Carmen, who had yet to descend from the upstairs bedroom.

"Geraldo, do we have to listen to that noise right now?" the grandfather, Robert, asked, practically shouting over the music.

"They're Charles' records," he said, pointing to his brother.

Robert went over to Charles, who sat in front of the stereo, looking absently into the cabinets of the credenza where his father kept his jazz records, which were now empty. The father, Seymour, had taken his jazz records, his clothes, and the food processor with him when he left. Robert tapped Charles on the shoulder. "Charles, could we please have some quiet?" Charles looked up at him. At first, he didn't register the words; they were just more sounds circling around his head, like gnats. "The music, if you can call it that, can we have a break from it?" Charles nodded and removed the needle from the record, making a loud screeching sound.

Geraldo went upstairs to check in on his mother. He knocked gently on the master bedroom door. A few years ago, when he was twelve, they added a second story to the house, which included a master bedroom, a second bathroom, and Geraldo's own room. Charles got the boys' old room downstairs. His parents let Geraldo pick out the color of the carpet and the paint on the walls. It was thrilling for him. He remembered being up in the room when the frame was built, but the walls had yet to be sealed. There was lightning and a thunderstorm, and the whole family—Mom, Dad, and Charles—watched from what was to be his bedroom. It was to Geraldo, an other-worldly event. It was better than the Fourth of July because it was caused by the forces of nature. What made it more memorable was that the whole family shared in the experience.

"Come in," Carmen's voice said quietly. Geraldo opened the door and stepped into a large room painted baby blue. Carmen was sitting on the king-size bed on top of a red and black printed quilt filled with geometric patterns they had bought from their trip to Mexico two years before. "Come here, darling," she said upon seeing Geraldo. She adored the boy. He had been so easy compared to the eldest son, who had been sickly and demonstrably eccentric. Geraldo was a cute baby, rarely sick, quiet, and contemplative. He liked soft and beautiful things. He thought about spiritual matters and would discuss with his mother how miraculous certain things were, like the colors in a painting or the sounds birds made, and how there had to be some benevolent force out there. From an early age, they had these kinds of talks. In the face of his father's outspoken atheism, he flirted with Christianity and even wore a crucifix for one summer. But soon, he concluded that the whole thing was far-fetched, and the criteria for heaven, which was what it was all about anyway, was the manifestation of a vain and unlikely god. Still, like his mother, he liked to entertain the possibility.

He sat down next to her, alongside a mountain of sodden pink Kleenex. She reached out and touched his hair and feigned a smile, then moved her hand to the glass of white wine on the nightstand, brought it to her lips, took a sip, and then took another. She held it close to her breasts. "Are you alright, Mom?" She smiled and thought that her boy did really care about her—maybe the only person in the world who did.

Eventually, Carmen made it downstairs before dinner. She sat on the sofa, clutching the wine glass to her breasts, when she wasn't sipping at it. Nana and Robert sat opposite in the arm chairs, and Charles was lying on the floor reading a M.A.D. magazine. Carmen pointed to Robert. "You must have known."

"I did not. I am very disappointed in my son."

"That's why we are here with you and the boys, dear. For Thanksgiving," Jesse said.

"To hell with Thanksgiving," Carmen disclaimed.

"Damn right," Charles said.

Geraldo came into the room with a glass of water. He held it out to his mother. "Thanks sweetie. But I'll just hold onto this for now." And she took another sip of her wine. Geraldo set the glass of water down on the coffee table and sat down next to Carmen. "Maybe you should stop drinking the wine," Jessie said with a concerned, maternal tone.

"I tried to hold this family together. I knew that he had affairs. I thought he had affairs. I didn't really know for sure. I guess I didn't want to know. When he bought the Porsche, I thought, 'Jesus, what a cliche'. But I never thought he would leave us. I thought I could hold this family together."

"Carmen. Have you ever heard of Dale Carnegie?" Robert asked.

"What?"

"He said, and don't forget, 'Every day in every way, it's getting better and better.'"

"Are you kidding me? Are you fucking kidding me? My god, white people have no feelings!"

"Now listen, dear," Jessie interjected. "I don't know what you mean. White, what white?"

"Every day in every way! I know why you treat me like you do. With affection but also with condescension. Because I am Mexican."

Robert stood up. "That's not true, Carmy."

"He condescends to everyone. Trust me. But he has a big heart," Jesse quipped.

"What?" Robert objected.

"I could have never imagined him treating you this way. We brought him up to be better than this. He's such a putz." Jessie said, getting up from the ottoman and sitting down next to Carmen, opposite Geraldo.

Carmen took a large sip of her wine. "His secretary. Can you believe it? It doesn't get more predictable."

"It's a shonda. Utterly shameful." Jessie put her hand on Carmen's back. "You know that we love you."

"I know, mom," Carmen said, calming down. "I never had a mom growing up. My mom died when I was just a little kid."

"I know. And you are my daughter. And we will always be here for you and the boys."

And with that, Carmen, embraced by Jessie, began to cry convulsively. Which was more than Charles could take. He got up and went outside to the patio. He sat down on one of the wrought-iron chairs. He pulled out a pack of Chesterfields from his jeans front pocket, extracted one, stuck it in his mouth, and with a lime green Bic lighter, ignited it. He took a small puff. Never a large drag. He did that once, and he never stopped coughing. The cigarettes were disgusting, he admitted to himself, but they adhered to the persona he was attempting to create. His father smoked cigars, and so he would smoke cigarettes—not just any cigarettes, not Marlboros, Camels, or Pall Malls, but Chesterfield or Gauloises. He wished he was Belmondo in Breathless, but he was aware enough to know that he was more like a post-adolescent Albert Brooks. Oh well.

He looked at the courtyard. He could remember when his father had it built, when he was thirteen. The cinder breeze block walls with decorative ventilation holes, the forest green metal gate, the patio furniture, and the flower garden with the roses Seymour fussed over on Saturdays, which were now all but dead. It was one evening, sitting out there having a cocktail while the jazz music blasted from inside the house, that a stray black and white cat jumped on Seymour's lap. The cat knew who to schmooze. Who was the patriarch. Indeed, as a result, he found a home. Seymour named the cat Groucho because of the pattern of the cat's facial hair resembling a mustache. This same black-and-white cat Charles gave a voice to. He would speak for the cat in a strange voice. Seymour, Carmen, and Geraldo got used to the voice and accepted the cat's running commentary on everything. For instance, if there was a commercial on television that Charles objected to, he would say in the cat's voice, which utilized the lowest part of his vocal register, "That was the most idiotic thing that I have ever heard." Or something like that. The grandparents thought the boy was a bit cracked because of the way he was always speaking in the cat's voice. Yet, even they got used to it. And now his father was gone. At least gone from this house, from this courtyard, probably forever. Everything changes and changes quickly.

Geraldo came out to the courtyard and sat down on a wrought iron chair next to Charles. Charles said, "What a shitshow," and threw his cigarette to the ground. He stood up.

"I hope Mom will be okay. It's terrible what dad has done to her," Geraldo said. He wanted to sound angry or indignant but could not muster any emotion. He felt nothing.

"No, it falls right in line with Dad's bourgeois aspirations. Mom is right. Typical. I just didn't think he was such a plebe."

April Weeks walked into the courtyard. She was Charles' girlfriend. The same girl had gone with him to the prom. She had almost the exact opposite personality as Charles. She was pleasant and usually tried to see the positive in most situations, while Charles was constantly lamenting the stupidity of not just situations but most human beings. April saw the good. And she loved Charles. She was waiting for him to grow up. She didn't know how long she was going to have to wait. Or how long she would be willing to wait. They had been going out for almost three years now. She went to UC Irvine and still lived with her parents. The parents liked Charles enough, though they thought that their daughter could do better.

"Hey Geraldo. Sorry to hear about, about, things," April said with sincere compassion.

"Thanks."

She went over to Charles, and they kissed. She made a face by scrunching up her mouth. "Disgusting."

"Sorry."

"It's okay. If there was ever a time to smoke, How's your mom?"

"She went upstairs to sleep," Geraldo said.

"Your mom is such a sweet woman. It seems like this kind of thing is happening more and more. If you need anything, let me know."

"Thanks."

Charles put his arm around April and said, "We're going inside to watch a movie. What are you going to do?"

"I think I might go over to the Griswold brothers' place."

"Griswold brothers? Barry Griswold?"

"Yeah."

"Tell Barry I said hi. That guy is a legitimate red."

Charles and April walked into the house. Geraldo watched them. He was amazed that his brother had such a cool girlfriend. This scrawny kid, who had no social skills and had no clue how to deport himself in society, had a girlfriend who was not only hot but just as brilliant as him. He was sweet to her in a way that Geraldo had never seen him be, not to anyone. He walked to where Charles' cigarette lay, still smoldering. He picked it up, put it between his lips, and started walking to the Griswold brothers' condo.

He walked past the oil tanks on Katella Avenue and then through the parking lot of the Safeway. In the condominium complex, he found the door marked 123 and knocked. He could hear a television blasting in there. It sounded like a science show, with a monotone voice like a low hum. Tommy opened the door and welcomed Geraldo with a big, genial smile. "Hello! Come on in!" Geraldo followed Tommy through the living room, where on a sofa lay an obese woman with 40-liter plastic bottles of diet soda scattered around her, watching on television a volcano spewing lava. "That's my mom. She's taking it easy. Day off from the DMV." They went through the kitchen, where there were dishes piled up in the sink and empty KFC buckets on the counter. "She's never been the same since Dad died."

They walked into the boy's bedroom, where there was a giant poster of Che' Guevarra, a record player and records, books in stacks and clothes scattered around the floor, and a black rat with white spots in a cage in the corner of the room. Geraldo looked around, amazed at the mess. "That's our rat, Leon Trotsky." Barry said, sitting at a desk in front of a typewriter. "Hey Geraldo. How go things?" Geraldo stopped himself from saying anything in regard to his father leaving. "Good. Pretty good. My brother says hi."

"Oh, cool. Hi back."

"We were just talking about you," Tommy said. "We want to make a manifesto and distribute it on campus, and we are thinking maybe you would want to be a part of our insurrection."

"It's not really an insurrection, Tommy, but people need to know about what is happening in Central America. About Nicaragua and how the Sandinistas overthrew the brutal American-supported Somoza regime and his savage death squads. And how those same death squads, now called fucking 'freedom fighters', are attempting to overturn a democratically elected government, terrorizing the people with Ronald Reagan's illegal support."

"And I told Barry you had just said as much in Calder's class!"

"So, what do you think, Geraldo? Want to be part of our movement?"

"I don't know."

"Think about Lennon."

"Yeah!" Tommy shouted. "Think about Vlad."

"Not Vladimir Lenin. John Lennon," Barry said. "He said, in the song Revolution, that if there was a revolution, you could count him in."

"Actually, on the single, he said, 'You can count me out.'" Geraldo corrected Barry.

"Oh."

"But on the White album, he says 'in.'"

"There you go!" Tommy shouted. "You're in! Now, what should we call the paper?"

"Maybe something about revolution. Like the song." Geraldo said.

Barry stood up. "After all. This country was founded on a revolution. Remember what Thomas Paine said? 'Tyranny, like hell, is not easily conquered — the harder the conflict, the more glorious the triumph.'"

"How about the Revolutionary Press?" Geraldo said loudly.

Chapter Twelve

With the hundred-dollar bill that her parents had left her on the dining room table in an envelope that had "Happy Thanksgiving!" written in blue ink, Sunshine paid for a taxi that took her to a French restaurant in Hollywood called Les Freres Taix. She wore a blonde wig, red lipstick, black eye liner expertly applied, her mother's mink stole, a black lace skirt, fishnets, and a pair of her mother's black high heels two which fit her perfectly. She entered the restaurant as if she owned it and asked the maitre'd for a table for one. She was told it would be a few moments and she could wait at the bar. Sunshine walked to the bar with aplomb and ordered a martini, "dry with a twist," which was then placed before her unquestioningly. She turned on her stool to face the room, which was fairly crowded. She was undoubtedly the best-dressed person there. The men looked ridiculous in their mullets, razor-thin ties, and sports coats with sleeves pulled up three a quarter of the way. The women in pastel dresses, had their hair either permed or feathered, and their faces adorned with dark eyeliner paired with bright eyeshadow and pink lipstick. This was the B-movie version of a French restaurant in Hollywood. She felt duped. But she was there, and she had a martini, which made her happy. One of the mullet men approached her.

"Hi there. Need another one of those?" he asked Sunshine.

"Almost," Sunshine said, and then she downed her drink. "Now I do."

"Are you alone?"

"Aren't we all?"

"I'm not. I'm with my friends over there," he said, pointing to the booth with his assortment.

"I meant in an existential way," Sunshine said dryly.

"Oh. That's funny. You know. We were talking. We think we have seen you in the movies."

"Is that so?"

"Yeah. But I can't quite remember which one."

"You speak like you and your friends share one brain."

"Are you in the movies?"

"Maybe," Sunshine said dishonestly.

The bartender put the drinks down in front of them. Giving the mullet man a dirty look, he took a crumpled ten-dollar bill from his pants pocket and set it down on the bar.

"I think I saw you in a movie at the Pussycat."

"The Pussycat?"

"Yeah. And in this movie." He looked around and then whispered something in Sunshine's ear. He pulled back and smiled lasciviously. Sunshine felt a mix of repugnance and power. She reached for her martini and threw it in the mullet man's face. They glared at each other. Frozen. Sunshine tried to understand exactly what she had just heard. She understood the parts of the anatomy the mullet man mentioned, but the idea of them doing the things he described in brevity was hard to comprehend quickly. The way he said it was intentionally demeaning and hurt her, as if he had stabbed her in the eye. The maitre'd came over to Sunshine. "Madam, your table is ready."

She ordered escargot and steak tartare. She thought of ordering a bottle of wine with dinner, but she didn't really like the taste of wine from the times she had snuck sips from her mother's glass. So she ordered another martini, and then another.

When the taxi pulled up in front of her house, the driver had to jostle Sunshine awake. At first, she thought he was her grandfather. He had the same mustache and the same Eastern European inflection. "Come on, little girl. You are home." Home? Oh yes, there it was—the hedge, the rose bushes, the courtyard. "That will be twenty-seven dollars." Sunshine opened her black leather handbag, her mother's handbag. There was just one crumpled five-dollar bill in there. She held it up. "That's all you got?" The driver snapped. She nodded her head as if it were partially untethered from her neck. "Don't cry! Can you please go and get your father to help you out?"

"I'm not crying," she said, holding back tears. "And. He is not home."

"How about your mom?"

She shook her head. "They went to Vail. I said I was going to sleepover with a friend. Ha! I don't have any friends."

"How old are you anyway?"

"Fifteen."

"Jeez. Don't you know that it's not safe to go around? Do you know what can happen to you? Terrible things. Terrible things could happen to you."

He turned his body so that he was facing her. His eyes were angry, and his lower jaw declinated; his open mouth presented a vortex of doom. Sunshine wondered if the implications of his words were actualizing, and this thought, along with her inebriety, caused her to feel as if she were in a dream. She was frightened.

"I'm sorry, mister."

"Sorry! Don't be sorry for me. It's my fault. I saw this whole scenario play out in my mind after you got into the car and told me where to take you. I thought, 'You're going to lose your shirt on this one, Joe, but what are you going to do? Let this kid pretending to be Marilyn get into trouble?' No! It's Thanksgiving, and I don't have any family. Except for the people who get into my cab."

"Thank you," Sunshine said, holding back her sobs.

"That's all right. Thank you too."

"Thank me?"

"I could only imagine what might have happened to you. I am glad I was there. My mitzvah for today. Listen to me, dumb-dumb; maybe take your time growing up. You have plenty of time for that other stuff. Okay?"

"Okay mister."

Sunshine walked into her house and was able to make it to the bathroom on the ground floor before letting everything out.

Chapter Thirteen

pril liked the feeling of Charles' lips on hers in the same way she liked wearing her favorite green fuzzy slippers. He placed his left arm across the front of her; her left arm was behind him, cupping his left shoulder; her right hand rested lightly on his half-erect cock, trapped and struggling beneath his denim jeans. She was thinking, as her chest felt a kind of incubated pressure, making her breathing rapid and her head goofy, "Is this love, or is this just passion and exuberance?" She pulled away and looked at his face. Sad eyes behind round wire-rimmed glasses, a large bulbous nose, and full lips when not sensual filled with irony. He was most definitely sensual. He instinctively knew where and how to touch her. And maybe more importantly, he knew how to make her laugh. Nobody could make her laugh like he did, except for her father.

And yet, she thought, why am I with a white boy? Well, for one, there were zero black boys in my grade—zero! So, if you take that away and add that I wanted a boy, I wanted a boy to like me, let alone love me. And Charles—you can see it in his eyes—adores me. And even though he seems to always have an erection, he never pushes. I like that about him. On the other hand, he is troubled and so full of himself, and many of his opinions are draconian. Not only that, half-baked. Somebody so smart can sound a bit like an idiot at times. This made her laugh to herself.

"What's so funny?" Charles asked.

"You're face."

"Thanks."

"No, I mean. It's sweet."

His eyes filled up with water.

"Oh Charles." She kissed his cheeks, tasting his tangy tears. "I'm so sorry."

"It's okay," he said, taking off his glasses and wiping his eyes. "I don't know why I'm crying," Forcing a laugh.

"I know why. It's sort of shocking. I know how much you looked up to your dad."

"I hate him. I really do. All that talk about doing the right thing. If this is the right thing, he did it the wrong way. A manila envelope. Jesus."

"Your poor mom."

"Yeah. Even though there were so many warning signs, it seems as if she had no idea."

"If my father did that to my mom, I'd kill him."

"It's predictable, really. Ok, maybe I am disappointed, I suppose. I am just glad that I won't be here for any of the fallout."

"Oh, that's right. Just Geraldo and your mom, in this big house."

"Poor kid."

Geraldo came into a darkened house. He went into the kitchen and turned on the overhead fluorescent light; it flickered and then came on, illuminating a spotless kitchen and casting a white neon glow. On the counter was a half-eaten apple pie. He cut himself a slice, put a dollop of vanilla ice cream on it, and carried it into the TV room. He found April and Charles canoodling. The fork fell off the plate and hit the brown shag carpet. The lovers broke apart. Charles at first felt annoyed at the sight of his little brother, but then remembered the situation. "Hey kid."

April sat up, straightened her blouse, and said, "Hi Geraldo." She reached over and turned on the light on the side table.

"How were the Griswold brothers?" Charles asked. He relinquished his hold on April.

Geraldo sat down on the recliner. "Good." He took a bite of the pie.

"I like Barry. He used to hang around me and my friends last year. God, I am glad to be out of that school. Nightmare in hell."

"Tell me about it," April said with an edge in her voice. "Try being the only black girl."

"Try being a Mexican-Jew commie."

"Seriously Charles. Not even close."

"Uh, yeah. True enough."

"True enough?"

"Totally true."

"Charles, I was wondering," Geraldo said. "Well, we wrote this paper that we want to distribute around the school, and we were wondering if you'd take a look."

"Paper?"

"Yeah, like a manifesto."

"And what are you going to do with this manifesto?"

"We are going to post it around the school. Some night."

Charles burst out in laughter. April gave him a look and whispered to him, "Don't make fun of your brother."

"You've got balls. Sure, I'll take a look."

Geraldo put his plate down on the seat of the recliner and pulled out a folded sheet of paper from his back pocket. "Here's the one duplicate. Barry really wanted to know what you thought."

Charles unfolded the paper and held it up. "The Revolutionary Press!" April chuckled as she looked over to read it with Charles. She thought, how sweet Geraldo was compared to Charles. Sweet and earnest, whereas it seemed to her that Charles' political opinions were more for effect than any actual consecrated belief. She thought both Charles and Geraldo would grow out of it; they were both questioning the status quo, and that was a good thing, but eventually they needed to get real.

Charles cleared his throat. "Looks good. I like your anti-imperialist agenda. I admire what you guys are doing, but let me tell you, if you get found out, the powers that be will make your life miserable. And the jocks will come after you, and they can do harm, physical harm, and they won't be held accountable. Believe me. And don't let Mom get a whiff of what you're up to. I think it's going to be rocky around here for a while."

Chapter Fourteen

After Geraldo brushed his teeth and got into his pajamas, he went to his mother's bedroom. Formerly his parent's bedroom. He knocked on the door. There was no response. He went in. The light of the television was flickering; silver and gray beams of light illuminated the darkened room. The sound was down low. He found her in bed, sitting up, in her nightgown. Her eyes were closed. She looked like she was at peace, especially in contrast to how she was earlier. She opened her eyes, smiled wanly, and patted the space next to her. Geraldo went over and climbed on the bed. Together, they stared at the television, which had an old black-and-white movie on. They had spent a lot of time when Geraldo was a toddler watching old movies on television during the daytime when his brother was at school and his father at work, before Geraldo began kindergarten, and before his mother had gone back to work at the hospital. "I love Humphrey Bogart," Carmen said. "Me too," Geraldo replied. Carmen put her arm around her son and folded him closer to her. "Did you get supper?" she asked.

"Yeah," Geraldo said, reflecting on a very awkward dinner with his grandparents and his brother. A dinner filled with bloated silences.

"Are your grandparents still here?"

"No, they left a while ago."

"Poor things. What a catastrophe for everyone."

It appeared to Geraldo that she was about to break down. Instead, she shook her head and emitted a long and low sigh. He took her hand and said, "You okay, Mom?"

"No. Not really. Así es la vida."

"Yeah."

"There's only so much you can do. You know?"

"I know."

"I keep thinking about our trip to New York City; when was that? Three summers ago? It was a big trip, not just to New York but to Boston, D.C., and Philadelphia. The bicentennial tour. But things never got stressful. He never lost his temper. He was inordinately affectionate. I remember it was so humid, but it was a nice trip. And then, in New York City, his secretary showed up in the lobby of the hotel. They were going to some kind of business meeting. What business? But off he went, leaving us. I never questioned it. Oh, he was a pro at explaining things away. Or sometimes you figure you would rather not investigate too strongly for fear of what you'll find."

"I remember Times Square, all the people, and we were following one lady who had panty hose falling around her ankles, and they were the fattest ankles that I had ever seen. They weren't even ankles. Just part of her leg. And holding your hand. So many people. It was kind of scary."

"Yes. You cried at dinner. It was all so overwhelming for you."

They sat looking at Humphrey Bogart getting shot as Ida Lupino watched in horror.

Geraldo said, "It's going to be okay, Mom." He was aware of what little conviction he had in his voice.

"Mostly, I just feel bad. I hurt all over." Carmen began to cry. Geraldo didn't know what to do. So many times, it was he

who had been crying and she would always know what to do,
what to say.

Chapter Fifteen

When things change in a person's life, in a momentous way, it is like all of the cells in your body and your brain are also recalibrated. This is what Geraldo thought as he walked out of his house and took in the colors of the block: the grass, the trees, the homes painted in pastel tints, the cars of various primary colors parked on the street and on driveways, the children on the way to school in their windbreakers and sweatshirts, wearing backpacks and rucksacks on this cool day in Cypress, California. All the colors and the kids in transit gave the street a kind of bloated and unsettled look. He looked up at the sun to ground himself, not directly into it, mind you, just at the orange haze of it, and remembered something he had read about the hydrogen bomb and how the intense heat and pressure in the sun's core caused protons to fuse together. This process releases large amounts of energy and a nuclear reaction, the same process that happens in a hydrogen bomb.

Lost in this thought, not sad but melancholy; what's the difference? One is in your blood, the other in your stomach. It wasn't a bad feeling. He had it before, but this was different somehow. He couldn't explain it. Not even to himself. He heard his name and a car horn that sounded like the Road Runner. He turned to see an old beat, faded gray Datsun, and in it, the Griswold brothers and Davy. Barry yelled out the open window of the driver's side, "Hey Geraldo, get in! I just got my license!" Geraldo began computing the significance of this moment. First time riding in a car with a friend driving, and first time to have a friend who drives; next year, I will be sixteen, and then I can drive. My father said he would buy me a car; it is written on the paper that was in the manila envelope that announced his departure from the household. That is if I maintain a B average. Piece of cake.

Geraldo got in the car and smiled at Davy, who said, "I didn't know you knew these guys."

Tommy turned around from the front passenger's seat and, with a huge grin, said, "Freaks got to stick together!"

Geraldo noticed that Tommy not only was wearing eyeliner but had something shiny on his lips.

Geraldo said, "This car is…"

"It's a piece of shit," Barry said, laughing.

"But it gets good gas mileage, which is important because of the crisis in the Middle East. Not to mention the environment, which just might be a foregone conclusion," Tommy said.

Barry slammed in a cassette of The Clash's "London Calling," everyone except Geraldo started violently bobbing their heads. "Come on!" shouted Tommy, and Geraldo joined the bobbing.

"Let's go to Mexico!" Barry exclaimed.

"Yeah," Tommy and Davy said in unison.

"I mean, why the hell not?"

"What about school?" Geraldo said.

"Fuck school," Tommy shouted, "It's not like we learn anything there except capitalist propaganda."

"We can get to Tijuana by 9, look around, get some tacos, and be back by the regular end of the school day. You can forge a note; we do it all the time. Nobody cares."

"Nah, I have an algebra test," Geraldo lied. "And I am on the verge of failing. I hate algebra."

"I don't," Tommy said. "It's the only class I like."

"He gets straight A's in everything. Always has, my genius little brother."

"Thanks, bro."

"Maybe another time," Barry said resignedly. "Well, let's at least get some donuts."

Chapter Sixteen

armen had been staring into a microscope for what seemed like twenty years. And she had. She thought, perhaps this is what causes those terrible headaches and intermittent flashes of kaleidoscopic visions. She lifted her head from the microscope and made some notes in a ledger. This one is an acute case of anemia. Then she saw squiggly lines that zig-zagged across her vision. She raised her head and looked around at the lab. It felt like she was on drugs. She thought the headache was like a drug, a bad drug, a bad trip. She had never been on a drug trip and hadn't even ever tried marijuana, though she suspected that her estranged husband had on occasion. "Oh god," she mumbled to herself. And just as quickly, the pain subsided, and the squigglies were gone.

She thought, all of these people, at their stations, doing their work, the same work as mine, I know them. I don't know them. But I know their domestic situations. They are all married, and now they are going to look at me with the pitiful look married women give to the newly divorced. Pathetic. She had read that almost fifty percent of marriages in the U.S. end in divorce. It was like an epidemic sweeping the land. But all of these women are married, still married except Phyllis over there. She got divorced last year. She chain smokes and talks to herself. That's me in a year's time. Except I can't stand the taste of cigarettes. Maybe I'll start smoking anyway.

Behind a large glass window was the new pathologist. Clive his name. He is good looking and black, and Carmen had overheard him speaking with an English accent. So very suave. He usually wore turtlenecks, red, black, olive green, and mustard yellow; he was as handsome a man as she had ever seen. She was thinking how she didn't care that he was black. She didn't care about any of that. She was a brown person, after all, first generation Mexican American. She could have married a handsome man. That Swede in San Francisco. He wanted to marry her. But she just didn't feel it. She didn't fully understand why she declined the Swede's proposal; he was a wealthy and successful jazz musician. That is until she met Seymour. Seymour made her laugh, and that was what really attracted her. He was very funny. Seymour got the last laugh.

She went back to work, examining blood samples. Blood, an endless flow of blood, would it ever stop? This is her life now: looking at blood five days a week, waking up at six in the morning, showering, dressing, making lunch for Geraldo, and leaving the house before he even wakes up. Gets into her blue Toyota Corolla and drives fifteen minutes to Los Alamitos Hospital. She puts on the white lab coat, goes to the bathroom, cries, fixes her face, buoys her spirits by summoning something inexplicable, and then to the microscope. She examines the blood. It is her job to detect disease, lymphoma, sickle cell anemia, leukemia, hemophilia, blood and inflammatory diseases, red and white blood cell counts, platelet counts, and hemoglobin concentration, like an accountant, numbers on paper; only these are human lives. It was amazing to her how she could detach herself, and she did detach herself from the sometimes-dire prognosis'; if only she could detach herself now from her own heartache and misery.

Chapter Seventeen

The Datsun pulled into the lot in front of Winchell's and slammed into the parking stop, lifting the back end of the car and then setting it back down brusquely. The boys dispatched from the car like freed hostages. "Got to work on your parking skills, Barry," Davy said snidely. They burst into the donut shop and went to the window next to the counter where all the donuts were on display. The glazed, the cakes, the rings, the fancies, the twists. Remarkably cheap, these donuts for just two dollars and seventy-nine cents you could get a dozen. Geraldo wasn't looking at the donuts; he was looking at the girl behind the counter moving trays of donuts. She was dressed in a mustard yellow short sleeve shirt with a triangle patch above her left breast that had the Winchell's logo. She wore brown polyester pants that seemed too tight. On her head she wore a red cap, also with the Winchell's logo. Her long black hair, tied in ponytails, protruded from the rear of her head. Save for those ponytails and modest bust, Geraldo thought she moved like a boy. She wasn't the one who took their orders. That was an older woman who showed very little interest in the matter.

Geraldo stayed at the counter, gazing at the girl as she brought a tray of cinnamon twists to the display window. She caught Geraldo's gaze, furrowed her brow, and then smiled. Her lips were full and pink, and right then, he could imagine kissing them. She removed an empty tray from the display window and then disappeared into the backroom. Geraldo went to where the others were sitting. Barry was talking, "I think the thing is, we go in at night and cover the walls with the Revolutionary Press!"

Davy said, "If the school finds out we did it, they will suspend us. Not that I care."

Tommy shoved a chocolate glazed into his mouth dramatically and said while masticating extravagantly, "How are they going to find out? There's no security guard at night. We already scoped it out."

"What do you think Geraldo?" Barry asked. Geraldo was staring at the girl who had returned from the backroom.

Tommy shoved him, "Geraldo?"

"What? Huh?"

"The plan! What do you think of the plan? And what Savior said about us getting suspended if we get caught."

"Oh, yeah. What's the plan?"

"Boy, you really spaced out. We put it up at night, late at night, on all the walls. Or my idea is that we put one in every locker."

"Every locker? It's like two thousand kids in the student body. Where can you get two thousand copies made?"

"At the copy shop," Barry said confidently.

Davy scratched the hair on his chin and said, "That would cost a lot."

"My mom will pay for it. She won't know what she's paying for, but she'll pay for it."

"Still, it would take all night. Let's be safe and post them to the walls," Geraldo said convincingly.

Tommy swallowed the glazed and said, "We could use dad's old mimeograph machine. The one he used to make the pamphlets with."

As the boys got up to leave, Geraldo lingered a little, pretending to have trouble zipping up his windbreaker. He took a glance at the girl. She was aware of him, she smiled, he wanted to say something to her. What would he say? Could he ask her out? He had never asked a girl out before. What do you even do when you go out with a girl? Something to eat, maybe a movie? But the other woman said something to her in Spanish, and she disappeared into the back room again.

Chapter Eighteen

Geraldo was thinking about the girl in the donut shop. He was so engrossed in the fantasy of her, the idea of her. He looked at girls at school all the time, and he fantasized about girls all the time, but none of those girls excited him, not like the girl in the donut shop. The girl in Winchell's seemed to be older than his classmates but still young. How old was she? Fifteen, sixteen- wasn't that too young to work? He would go to see her after dinner. But no, she would be off by then, wouldn't she? Maybe not; after all, the small sign underneath the big yellow sign out front says open 24 Hours. If he rode his bike after dinner, he could get there by 7; she might get off by 8:30. A 12-hour shift? No way. I'll just go tomorrow, but not with the others; I can't talk to her if they are around and…

"Hey!" Carmen shouted.

Geraldo came out of his revelry. "Oh, uh, what?"

"I asked you how school was today. I asked you three times, to be exact."

"It was fine." Geraldo tried to think of something else to say but nothing came. School was fine. It wasn't fine, it sucked, but it sucked the way it usually sucked, and that was fine. Nothing terrible happened. Something great happened, but not at school. Seeing that girl at the donut shop. That was great. That was more than fine.

Carmen felt the anger accumulating in her chest. She wanted a glass of wine, but it was Monday and a work night, and, well, she was aware of how she let loose on Thanksgiving.

She had never been like that before, never drunk like that, and never angry and mean like that. She felt bad about how she spoke to her in-laws. She felt bad but also good because it was something that she had thought about for a while, and so she finally said it. She didn't know how she felt, or she was of two minds, maybe more. True, they were her in-laws; they were more than that; they were her white parents, the white parents she never had.

She had been on her own since she was a kid, first in the Crippled Children's Home because she had tuberculosis in her hip and couldn't walk for a few years, and her Papa was too poor to take care of her properly. So, the nuns at the home were surrogate parents; they were white, and because she spent so much time with them, her English was perfect, unlike her brothers and sisters, who had strong accents. At the same time, she felt alienated from her family. She went to college and medical school. She was told she couldn't be a doctor because of her hip injury which had caused a pronounced limp. She didn't have the mobility to be a doctor, they told her. Later on, she felt she was discriminated against because she was Mexican and a woman. Her limp wasn't all that bad. So, instead, she studied hematology. After graduating from Arizona State, the first in her family to graduate from a university, she moved to San Francisco and lived a wonderful and glamorous life at the height of that city's most beautiful era, the late fifties. So, she had spent most of her life around white people, had married a white man, and, for all practical purposes, had white children.

"Okay, if you don't want to talk, that's fine," Carmen said angrily.

"I, well, just not much to say. School is school. You know."

"Whatever."

Geraldo felt powerless. He wanted to say more about his day. He wanted to give details about his class, or his friends, maybe even talk about the girl at the donut shop. He went so far as to open his mouth, but nothing came out. His mom was looking down at her food. And for the first time, he noticed the empty chairs. He hadn't thought of them before. The two other chairs where his father and brother used to sit were empty. Geraldo sat to the left of his mom; to his left would be where his father sat, and so if Carmen looked straight ahead, she would see an empty chair. Across from where Geraldo sat was the chair where his brother used to sit. He imagined the way Charles opened his mouth and showed Geraldo a mouth full of half masticated food when he was sure his parents were not looking. It disgusted Geraldo but also never failed to make him laugh.

"Do you want to go and live with him?"

"What?"

"Do you want to go and live with your father?"

"No!"

"You probably do. I can sense it in your body language. And the way you are not talking to me. The silence is deafening!"

"Mom. No. I don't want to live with him. Not at all. I don't even know where he lives, and I don't care. I think that he is, he is..." Geraldo began to cry. First, a few tears, then more, and then a cathartic wail. His mother reached out her hand to his.

"Oh, it's okay. I'm sorry, dear. I'm sorry. This is so hard."

"I want to stay with you." When he said it he realized how happy he was to be just with his mom. How happy he was now that his father and brother were gone. He felt liberated from the two arrogant, didactic, and domineering personalities, who, if someone had a different opinion from them, were labeled stupid. Or idiotic. Now, he could listen to the music he liked to listen to, free from any judgment from his father, who thought rock music was mundane and for the soft-headed. He could watch the shows he liked, Charlie's Angels One Day at a Time, without being castigated by his brother as a plebe.

Carmen stood up and then knelt down and took her son into her arms. "There, there. There, there," she said while patting him on the back.

Chapter Nineteen

It wasn't that Geraldo was stimulated by watching the women who were Charlie's Angels. It wasn't like they aroused him. They did, but not especially any more than, let's say, his biology teacher, Miss Canshaw. Geraldo was not good at guessing a woman's age; whenever he asked his mother her age, she would say 28. He stopped asking. This made his ability to gauge a woman's age a bit askew. That said, Geraldo ventured to guess that Miss Canshaw was somewhere in her forties. And she was by no means good-looking by the standards that his peers or the magazines applied, yet she aroused him. He would sit the entire class thinking about her naked. That was the extent of his fantasy. Miss Canshaw naked, at the chalkboard, Miss Canshaw naked behind her desk. Miss Canshaw naked, at the microscope.

Geraldo sat next to his mother on the sofa in the TV. Room. They were eating ice cream sundaes that Geraldo had made for the both of them: three scoops of Knudson vanilla ice cream, Hershey's chocolate sauce, a mountain of Reddi Whip, sprinkles, and a maraschino cherry on top. Just like they made and served at Farrell's Ice Cream Parlor, where they hadn't gone in a long while, not since his thirteenth birthday. It was nice and cozy to be next to his mom, watching Charlie's Angels. Carmen seemed to be enjoying both the sundae and the television program. It seemed to Geraldo that she was pleasantly distracted, which made him glad. The first time he had seen her somewhat enjoying herself since before Thanksgiving. When the commercial came on, Geraldo set down his finished bowl on the coffee table.

"Mom?"

"Yes?"

"Oh, nothing."

"What is it?"

"How do you…"

"How do you what?"

"Well, there's this girl."

"And you like her."

"Yeah."

"That's nice. I guess."

"And I don't know. How do you, you know, um, tell, talk…"

"If you like her. Maybe show her. Girls aren't detectives. You have to express yourself."

"Express yourself?"

"You can say that you think she is pretty. Or just come right out and tell her that you like her."

"That's all?"

"Everyone likes to hear that."

"That's it?"

"That's not *it*, not all of it, but it's a good start.

Chapter Twenty

In the Griswold brother's bedroom, the stink of the blue ink was almost unbearable. Tommy was spinning the barrel, staring into space as he did. He was thinking about something that he realized was totally possible, but he also realized it would be something that could be addictive, and once he started, he doubted that he could stop. All his free time, every private moment might be spent doing the thing that he realized he could now do. He discovered yoga by way of one of the books in his father's library, a book called The Yoga System by Yogi Vilthadas. By reading the book, he learned various exercises and techniques for stretching and relaxing his body. He was doing things with his body that he didn't think possible, and he was becoming more centered in his mind, and this was leading him to certain revelations about himself.

"Tommy. What are you doing? Tommy!"

Coming out of his cloud of thought, Tommy said, "What? Huh?"

"You're out of paper," Barry said.

Geraldo and Davy, sitting on the bed, started laughing.

"You've been cranking that thing for five minutes without any paper. We were going to see how long you'd go before you'd notice but we haven't got all night," Davy said.

Tommy looked serious and then had a chuckle at his own expense. "Let's load more paper,"

"That's okay, Tom," Barry said, patting his brother on the back. "I think we've got enough. Plenty enough."

"How many do we have?" Geraldo asked.

"We got about one hundred." Barry picked up one of the copies, held it up, and showed it to the group. THE REVOLUTIONARY PRESS Vol. 1.

"There it is."

"Looks great," Geraldo said, not without a little pride; after all, it was he who came up with the name.

The flip clock flipped three of its flaps from 11:59 to 12:00. Geraldo flipped his covers over and got out of bed fully dressed. He laid down his beat-up copy of Catcher in the Rye, given to him from Charles, on his nightstand, stood, picked up his sneakers and walked out of his bedroom. He stuck his head into his mother's bedroom. She still had the television on, but she was asleep. He walked over and turned it off. There was an empty bottle of Chablis on the nightstand. Geraldo shook his head. It was terrible what his father had done. Terrible. Yet it seemed his was like the fourth house on the block in which such a thing had occurred. In all but the Garvey's it was the father who left. Mrs. Garvey was another case. She left her husband, left the children, and was gone. Moved out of state. That's all Geraldo knew about what happened over at the Garvey's. The other families, the Thompson's, the Fielder's, and the Reiner's, it was the dad who left. Just drove away in their fancy new sports car.

The Datsun was waiting at the curb outside of Geraldo's house. Geraldo got into the back seat next to Tommy. "Hello, comrade!" Tommy's face was exuberant. His eyes were wide and his mouth agape, spittle gathered at the corners of his mouth. "It's a good day to die," Barry said at the wheel. "Oh Jesus," Davy muttered. It was quiet on the streets. Very few cars. Geraldo rolled down his window. The air was cool and crisp, and it made him feel calm. This was simply something that had to be done, like anything else, like mowing the lawn, which was his chore to do, both front and back, now that Charles was gone, or like writing a paper on Francis Bacon's essay about the three most important inventions in history: gunpowder, the magnetic compass, and the printing press. It had to be done. Not just done but done properly by injecting his own inductive reasoning. With the writing of the Revolutionary Press, it had to be disseminated, and it followed. That was the whole purpose, wasn't it? It had to be done.

Barry parked the Datsun on a side street a couple of blocks from the school on the other side of the football field. The boys walked across the field humming the theme song from A Bridge Over the River Kwai. Barry carried the copies of the Revolutionary Press in the knapsack draped over his shoulder. This was Army Surplus from his father. They got to the plaza. Barry raised his hand. The boys stopped humming. The campus of the school was almost in complete darkness. There were no lights, just the light from the moon and the stars, which were ample. Barry handed each boy a stack of papers and a jar of rubber cement, which included a little brush attached to the lid. They went about pasting the Revolutionary Press to the walls of the school.

Barry was cognizant of the fact that he was experiencing a kind of satisfaction that had been missing in his life. A sense of fulfillment. He thought of his father, this his knapsack. His father did covert operations for the CIA. Not necessarily like this but perhaps things similar. Yet, what was the point? Was this country even worth saving? Was it possible to make these kids aware of what was really happening, and was that the point? Or was the point just to tweak authority? Barry settled on a combination of both. There was no doubt that the moral imperative was to say something, to do something in the face of such egregious acts of barbarism by his government. Even if it came to nothing at least he had known that he did what he could.

Tommy came over to Barry and whispered in a rasp, "I think I heard someone." Barry looked at Tommy and then into the darkness. He made a whistling sound, two tones, one high and one low. It was supposed to sound like a mourning dove. This was the signal. Geraldo and Davy appeared. Davy said, "What is it?"

"I thought I heard someone," Tommy said as quietly as he could, attempting to hide his fear.

Geraldo looked around. Entertained the idea that they could get caught and wondered how that would sit with his mother, who was already a basket case. "I thought you said that there was no security guard."

"There isn't," Barry said defensively. "I thought."

They heard footsteps, heavy footsteps. Slow yet determined. Out from the shadows stepped Sunshine. "I want to be a revolutionary too."

Chapter Twenty-One

In the car, there was the distinct aroma of teen perspiration. Because the car was so small, the only place for Sunshine to sit was on Tommy's lap in the back seat next to Geraldo. She could feel Tommy's erection jabbing her behind. She didn't mind, and he didn't seem to even notice he had a boner; he was just jabbering away about how, in the morning, the school was going to wake up to find their revolutionary message covering the walls. Wait until Calder sees Duane and all the other jocks and jerks. He kept jabbering with his mouth even as his pecker was jabbing her butt. It made her laugh. It was Davy who told Sunshine to join them that night. She approached him at school to tell him that she thought his Jesus act was kind of cool and that he had balls. Even if he was going to get himself killed just like Jesus did, so, he invited her. He didn't think she would show up, and that's why Davy didn't tell the others. But she did show up. And now they were all riding back at three o'clock in the morning, exhausted and exhilarated.

The exhilaration was soon deflated when, the next morning, upon arriving at school, they found the walls barren. All the Revolutionary Presses had been taken down, only fragments of the paper adhered to the walls. "Fucking fascists!" Barry exclaimed. Tommy let out a wail and let his head slump. He thought he was going to cry until Sunshine took hold of his hand. He turned to her, looked into her pale green eyes, and something shifted in his heart. Geraldo shook his head but, in some ways, felt relief. He knew that he would have been called in; he knew that Magg would accuse and berate him. But then he thought, just because they tore them down doesn't mean he won't get called in. And he was right. First thing, first period, he got pulled out of trig and into Magg's office. It was the same song and dance, the same sanctimonious lecture about Vietnam, but ultimately, Magg had no proof to substantiate anything, so he let Geraldo go.

After school, they stopped at Winchell's. Geraldo trailed behind the others as they went into the donut shop. Maria was cleaning the front window; she could see Geraldo in the parking lot talking to himself. She liked the boy and thought that he was cute. But the way he was muttering to himself she was wondered if he was not a little crazy. He looked up to notice Maria looking at him. He frowned and then smiled and then waved at her. She shyly waved back. When he entered the shop, the others had already gotten their donuts and were sitting at a booth. Geraldo walked to the counter. Maria, finished with the windows, was behind the counter. "Hello," Geraldo said to her. She looked at him. Was he talking to her? Should I say hello or hola? She wondered to herself. If I say hello, then he will think that I speak English, and then he will start talking to me, and I may not understand what he says. But, what the hell. "Hello."

"I was just trying to figure out which donut, you know, Boston cream, glazed, jelly roll, or maybe an apple fritter. Do you, do you have a favorite?"

"Que?"

"Do you have a favorite donut?"

Maria shook her head and felt a little stupid. She thought that maybe she would get into trouble talking to this boy instead of heading to the back, but the other worker was staring absently out the window and wasn't paying any attention to her.

"I was in the other day. With my friends."

"Si. Amigos."

"Yeah. No habla English?"

Maria shook her head. "Poquito."

"That's okay. I knew I should have paid more attention in Spanish class."

"Que?"

Pointing to himself, he said, "My mom is Mexican. But I never learned Spanish very well, and she doesn't speak it much around the house except to say 'quiete la boca!'"

Maria was taken aback. What is this crazy gringo saying to me?

"No. Not you. Mi Madre, to me," Geraldo said and laughed awkwardly. Maria thought that she understood what he was saying. His mother would tell him to shut up in Spanish. She smiled and nodded her head.

"I know. Funny. The only other thing that she says to me is dame un besito."

Now, this boy wants me to give him a kiss. She furrowed her brow.

"Oh. No. I didn't mean for you to. Mi madre to me. She is very nice. A little sad right now. But. Muy bonito. Eres muy bonita."

"Gracias."

Geraldo laughed, and Maria laughed as well. They were not speaking the same language, but they were communicating. Geraldo pointed at the donuts behind the glass.

"Well, what should I have?"

"Chocolate acristalado con espolvoreadas."

"What? Que?"

"Chocolate glazed with sprinkles."

Chapter Twenty-Two

Red blood cells look like donuts, lopsided donuts with asymmetrical holes. White blood cells turn light pink or purple, as a result of using Leishman's stain. Otherwise, you wouldn't see them at all. Carmen sometimes thought of these blood cells as beautiful, like abstract art which she quite liked even though when she would go to museums with Seymour, he disparaged it. He said of Rothko that he did it with a roller brush and that anyone could do it. Carmen thought, if anyone could do it, then why didn't they? When she looked at a Rothko, she felt both sad and somehow comforted. She got lost in it, the cross-section of two or three colors, the balance, the composition; Rothko nailed it, always. And she thought her husband was a bit of a blowhard, not just about abstract art, but also about politics and religion; even though she mostly agreed with him, often his didacticism rubbed her the wrong way, to the extent that she started going to the Unitarian Church, almost out of spite. And much to his disapproval, she took the boys.

Carmen took the slide from the microscope, put it in a tray, and made notes in a spiral notebook. She felt an odd sensation like someone had touched her back with a feather. She turned to find the pathologist standing there. He smiled and said with his charming English accent, "Hello, I'm Clive, the new pathologist." That was true enough. It had been about a month since he came. It seemed longer because he stood out; so suave, so friendly, so well dressed, those turtlenecks; the opposite of the previous pathologist Mr. Conklin, who was decidedly not friendly, had a cigarette forever dangling from the fat lips that protruded from a gangly gray beard. If the women of the lab, and they were all women, the hematologists, were talking too loudly or had the radio on, Conklin would let out a long, dire moan, filled with all kinds of dark tones and vibrations, even from behind the glass it could be felt. It wouldn't necessarily silence the talk or radio, but it might quiet it down. Yet, Carmen had a soft spot for him, he looked like a homeless Santa Claus, and he had kind eyes. He collapsed back there with a kidney on his table. He never came back. She found out later that he had a heart attack and died shortly thereafter.

"Hello," she replied to the pathologist. "I'm Carmen."

"Hello, Carmen. How are things in hematology today?"

"How are things?"

"Yes, bloodwork, you know, red blood cells, white blood cells, platelets, and plasma, examining, counting, analyzing."

"Everything is fine in hematology today. That is, except for *this person*, it looks like an unfortunate case of sickle-cell anemia."

"That is a shame."

"How are things in pathology, Clive?"

"It's so strange, don't you think, how we examine blood and tissue and discern exactly, or as exact as we can, the analysis of what will undoubtedly be a verdict of sorts, or a cause, that either rules some things out or comes to the conclusion that the person, whose blood or tissue it is, has little or no time left to live. Or must live with some terrible disease. And what is odd is how removed we are. For us, it is just a matter of numbers really, and therefore, we are insulated from their tragedy."

"That's how you view it? I view it as we examine his or her blood to be better able to enable the proper course of treatment to ensure recovery. You are kind of dark. You think too much, Clive."

"Yes. True. I have too much time to do that. There, behind the glass, all alone."

"Well, Clive, is there anything else?"

"Uh, no. I guess not. Nice meeting you. Carmen."

Clive smiled and then walked away. Carmen went back to the tray, pulled out another slide, and put it in the microscope. Was that black Englishman flirting with me? Who is this guy? How does he know that I am not married? Although I did take off the ring. Still, nice to be flirted with. When was the last time that happened? Oh yes, at Seymour's office holiday party, his partner, Frank, what an ass. She must have been there, Seymour's secretary. Jane. Could she be more white? Jesus Christ. She was so nervous. I wondered why. She must have given him hell seeing me. Threatened to break it off, which she did, because, for a few weeks, he didn't have so many meetings in the evenings. And he was sulking. No fun. But then they must have started up again; his spirits perked up, and then a few months later, the manila envelope. The fucking manila envelope. I mean Jesus Christ. After all those years, raising the kids and working here, practically supporting the family while he got his business off the ground. And he is cheating on me with God knows how many. This whole sexual liberation thing only works in the men's favor, giving them carte blanche to galivant while women, wives, and mothers are fucked!

She lifted her head and spun around on her stool; she needed air. There was Clive again.

"Excuse me, Carmen."

"Clive."

"I was wondering, if, when you have your lunch, you wouldn't perhaps have it with me in our lovely cafeteria."

Chapter Twenty-Three

The thing with the hamburgers that were served in the cafeteria at the high school is that they came wrapped in a kind of paper foil, and something about the temperature of the thing in the paper foil caused the inside part of the bun to liquefy so that when you bit into the burger you were biting into something soggy, and if you chose to lift the bun to apply ketchup to the burger you were exposed to a strange grayish blob, this would more than likely put one off their appetite. Tommy carried one of these burgers on his plastic tray, along with a paper plate of tater tots and a carton of milk. He saw Sunshine and sat down next to her. He looked at her and smiled. He looked down at his tray and said, "I can't eat this."

"I can't blame you," she said, opening a brown paper bag and extracting a handful of cherries. She put one in her mouth between her teeth and then pulled the stem from it as if she were removing the pin from a hand grenade. She chewed the cherry purposefully and then spat the pit into a cardboard paper cup. "Want some cherries?" she said to Tommy. He nodded, and she pushed the bag towards him.

"Where is everybody?" Sunshine asked and then spat a pit, missing the cup entirely."

"Geraldo and Davy are in the band room, and Barry went to take the Revolutionary Press to the copy store. So glad we made the grammatical corrections that we missed on the first run."

"How many copies?"

"Three thousand kids. Three thousand lockers."

"We are going to put one in every locker?"

"That's the plan."

"It will take all night."

"Yep."

Sunshine spat a cherry pit at Tommy, hitting him in the cheek. He rubbed the spot. "That kind of hurt."

"So," Sunshine said, "What are you anyway?"

"What do you mean?"

"Are you queer or something?"

"Why do you ask?"

"Something about you. Plus, you wear mascara and lip gloss."

"I guess, or something."

"Mmm. I get it. Have you ever had a martini?"

Chapter Twenty-Four

Clive came by Carmen's station at noon, and they walked over to the cafeteria together. Carmen was thinking about what the others would be saying about her going to lunch with Clive. It amused her, but that was about all. She and Clive made perfunctory talk about the weather. How nice it was, especially compared to London. They sat across from each other. Their trays looked remarkably similar. Salad with thousand island dressing, fruit cocktail, cottage cheese, and a cheese sandwich on whole wheat bread. Clive was drinking pineapple juice and Carmen tomato juice; that's where the difference was. "When were you last in London?" Carmen asked obligingly.

"Oh, last summer. I try to get back once a year."

"And how do you like it here, at Los Alamitos?"

"Very much. I was working at Hollywood Presbyterian Medical Center before."

"Sounds glamorous. The organs of the rich and famous."

"Yes. Sometimes. But it was so far from where I live, and the traffic was terrible every day. I practically lived in my car."

"Do you miss England?"

"Oh, sometimes. Not really. What about you? Are you a native? Of California?"

"I was born in Arizona. Then, after college, I lived in San Francisco for a while, which was nice, and then came back to Arizona to be with my dad; he was kind of sad, empty nest and all. That's where I met my husband. And then we moved to

Southern California, had two children, and after twenty years, he just left me."

"I'm sorry. Oh, my goodness. I'm sorry." Clive happened to have a perfectly folded hankie in his back pocket, which he procured and presented to Carmen, who took it from him, wiped her eyes, and blew her nose.

"I'm sorry," she said, handing the hankie back to Clive. "Well, there's my life story!" she said, barely suppressing an almost maniacal laugh.

"So far, Carmen. So far."

Chapter Twenty-Five

Agiant boom box that Sunshine got for Christmas the year before sat on the glass top of a white iron table in her backyard. Elevating from a hole at the center of the table was a pole that featured an aqua-blue umbrella with bulbous bright red cherries painted on the inside of the canopy. The "Ghetto Blaster" was not given to her by her parents, but she had bought herself with the money that they had given her. They would have hated it if they heard the Buzzcocks stream forth from the large vibrating speakers, "Orgasm Addict."

> *Well, you tried it just for once*
> *Found it all right for kicks*
> *But now you found out*
> *That it's a habit that sticks*
> *And you're an orgasm addict*
> *You're an orgasm addict*

Tommy couldn't believe there was a song that described his particular predicament. He felt that not only did Sunshine read his mind, but she was perhaps going through the same things. They sat on the chaise lounges sipping martinis, which, to Tommy, tasted almost like water. Compared to the other times he had drank from his mother's liquor cabinet, from the brown liquids, which were strong and almost impossible to get down, this was unbelievably smooth and refreshing. He could see why Sunshine liked them so. They made you feel good. They made you feel settled. They made you feel in control of your destiny.

"You like the martini?" Sunshine asked Tommy, hoping that he would, hoping that he would like the thing that made her so very happy.

"I think that it is perhaps the greatest thing that I have ever drunk, or drank, or drinkened."

"I think you're getting drunkened."

She reached over to the side table and, from the tumbler, refilled both of their glasses. The sun was a head above the horizon, creating that wonderful orange haze of waning sunlight and smog. Tommy couldn't remember the last time he was at another kid's house and certainly never one as nice as this. The verdant neon grass cut tightly like the gardeners used a scalpel, and the hedges and flowers manicured so precisely they looked like still life, and the swimming pool that glistened like it was illuminated by something other worldly. It was all so perfect. And yet, there was something missing.

"Where are your parents?" Tommy asked.

"They don't get home until late. They both work in Los Angeles. They keep saying that we should move there, that the commute is killing them, but then they say it is not a 'good time.' Too busy. They are hardly ever here. Except on the weekends. But not even then, sometimes."

Tommy pointed to a large black disc elevating above ground in the corner of the yard. "What's that?"

Sunshine followed his finger. "That's a trampoline."

"A trampoline!?"

"Yeah. My parents got it for me. Said I needed to lighten up."

"Do you like it?"

"I've never been on it."

Acquiescing to Tommy's insistence, Sunshine agreed to try the trampoline. They took off their shoes and socks and got on. They bounced up and down in sync, holding hands. Sunshine dropped her dour demeanor and smiled intently at Tommy. He had wanted someone to notice him, and she did, and more importantly, she was cool. Almost too cool. She was pretty when she was dour, and she is pretty now. Tommy thought of that song in West Side Story: *I feel pretty, oh so pretty, I feel pretty and witty and bright. And I pity any girl who isn't me tonight.* Not quite "Orgasm Addict," but still, he loved the song and the musical. In fact, he loved almost all musicals. From Jesus Christ Superstar to his namesake Tommy to the great big MGM technicolor ones, Oklahoma, Seven Brides, and State Fair, he didn't care how hokey. Whenever they were on Television, he insisted they watch. He started humming the song as they bounced. Sunshine picked up on the melody and started singing the song. Tommy joined in at the second verse. *I feel charming, oh so charming; it's alarming how charming I feel. And so pretty that I can hardly believe that I'm real.* They let go of each other and traded the next few lines, bouncing out of sync. Sunshine: *See the pretty girl in the mirror there.* Tommy: *Who can that attractive girl be?* Sunshine: *Such a pretty face.* Tommy: *Such a pretty dress.* Sunshine: *Such a pretty smile.* Together: *Such a pretty me!* And they fell down on the trampoline laughing.

"Let's go swimming in the swimming pool," Tommy shouted.

Sunshine got serious. "No. Let's not."

"Why not?"

"Just don't want to."

"Come on!"

"You don't have a swimsuit."

"Let's go skinny dipping."

"No way."

Sunshine walked over to the chaise lounges with Tommy following her. She finished the liquid in her glass and poured herself more martini. Tommy did the same and then said, "What's wrong?" Sunshine and Tommy sat down. "Do you really want to go skinny dipping?" Sunshine asked. Tommy thought about it. He had just blurted it out before, but now confronted with the possibility of taking off all of his clothing and jumping in the pool, he felt inhibited. But just for a few seconds. "Yeah, sure!" Tommy stood up and took off his shirt and then his pants, and then his tighty whities. Sunshine looked at him. His body had very little hair, but his penis was kind of big. Bigger than she would have thought. "Your turn," he said, pointing at Sunshine. She stood up and unbuttoned her blouse; she wore a small black padded bra. She took off her skirt, and now she stood in a bra and panties. "Go ahead," Tommy said. She undid her bra, and Tommy noticed she was pretty flat-chested, but he didn't care. Then she pulled down her panties, revealing a perfectly pink penis with a crown of auburn pubic hair.

Chapter Twenty-Six

April's room was above the garage; it had a separate entrance. Her father had it built in her senior year of high school in the hopes that she would go to college nearby and still live at home. He had also built a study in the backyard to work on his memoirs and a sun porch off the back for his wife. It was the summer of renovations. Also, the summer that April and Charles started having sex, firstly on the beach, then in his car, a 1965 Dodge Dart that he had indirectly inherited from his grandparents. When her room was completed, they would meet there. April's mom liked Charles but had her qualms. He was weird; it could not be denied. With his eccentric Einstein hair and distinctive mannerisms, but since she was originally from New York City and had lived there through high school, his personality type was familiar to her, the aspiring intellectual. Pretentious at times but earnest. She missed New York City and so she liked Charles. April's father was mostly ambivalent in regard to Charles admitting that he didn't know quite what to make of him; that is when he gave it any thought.

April was an undergraduate at UC Irvine majoring in Economics. She was working on a paper on Keynesian macroeconomics. She was listening to Gabor Szabo on her turntable when there was a knock on her door. It was Charles. He entered and dramatically fell on her bed. "Charles, what are you doing here?"

"I don't know. I wanted to see you. I wanted to see your room. I wanted to see your bed. I wanted to see your face."

"What about your classes?"

“I’m sick of school. I’m sick of everything.”

Charles unzipped his black leather jacket and pulled from an inside pocket a silver flask. It was his father’s. He found it in the back of the liquor cabinet when he was home for Thanksgiving. He unscrewed the cap, took a mouthful of gin, and then held it out to April. “Want some?”

“Are you crazy? I have to finish my term paper. And so do you, from what you told me on the phone.”

“Let’s go to the beach and get drunk.”

“No.” She sat down on the bed next to Charles. He held out the flask to her again. She took it this time, put it to her lips, had a little sip, grimaced, and then handed it back to Charles, who took another draw, screwed the lid back on, and then put it back into his pocket. He stood up, walked over to her desk, and looked at her typewriter. “Well, how is old John Maynard Keynes?”

“No longer the shining star.”

“What is this shit?” Charles picked up a book next to April’s typewriter, Milton Friedman’s ‘Capitalism and Freedom.’

“Friedman is the architect of Reaganomics. So, they say. Times have changed. Old Keynes has fallen out of favor. Nobody wants to hear that ‘expectations involving an uncertain future affect aggregate demand decision.”

“Meanwhile, we are in the biggest recession since the Great Depression. Fuck Milton Friedman.”

“Yes, well, that’s debatable. I’m no fan of Freidman. But things have changed since Keynes’ time and his theories are short on mathematical models. Still, Reagan’s ‘trickle down voodoo economics’ is a mirage, an excuse for more wealth disparity.”

"You mean the consolidation of wealth. Is that what you're going to put into your paper? The part about voodoo economics?"

"I wish."

Charles sat down next to April and rested his head against her breasts.

"Have you spoken with your father yet?" April asked, patting his hair.

"My father? Why would I do that?"

"You'll have too eventually. You know, it was terrible what he did, but he's a human being, and humans, well they're flawed. Especially men. No offense. It's how you're churned out. As Keynes said, 'Markets are moved by animal spirits, and not by reason.' You should return his calls."

"How would you feel? If your father was having an affair and then left your mother without warning. He always acted as if he was so morally superior to everyone."

"My father would never do that. He's not like that. But. I guess I would forgive him."

"You're nicer than me."

"You're nice enough."

"Thanks."

Charles could hear April's heartbeat. He was thinking how steady the beat was and how he had never listened to someone's heartbeat before. Were they all like this? The thing of it, the machine of it, powering the person whose flesh he had known, powering the brain he respected, more than any person he had ever known. All the power, all of her beauty, was a result of this contraption. He didn't believe in god. Or did he? Not god, but something. How else is this? His father was an atheist, and look at him, a bloody bastard. Maybe his own thinking was all wrong. Maybe he ruled out too much and made too many blanket pronunciations. Yet, rational thought was the foundation for everything. Everything that mattered to him. Even his love for April was rational. She was beautiful and smart, and she was attracted to him. That was maybe the most attractive thing about her that she was attracted to him. She was so beautiful and lovely and kind; it made one think that perhaps there was some kind of divine force. You just can't know, and what you can't know doesn't exist. God, she smelled good, and her breasts against the side of his face were so soft. The heartbeat. He felt that since he was there, in her bedroom, he should try to make love to her. He raised himself and turned to face her.

"You're crying."

"I am?"

She took his face in her hands, smiled lovingly, and kissed him.

Chapter Twenty-Seven

Tommy kept his head still, but his mind was moving fast. Sunshine was using a special technique that she invented using hair spray and a hardcover book to make his long brown hair go up and back like a cantilever. With expertise, she applied angel wings to his eyes with her mother's eyeliner pencil. Tommy searched in Sunshine's eyes, searched for the answer, for the question, for the solution. She was a girl; he had no doubt. She was a girl, but she had a penis. He thought, *I am a boy*, but not just because I have a penis. There was more to it. Yet Sunshine seemed pretty sure of herself; even if she had a penis, she seemed very confident regarding *her* identity. Sunshine brushed purple glitter eyeshadow on Tommy's eyelids. She stopped, stepped back, and said, "There. Why don't you look." Tommy stood up and went to the mirror above the dresser next to Sunshine's bed. He was amazed. He looked like David Bowie. He turned around, Sunshine threw her arms around him, and they kissed. Tommy lost his balance, and they fell onto the bed. They lay next to each other like otters holding hands.

Sunshine got up, went over to the Philco record player that she had taken from her father's study, and put on The Stooges 'No Fun.' She twirled around and around until she fell onto the bed and right on top of Tommy. She put her hand on his stiff member. "Do you always have an erection?" He nodded. "Do you want me to touch it?" He nodded again. She put her hand on his pants and then rubbed it. "Does that feel good?" He nodded. He thought he was going to cry. It felt so good. The other thing, the thing that he did when he was by himself, kind of felt better, in some ways, but this felt more than just physically good; it felt good to be there, and it felt good in his chest and in his eyes. He let out a moan and ejaculated. It lasted almost a whole minute.

"Do you have a change of underwear?"

"I have panties."

"Yes. It's okay. I mean, no, that's alright. I was wondering. What is the deal with you?"

Sunshine thought, here we go, he can't comprehend; how could he comprehend something I can't fully comprehend? "What do you mean?"

"You know."

"No, I don't know."

He took her hand in his. "You're a girl. The best girl I have ever known, but you know, you have a dick."

"Oh, that. Well, yeah. Don't remind me."

"Do you wish that you didn't have it?"

She laughed. "Yes. Very much."

"Oh." Tommy laughed, too. "Isn't it funny?"

"What?"

"All of it. Sexuality. Not just humans but animals, insects, all of it. The Praying Mantis decapitates its male lover during sex, the male bee's dick falls off during sex, the male cat has these needles on his dick, and when he pulls out, it is excruciating for the female, and more. Humans are weird, but maybe not the weirdest."

"I don't feel weird. I feel normal. It's the whole world that seems weird to me."

"Before I met you, I thought that I was going to lose my mind. I really did. I didn't know what was going to happen, but

I knew that something bad was going to happen, something bad, that I was this rubber band being pulled, and I was going to snap, you know. But being with you makes me feel as if there is some logic to why I am the way I am."

"I love the way you are."

"You do?"

"Yes. Do you love me?"

"I love you. And not in a fake Hollywood kind of way. I love you because you are the most beautiful and interesting person I have ever known."

"Oh wow. Really?"

"Yes. I'm not lying." Tommy took his hand back and put his head down.

"Then what's wrong? You look sad."

He stood up, walked a few paces, and then turned to face her. "There is something that I have to tell you. I have to tell someone. I have been carrying it around for over a month now, and it has been driving me crazy."

"What is it?"

"I don't know if I should be embarrassed or proud of myself or what. I don't know. But, you see, I found this book about Yoga in my father's library, and I was reading it; it's called The Yoga System and Relief from Tension. Sounds good, right? And it shows you all of these positions and postures and it helps you get really relaxed and flexible. Really flexible. And. It happened, and now it has taken over my life."

"What the hell is it?"

"I can suck my own cock."

"What! You're kidding?"

"No, I'm not. And I can't stop. It's all I do when I can and all I think about. That is until I met you, and we started hanging out. And now I don't want to do it anymore. But I don't think I'll be able to stop."

Sunshine wasn't sure what to think. If they started going together, would it be like he was cheating on her if he gave himself a blowjob? Yet it wasn't really different from masturbation. So, it was fine. And yes, kind of ingenious. Just like Tommy to be smarter than everyone else, so smart that he figures out how to pleasure himself in the most sensual way. She tried to picture it. Tommy sitting with his legs crossed, naked, and then stretching over and taking his member in his mouth. The image was too much, too much to take in. She put her hand to her eyes and, with her thumb and forefinger, pushed down hard on either eye as if the pressure could help her make sense of it all and help her keep it in. She really tried to hold it in, but she could not. She burst out laughing. Laughing hysterically.

Chapter Twenty-Eight

Because of Jim Morrison, he read Nietzsche; because of George Harrison, he read everything he could find on Hinduism, Buddhism, and meditation; because of Black Sabbath, he read Anton LeVay; because of The Clash, he read Karl Marx; because of Bob Dylan he read The Beats, and when Dylan became a born-again Christian, he read the bible; starting with the Old Testament and then the New. He was amazed at what he read. The language in the Old Testament was beautiful, poetic, almost pornographic, and terribly violent in places, but mostly, it espoused a kind of deadly and malevolent intolerance. The New Testament ran contrary; it was all about Jesus, Jesus' apocryphal message, Jesus and the Romans, Jesus and the Jews, Jesus and the impoverished. He never read the two books of the bible in their entirety; he sped read them, gleaning this and that, and still, it took him the whole summer. He wanted to get a feel for it, and he knew, he just knew, that he wanted to be like Jesus. He wanted to look like him, he wanted to talk like him, he wanted a chick to wash his feet with her hair, and he wanted to be worshiped like him. He even wanted to be crucified like him.

He didn't go so far as to believe that Jesus was the son of god or that he had died for our sins or any of that. In fact, he thought of him as more mythic than divine. It was D.H. Lawrence's short novel *The Man Who Died* he thought might have best captured the story of Christ's crucifixion. "They took me down too soon," Jesus says. It is not three days, but almost immediately when he comes to and gets the hell out of dodge. His followers hope that he will resume his previous role as savior, but he says, "No, thank you." PTSD is real. He leaves town and runs into the Egyptian pagan goddess Isis, and they have sex. He hopes that she will do her thing and help him make it to an afterlife. The whole point of the story is that life is enough and that there is no need for a higher authority.

Jesus is a commie, punk rock, narcissistic rockstar. He is not afraid of the Romans. He castigates the rich. He harangues the crowds gathered to hear him speak. He ridicules his followers. He has his groupies, female and male. He likes prostitutes and outsiders. He turns water into wine. He brings eyesight back to the blind, and he is hated, with a kind of rich, unstable hatred, hated by his own people, hated by the Romans, almost universally hated. Davy liked that most about Jesus.

He strummed his guitar, his father's old black with silver sparkled Danelectro electric. These guitars were considered maybe the cheapest guitars ever made. The bodies were made of Masonite board, lipstick tubes served as pickups, and the edge of the body was wrapped up in white Naugahyde tape. Jimmy Page used one on *When the Levee Breaks*. Davy strummed the chords to Lou Reed's song *Jesus* and sang in his sweet falsetto the words, *Jesus help me find my proper place.* He wondered if his voice sounded as good to others as it did to himself. Was his voice good enough to get the attention of girls? Wasn't all of this to get the attention of girls? Not just any girls, but cool girls, of which there weren't too many in his school. Sunshine was cool, but obviously, she liked Tommy. That was okay; they seemed right for each other, and he was glad that he had a hand in bringing them together. Still, he wanted a girl, and it was kind of killing him.

He got out his baby blue Panasonic tape recorder. He found a cassette tape of Queen. He put some scotch tape over the punched-in tabs on the top corners of the cassette so that he could record over it. He put it in the machine and pressed the red record button. He strummed and sang *Jesus*. He sang the whole song, pressed stop, then rewind, and then pressed play. What came out of the little six-inch speaker was a voice that he barely recognized. It didn't sound like himself. Not the way he heard himself. It sounded like an actual recording, like an actual rock and roll singer. It sounded as if he had reinvented himself, and he knew that, as a result, everything had changed. He knew that with this voice, he was, for the very first time, going to get laid.

Chapter Twenty-Nine

Geraldo hated Catcher in the Rye. What an arrogant idiot Holden Caufield was. The first-person narration was annoying and not believable. His voice was grating; Geraldo could hear it in his head. It squeaked. Morbid curiosity. Morbid curiosity was the only reason he was reading it. That and his brother told him that it was a "must-reading," along with Clockwork Orange and Death On the Installment Plan. Mark David Chapman had a copy of Catcher in his coat pocket when he shot and killed John Lennon. The disaffected youth syndrome, or what have you, was a crock. You can't blame the corrupt conditions of the world for your own unhappiness. This is what Geraldo felt, and he felt that John Lennon symbolized action, action over simply bemoaning the state of things. It is true that the powers that be seemed to be without any moral center, but that is abstract, not relatable. Chapman killed Lennon because Lennon was famous because he was a phony because he thought that Holden Caufield would have done the same. Chapman killed Lennon because he was insane. He took the book and tossed it in the green metal wastebasket in the corner of his room. "Fuck that!"

"Fuck what?" Carmen said as she entered Geraldo's room.

"Oh. Sorry, mom."

She sat down on his bed. "What has got you so upset?"

"Oh, nothing," He said. Carmen looked at her son with one arched eyebrow; he remembered that he was going to try to be better at communicating, "Oh, that stupid book Catcher in the Rye."

"Why is it so stupid."

"The protagonist is annoying. You know the guy who killed John Lennon was reading it when he shot him."

"So was the guy who tried to kill Reagan."

"Really?"

"That's what it said in the newspaper."

"What is up with that book? Does it have some kind of magical power that makes you need to kill people if you read it?" Geraldo lamented.

"I read it, and I didn't want to kill anyone. I also didn't much care for it. But I did like one of his other books, Franny and Zooey. I could relate to that one. It is about a young woman in college looking to find spiritual meaning and how prayer and meditation can help. It also speaks to how everyone needs love, the cruel and the kind alike."

"That sounds better."

"Good to remember. I think I have lost touch with those ideas of late. So, tell me, how was school today? Did you talk to your friend?"

For a few seconds, Geraldo was confused. Which friend? He didn't have any friends for so long and now he had a few. "Friend? Oh, my friend. Yes, I did. I kind of did what you suggested."

"And?"

"And we are going out."

"On a date?"

"I guess so."

"Whoa. Well, you see, there you go. And you'll never guess what, I have a date too."

"You have a date? With who?"

"Oh, just someone from work. No big deal, but I thought I would at least try to have fun. But, listen, your father wants to see you this weekend."

"No way."

"Well. I think you should. He's going to take you to lunch. It'll be alright. You have to see him sometime. Okay?"

"Do I have to?"

"You don't *have* to. But I think you should. Okay?"

"Okay. But mom."

"Yeah?"

"I hate him. I really, really hate him."

"No, you don't. But thanks for saying so."

Chapter Thirty

Maria stood on the corner of Moody and Bell, waiting for Geraldo. She was humming the Blondie song *The Tide is High*, watching the busy Friday evening traffic, thinking how strange it was that she was here in California, so far from her home, so far from the mayhem and violence that was decimating her country of origin. She was only fifteen years old, but she had known death; she had experienced coming face to face with it in the form of bullets ripping through her home, missing her by inches, but not her mother, not her sisters. She had not time to grieve. Only time to flee, and she was lucky not only to be alive but to have an uncle who brought her with him and his comrades on the long, arduous journey, first by an old leaky schooner from Guatemala City to Mazatlán, then in the back of a pickup truck to Nogales and then to Tijuana. The whole trip was herself and nine young men who all had stories, who all knew how to tell a story. That's what they did to pass the time. They told heartbreaking stories. And yet they were always kind of funny, these stories. They got through the border in the cover of darkness and were met by people who helped get her and her uncle to family in Cypress. She was ushered into the job at Winchell's. No questions asked. Her uncle went to work on the oil rigs outside of San Pedro.

The whole of her past was a blur. What had happened? Was it really real? Her mother, not just a memory, not just a mother. Not just another death in a never-ending war. Was that real? Memory was just a contrivance, her past populated by mere phantoms who, with every passing day, fade. Now, here in the peaceful dusk of Orange County, waiting for a clean, sweet boy. What did he want? What did it matter? He was nice and had mist in his eyes. These Americans have everything, and they don't know it; they don't appreciate it. She envied them that. She watched them come into the donut store, the boys, the same age as the ones who she traveled with; she watched them with their lanky movements, their hands bringing from pockets, crumpled dollar bills, coins, slapped on the counter, and then from a white paper bag pulling out the sweet thing, holding the sweet thing in their hands, putting the sweet thing in their mouth, licking their fingers for the residue of the sweet thing.

Geraldo was whistling the Beatles song Ob-la-di, Ob-la-da. He felt his armpits moisten. It made him laugh. Not usually one to use deodorant now of all times. It might have been a good idea. He is going to have B.O. on his very first date with a girl. Sure, she wasn't one of the girls from school. Not they would go out with him anyway. Except for Risa Rose Cooley. Freshman year in high school. She liked Geraldo. She always wanted to spend time with him, and he liked her. She was funny and played saxophone and was very pretty. At least, that's what everyone said. How *foxy* she was. Tall, blonde, always the peeling pinkish-red tip of her nose from spending so much time at the beach. Nobody could believe that she wanted to hang out with Geraldo. *He* couldn't believe it. They would go to the park after school and skate around or go to Tastee-Freez for cones. When they said goodbye, she would put her arms around him, pull him close, and then rub her nose on his. Only when he saw her with her boyfriend, some surfer dude, did it make sense to him. He was her toy. He didn't hold it against her, but he didn't want to spend so much time with her anymore. And truth be told, even though everyone said she was so hot, he didn't feel any attraction to her.

But Maria, the first time he saw her, he thought she was the most beautiful girl he had ever seen. It wasn't just that she was beautiful, with her long dark hair and sanguine eyes, tawny skin, delicate nose splattered with dark brown freckles, whimsical mouth, pert breasts and sharp shoulders and fleshy bottom and thin legs, he noticed all of that, and it made an impression, made his heart race, but it was her sense of humor, her confidence, her apparent attraction to him and curiosity about him which were the things that made it. This was their story, and they had begun writing it together. But it was him; he was the one to put it in motion. He was proud of himself for this.

He saw her on the corner in her yellow, orange, and gold sundress. There is this thing that happens when you see someone, and they don't know that you are looking at them; you are catching them in a private movement, almost like you are infringing on their privacy, like one of those Degas paintings that Geraldo saw when his art class took a field trip to the Norton Simon Museum. Degas spying on a ballerina as she worked out. Catching her unawares. Geraldo wanted to stop, maybe hide behind a bush, and just watch Maria. She was lost in thought. She held part of her dress and made it slowly sway back and forth. The fading light of the sun setting behind the mall backlit her; she was illuminated by the orange haze, and as he got closer to her, she became even more of an idea, an idea of what he thought was the thing that made two people come together, the idea of it as it was in reality, not in a book or in a movie, but in reality. She was real, and she had agreed to meet him even though they were perfect strangers because of this very idea.

When Geraldo was ten feet away, he shouted, "Hola!"

Maria came out of her daydream, saw Geraldo, and smiled, "Hola," she said back to him as he stepped into her space. "Hello."

"Como estas?"

"I am good. Thank you. How are you?" she asked him.

"I'm good. I'm glad it's Friday."

"Thank god," Maria said.

"Why? You have the weekend off?"

"Weekend off? Oh no. I have work. Donuts."

"Then why, thank god?"

"The song," she sang, "Thank God it's Friday."

"Oh yeah. The song. I hate disco. But. You have a pretty voice."

"Gracias. Thank you."

They started walking side by side. They hadn't a plan, at least a stated one, but they walked away from the sun; that was a plan in and of itself. He was trying to think what it was that she smelled like. It was so familiar; it was on the tip of his mind. Cocoanut. Something cocoanut. It didn't matter. It smelled nice. They stopped at a light. Geraldo thought about her singing that song. So cute. It made him laugh. He looked at her. "That was funny."

"Funny?"

He sang, "Thank God it's Friday."

She smiled, not knowing for certain if he was making fun of her.

"My father is an atheist."

"Atheist?" she said, confused by the word and by the seemingly abrupt change in the direction of the conversation.

"He does not believe in a god to thank."

"Oh. I see. Do you? Do you believe in a god?"

"Well, Marx says religion is the opiate of the masses. And surely that's true. Just look at that disgusting Crystal Cathedral. But a god? Is there a god? I don't know. How about you?"

"I don't know too."

They walked past the Safeway. He wondered what Barry and Tommy were doing. Maybe they should go there. That was a stupid idea. The whole point was to be with her. To get to know her. Here he was having a conversation in his head when he should be having a conversation with her. He just couldn't think of what to say. This happened to him; what made his mother angry at times was this inability to speak. To even come up with something to say to another person. God, it was aggravating.

"Are you hungry?" Maria asked him.

"Yes! Great idea! Yes. Let's go get something to eat. Thank you. Gracias"

"No problem. Donde esta?"

"The Copper Penny. Come with me, and I will take you to one of the worst diners in all of America. I don't know why, but almost all of the food there is so bad. Comida mala. How can you mess up diner food?"

"Then why we go?"

"Ah, not all of the food. The apple pie, the apple pie is to die for."

"To die for?"

"Yes!"

Chapter Thirty-One

Isn't it a lovely evening? Carmen said to herself. And it was. It certainly was a lovely evening. Did I put on too much perfume? Well, nothing to be done about it now. Besides, who doesn't like Chanel No. 5? God, why did I put that on? Seymour bought it for me on our anniversary last August. Well, I can't keep track of everything that is associated with my failed marriage. Failed marriage. Jesus. That is awful. That is an awful way to put it, Carmen. Well, that's what it is. Might as well face up to the facts. And now what? Divorce, of course. Divorce court. Division of property. What did he mean by waiting until Geraldo goes to college to sell the house? I'm not selling the house. He can't make me sell the house. Or can he? I have to get a lawyer. Maybe I can ask Phyllis in the lab who she used. I need a good one. I want to make Seymour pay.

Clive pulled up in his copper 1978 Mercedes Benz 380. He was going to beep his horn, but that was the one thing about this car that he didn't much care for, the horn. It had a high pitch, slightly comical sound. Didn't match the classiness of the car. Almost made him not buy the car, which he got second hand from the dealer with only thirty thousand miles on it. Still quite expensive, and the subsequent repairs, but now it was running like a top. After all, it was a Mercedes. Instead, he pulled up to the curb and rolled down his window. "Carmen. Hello." She turned towards Clive and his car. He took a deep breath, she was radiant. She looked at him quizzically, barely remembering who he was and what she was doing. But it all came back to her. She smiled and walked towards the car. Clive put the car in park, got out, went around, and opened the door for her.

They drove along, exchanging pleasantries, the weather, and such. He got on the Pacific Coast Highway and headed south. "Where are you taking me, Clive?"

"That is a surprise."

"You're not a serial killer? Lots of that going around."

"Now, if I were a serial killer, would I tell you?"

"No. I guess not. Not at this point."

He laughed heartily. She chuckled a little. "You're right," he said. "Does seem to be a lot of that going around."

"Yes, and the newspapers seem to give them all that free publicity."

"And the names: The Hillside Strangler, The Golden State Killer, The Zodiac…"

"The Manson Family."

"A family that slays together stays together."

"Clive. Did anyone ever tell you that you have a wicked sense of humor?"

"Did anyone ever tell you that you are incredibly beautiful?"

"Not for a while. Not for a long while."

Chapter Thirty-Two

On the paper placemat was an image of an American penny and Abraham Lincoln's iconic profile. The plate containing an apple pie ala mode, the exact same circumference as Abraham Lincoln's profile, was placed before Maria rather brusquely by the waitress which made Geraldo and Maria laugh. Geraldo looked at Maria expectantly. Maria looked at Geraldo and felt oddly inhibited. She felt pressure to find this piece of pie the best that she ever tasted. That wouldn't be difficult because she hadn't had any apple pie. There were many Guatemalan desserts that she loved, champurrados, arroz con leche, torrejas, bunuelos, but somehow, the American desserts had an aftertaste that she didn't much care for. Something about the sugar, too much, and the taste of artificiality. Nevertheless, she had to try it and do her best to act as if she enjoyed it. She lifted her fork and took a bite. It was okay, in fact, pretty good. She took another bite and then put her fork down. Geraldo was staring at her with a very serious expression; it was unnerving her.

"What you looking at?"

"You're really pretty," he said.

"Why you say like that?"

"Like what?

"Um. You're really pretty. You do not smile."

"I smile. Sometimes."

"I never see."

Geraldo tried to smile. It was awkward and contrived.

"You no have to. If you no want to. Maybe, um, you no happy."

"I'm happy."

"You no have to be happy."

"I'm happy to be here with you."

"Me too."

"So, what do you think?"

"Think?"

"The pie."

"Muy bueno."

For some inexplicable reason, it was of great importance to him that she seemed to enjoy the pie. The tightness in his chest relaxed. There was still a tightness, a feeling like perhaps he needed to put a brown paper bag over his head. He leaned over the table and, with his fork, took a bite of her pie. Not quite as great as he remembered. Why did he think that this was the best slice of pie he had ever had? When did he have it last? Oh yes, with his brother. What was different was that he had his first cup of coffee with it.

"Would you like a cup of coffee?"

Maria thought about it. A cup of coffee sounded like the best thing in the world.

"Yes. Thank you."

After the waitress brought the two cups of coffee Geraldo picked up a pod out of a little jar next to the plastic flowers and poured cream into his coffee. He looked to Maria, who nodded. He opened up one for her and poured it into her cup. They both took a sip and then made a face. He grabbed the jar of white sugar and poured sugar into hers and then his. They both took spoons and stirred. The coffee was both bitter and sweet and now, almost good.

Geraldo, looking at Maria, a real live girl sitting across from him. He tried to think of something to say. "How do you like America? A lot different from Mexico?"

"I am not from Mexico."

"No?"

"I am from Guatemala."

He talked slowly because he wanted Maria to understand what he was saying. "Oh. Yeah. I have been reading about what has happened there."

"Yes. Many very bad things happened."

"I read about the death squads."

"Yes. Escuadrón de la Muerte."

"Is your mother and father here too?"

"They were of the land. Farmers. From Zacapa. Means river of grass. They are no longer living. All are gone, except mi hermano. And he is hiding."

"Oh. I'm so sorry. That's just awful."

"People come into your life, and then they go."

"It's all because of this country. The C.I.A. They're the ones who put Osorio and his death squads in power. All for the sake of United Fruit."

"You know mucho of my country."

"Me and my friends. We are revolutionaries. We are communists."

"Que? You are a revolutionary?"

"Yes."

"You are a communist?"

"Yes!"

Maria started to laugh. A little at first, but then she got louder and louder and louder with it. She had to hold her belly as water leaked from her eyes.

"What's so funny?"

"I am sorry. I am sorry. If you say, you are a communist. In Guatemala, they will kill you, and they will kill you and your whole family."

"Well. I am!"

Maria's laughter subsided, and then getting more serious, though a bit incredulous, she asked, "Really? You are, you are a, a...?"

Geraldo slammed his fist on the table and shouted, "I AM A COMMUNIST REVOLUTIONARY!"

Everyone in the restaurant turned to look at him.

Chapter Thirty-Three

The restaurant was nice with the requisite white tablecloths, candles in red sterno jars, waiters in white button-up shirts, black half jackets, and black bow ties. It smelled like clams and tomatoes and garlic and broth. There was an old fellow walking from table to table with a pronounced limp holding an accordion, playing songs like *Mona Lisa* and *Misty*. Clive and Carmen had a table next to a wall-length window that overlooked the ocean. The stars, slightly muted by fog and a moon almost full, hung like a lost kite high above the water, illuminating the dark ocean and the oil derricks on the horizon.

Carmen was surprised that Clive had taken her all the way to San Pedro, but the restaurant was quite lovely and had a wonderful, if not fulsome, romantic ambiance. "This is nice. I have to admit, I was wondering where you were taking me. Not that I thought you were a serial killer. Though I didn't rule it out."

"One of my favorite restaurants. And I think worth the drive."

"I love the ocean. I grew up in the desert, so I find it very relaxing. The sound of the waves breaking, the smell of the salt water, and the way the sun slowly descends behind the horizon," she said, seeing if Clive would pick up on her bullshitting.

He made a big sigh and said, "That's beautiful. I like it too. I like you too, Carmen. I like you very much."

He did seem sincere. However, something was not right with him. Even pathological. Afterall, he was a pathologist. She smiled, feeling the Chianti, and said, "Thanks. That's nice to hear. Especially right now." And it was. It was nice to hear.

"It's been hard?

"Yeah. It's been hard. I just can't fathom it." Carmen said, feeling herself opening up against her will. "You never think that you'll join the club, you know. The divorce club. And then the lies, the betrayal. Hurts much more than you would have thought it would. You love a person, you know, for what they are or for who you think they are, but then it turns out they were somebody else entirely."

"I guess you can just never know somebody."

"That's a sad thought."

"Well, you certainly deserve better."

"Thanks, Clive."

"The seafood here is marvelous. Are you hungry?"

"I'm starving."

*

They drank a bottle and half of chianti with dinner which was delicious even if it was way the hell in San Pedro. As they drove along the Pacific Coast Highway, listening to Oscar Peterson on the car stereo, Carmen was feeling imbued with a kind of reasonable interior convection. She was ready for anything and wondered what would come of this date and what this man might try when the car was parked in front of her nice suburban home. She certainly was not going to invite him in. When they got to her block, he pulled the car over, put the car in park, and turned off the engine. Carmen looked at Clive, who smiled nervously; she looked down and then out the window. She noticed that the lawn was looking quite unruly. Geraldo

108

hadn't mowed it in weeks. God, she hated to nag him, what with those monumental sighs, but what could she do, she wasn't going to mow it herself.

"Carmen?"

She shook herself from her thoughts and turned towards him. "I had a lovely evening," she said as if she were an actress in an old movie.

"I did, too. I can't remember the last time I had such a lovely evening."

Gathering her purse from the floor she said, "Well, I guess I'll see you at…"

"Carmen, may I ask you a question?"

"Of course, Clive."

"May I kiss you?"

"You're so formal."

"It's the Englishman in me."

There he was. So polite, taking no chances, making sure the coast is clear. And indeed, the coast was clear.

"Alright, Clive, you can kiss me."

Clive leaned over and kissed her. He pulled away and looked into her eyes and then put his arm around her, pulled her closer, and kissed her more passionately this time. Carmen felt almost like swooning. He pulled away and then let out a breath accompanied by a quiet whistle. Carmen, breathing heavy said, "I always wondered what that would be like." Clive was taken aback by her comment. "What? To kiss a black man," he said, chuckling.

"No. You idiot. To kiss a married man. I've never done it before. Unless you count my husband."

"But, but, how did you, why do you…"

"Oh, Clive, men are such imbeciles."

Chapter Thirty-Four

Seymour was nervous to meet his son for the first time since he left. He was glad that Geraldo had agreed to see him. But God damn that. He was his father. He ought to see him. It was bad enough that Carmen had changed the locks on the front door. Of his own house! He wanted to think ill of her. God knows his girlfriend degraded her often. He was somehow powerless to come to Carmen's defense. There was the time when he told Jane that he still loved Carmen. You don't stop loving the woman you raised two children with. He wasn't in love with her anymore. Of course not. But he loved her. That was a huge argument. When Jane lost her temper, it was god damn scary. He never said anything like that again. But when he thought of Carmen, he only thought kindly of her. She was a sweet and generous woman. He had rarely heard her say a negative word against anyone. He was grateful to her for loving him way back when, when he was such a schlub. She was a beautiful, intelligent woman when they met, and he was a nebbish ne'er-do-well. And she was *still* beautiful, just, well, he was no longer in love with her. Did he love Jane? He couldn't say. The whole thing was a mess. Mostly, he was relieved that he could stop lying. In a way, that was the main reason that he left so that he could stop lying. Not that he was in love or not in love with Jane. He was attracted to her. She was sexy, and she was great in bed, but it wasn't because of her. He knew well enough that he had ruined the marriage by being unfaithful. And he knew it couldn't be repaired. And he hadn't the will power to cut things off with Jane. And again, he couldn't go on lying. So he left.

The Porsche pulled up, and Geraldo got into the car. His father looked older than he had remembered. When was the last time he saw him? Maybe two months now. His thinning red hair was graying at the sideburns. Always a bit chubby, he seemed a little fatter. But it was him. Still, his father, just not someone he revered any longer. Did he revere him before? Yeah, sure, maybe. Hadn't really thought about it. He didn't really feel anything. One way or the other. The car drove off. His father was speaking. He wasn't hearing the words. He was smelling the smoke from the cigar burning in the ashtray and listening to the jazz music on the radio. He couldn't wait for this to be over with.

"How about Japanese?"

"What?"

"How about Japanese food?"

"Okay."

"How's your brother? He won't return my calls. I'm going to cut him off if he continues to ignore me. You tell him that when you talk to him. Okay?"

"Okay."

"And how's, how's your mom?"

"Okay."

Seymour took the cigar out of the ashtray and put it between his lips. It had gone out, and so he punched the lighter, and when it popped out, he put the glowing orange end to his cigar and took a few puffs to get it going again. That was one thing that Geraldo missed, maybe more than anything, of his father. The smell of his cigars. The sweet, dark, smoky smell of his father's cigars.

They sat across from each other at a Japanese restaurant in Long Beach. His father seemed nervous. Geraldo had never seen him unsure of himself. It made his father seem even more of a stranger to him. He was the man who had hurt his mother so much, *that* was what made him a stranger to him. Geraldo looked at the menu. He didn't know the things on it. Seymour set down his menu and said to Geraldo, "So. What are you going to have?"

"I don't know. I have never had sushi before."

"Well, they don't just have sushi. They have tempura. I know you like that."

"I've never had that."

"Yes, you have."

"I don't think so."

"A few years ago, when we took that trip to San Francisco."

"I don't remember."

"Well, I'll order. And you can try a lot of different things."

"Whatever."

"Whatever?"

"Yeah. Whatever."

"Okay. So. Let's get this out of the way."

"Get *what* out of the way?"

"You obviously have an attitude of some kind."

"It's not an *attitude.*"

"Or whatever you want to call it."

"Well. Since you brought it up, you have been cheating on Mom for years. And that pretty much sucks."

"Listen, Geraldo. It's not as easy as that. I don't think it's something that you can understand quite yet."

"What can't I understand? That, that, you're a…"

"Watch it now. I know you're angry. But you have to understand. I didn't mean to hurt your mom. She's a good person and a great mom. But, sometimes, people grow apart, and, well, there are just some things you don't know about."

"I know about it. I know about it plenty. I just don't think you have to let it control you."

"You mean sex. It's okay to talk about. We have never really talked about it."

"I'm good."

"It's not that it controls you son. But. It sort of does. A little. And. Well. Things happen. Yet, like I said. We grew apart."

"Yeah. Whatever."

The waiter came over. Geraldo didn't really pay attention to the things his father ordered. He was more concerned with managing his anxiety, which felt like it was spreading from the middle of his chest down his arms and up his neck. He could imagine his head and hands exploding like in that movie Scanners, which he had just seen the weekend before at the Cypress Cinema. He was so surprised that his mother agreed to go with him. She usually hated gory movies, let alone a movie where a person's head explodes. She said she liked it and found it "cathartic." Thinking about his mom and seeing the movie with her somehow calmed him. Is my mom my best friend? He asked himself. So, what if she is?

They talked about baseball until the food came. The conversation was marked by palpably uncomfortable moments of no conversation. Geraldo realized that he couldn't remember having a meal alone with his father. Ever. Always his brother and or his mother were also there. This thought made him feel less uncomfortable somehow. The food came, and it looked cool how the piece of pink and white fish lay on little logs of rice.

Geraldo was all too happy to try something new, and he enjoyed it. What he loved most of all was the unagi. If someone had told him that eel could be this delicious, he never would have believed them.

"Looks like you like the food."

Geraldo nodded as he shoved yellowtail sashimi in his mouth.

"So. What have you been up to? How's the old gang?"

"What old gang?"

"You know. Your friends from the neighborhood."

"I don't have any friends. *From the neighborhood.*" Geraldo said with his mouth full of sushi.

"You don't have any friends?"

"I didn't say that."

"So you *have* friends?"

"I have comrades."

"Comrades?"

"Yes. Comrades."

"Okay. What, are you a communist now like your brother?"

"Yes. In fact, I am."

"Are you serious? Is this just some anti-establishment stance you're taking because you're pissed off at me?"

"Not everything is about you."

"Do you even know what communism is?"

"I am for a classless society where there is no private property, and the means of production is controlled by the proletariat."

"The proletariat? The proletariat in this country largely supported Richard Nixon and Ronald Reagan. I don't think that it's realistic that they would suddenly embrace Marxism."

"When the economy collapses and the means of production…"

"Listen, son. I know that this is coming from a good place. I used to be idealistic when I was your age. You need to know whenever there has been any attempt at a "classless society" you speak of, it has ended up a bloodbath. And then fascism."

"You don't understand. You don't understand anything."

"I understand one thing."

"What's that?"

"That you're petulant and talking like a jackass."

Chapter Thirty-Five

In Davy's garage, the band was practicing an Elvis Costello song, *Watching the Detectives*. Davy was playing guitar, Geraldo was playing bass, and Sunshine was on the drums. It was sloppy. Sunshine wasn't much of a drummer, let alone one who could play a convincing reggae beat like how the band on the record recorded it. Geraldo, being left-handed, like Paul McCartney, his hero, played a cheap upside-down Hohner bass. He hadn't quite learned the bass part and was fumbling all over the place. Davy was a decent guitarist but not yet a convincing singer. He had trouble hearing himself, considering how hard Sunshine was hitting the cymbals. Yet, after a little while, they started settling into a nice groove. The garage door opened, and Barry and Tommy walked in. Sunshine played a mini drum solo, threw her sticks in the air, and ran into Tommy's arms.

Davy shouted, "Sunshine, what the fuck!"

Tommy and Sunshine flopped down on the old leather sofa, which was against the wall of the garage, and started to make out. Davy looked at Geraldo and shrugged. "I guess practice is over." Davy took off his guitar and walked over to Barry, who was holding a six-pack of beer. Davy said, "Where'd you get that?" Barry pulled a can from the plastic tabs and handed Davy one. "Dear old mom."

"Very nice of her."

"Geraldo. Care for a Coors? I know we shouldn't be drinking these fascist beers because of their union-busting policies, but nobody has yet elucidated my mother on the issues."

"I don't know," Geraldo said, fiddling with his bass strings.

"Go ahead, Geraldo," Tommy shouted. "Coors is barely anything more than water anyway."

Geraldo took off his bass, leaned it against the drums, and walked over to Barry, who handed him a Coors. He opened it and took a sip. It wasn't bad, kind of bland. He took another sip.

"Hey Tommy, want a beer," Barry shouted at Tommy who was in the process of French kissing Sunshine. "Ah, forget it."

"Speaking of which, Geraldo, how was your big night with your Mexican donut queen?" Davy said, playfully punching Geraldo in the ribs.

"She's not from Mexico; she's from Guatemala."

"Whatever. Did you, you know, get some?"

"Davy, give him a break," Barry said.

Sunshine came up for air and said, "Yeah, it was only his first date. Though on our first date, we got naked!"

Tommy shouted, "Getting naked is the best! Listen, Geraldo, you're lucky you found someone you like. Not always easy to do. I highly recommend exploring your erogenous zones. Hers too."

"Oh, Jesus," Barry said and then took a long pull from his beer.

"I miss Marcia," Davy bemoaned. "I miss having a girlfriend."

Sunshine walked over and grabbed a beer from Barry, "You had a girlfriend? A girlfriend named Marcia? Like in the Brady Bunch?"

"Yeah, well. Ever since she became a born-again Christian, she'll have nothing to do with me."

"I would think she would go for you. What with your Jesus look and all. But you're better off. Seems like all those born-again girls are getting pregnant."

Barry put down his beer and said, "Enough chit-chat. Tomorrow is the night. Thousands of Revolutionary Press ready to be disseminated. We are going to have to be efficient to get one in every locker before sunrise. I know it can be done. And then, on Monday morning, the entire student body will be in for a big, red surprise. This is huge. I mean, we're really taking it to the man. We're really doing something. Not just talk."

"I wish Dad could see us now," Tommy said.

"Yeah, well, I don't know if he would dig our anti-capitalist message."

"No, but he would dig our stealth operations."

"That's true."

Tommy turned to Sunshine and said, "My dad was in the C.I.A. But when he found out about the illegal bombings in Laos and Cambodia, he raised a stink, and next thing you know, he is dead."

"Oh, babe."

"Okay. We're going to have to talk about something important," Barry said, getting serious. "What happens if the police come? I don't think they will, but if they do show up, we need to have a plan."

Davy laughed, "I know the plan. Run away!"

"Yes. But do we run in different directions, or all run together? And what if they grab one of us? What then? Does that person keep quiet, or do they name names?"

"We should all go down together," Tommy said solemnly.

Davy raised his hand, "I don't want to go down at all."

"Whoever gets caught will be expelled, and or we will all be expelled," Barry said.

"We should just not get caught," Davy said, getting exasperated.

"I say," Tommy said. "If someone gets caught, then we all go down together."

Sunshine lowered her head and said, "My parents would kill me."

Barry said, "Realistically. It could affect getting into a good college."

"I never thought of that," Tommy said sadly.

"Nobody said that there weren't risks. You can't be a revolutionary without taking a risk. Jesus Christ. We must be willing to pay the price," Barry said, sounding annoyed.

It had not occurred to Geraldo that he would get in trouble for his revolutionary activities. It would further wreck his mother. "I have to think about this," he said.

"What's there to think about?" Barry shouted. "Think about Che Guevarra, Leon Trotsky, Emma Goldman."

Tommy chimed in, "Jerry Rubin, Abbie Hoffman!"

Sunshine sang, "Johnny Rotten, Sid Vicious, Joe Strummer!"

Davy shouted, "Yeah! Good old Joe Strummer."

"And don't forget John Lennon!" Geraldo said quietly.

"Yeah, Geraldo," Barry clapped him on the back. "Don't forget John Lennon. He died for our sins."

Chapter Thirty-Six

There was a layer of fog about three feet off the ground of the football field; the group waded through it, marching in lockstep, grim and determined and convinced that what they were doing was essential to fulfilling their personal obligation to humanity. Geraldo looked to his comrades. Each one had an angelic glow about them. Barry, the chief, the captain leading the squad, it was Barry who inspired them, who instigated the operation and who took care of the actual manufacturing of the document. And it was Barry who had the car to transport the group to their destinations. There were Tommy and Sunshine, like Jack Reed and Louise Bryant in the movie Reds, as portrayed by Warren Beatty and Diane Keaton. Romantic purveyors of the truth. True to themselves and to their love and true to truth. And lastly, Savior, the odd ball, the eccentric, perhaps the bravest of them all, willing to antagonize the brutes who run amuck on campus. He was the one who wore a giant smile, a pink suit, and flowers in his hair the day after Reagan was assassinated. Yes, quite a group. Geraldo was the quiet one, the poet of the revolution; at least, that is how he saw himself.

They stopped at the edge of the field. Barry removed the rucksack from over his shoulder. Davy pulled a large backpack off his back. Both extracted piles of the Revolutionary Press, handing a stack to each one in the group. Barry passed around plastic whistles to each kid and said in a loud whisper, "Okay. If you see anyone coming, blow that whistle, and then we all head for the entrance to the music room. We will make a plan to escape from there. All right then. You know which block of lockers you've been assigned to. Let's do this!"

The 8 x10 papers fit easily through the slit at the top of the locker. Still, it was not a quick process, and Geraldo was quite sure it was going to take all night. He was glad he brought his corduroy coat with a faux fur lining, the one handed down from his brother. He envisioned his brother being proud of this operation. Charles never tried anything nearly as daring during his time as a high school communist insurgent. Yet, it was his brother's example that inspired the group and his expert copy editing that got the Revolutionary Press looking good. He was most definitely an honorary member of the CCCP- Cypress Centurion Communist Party.

Some kind of bird was singing in the distance. Strange kind of singing. Not just one song but many different melodies. Short melodies, longer ones, melodies that went up and down rapidly, melodies that were nothing but a long tone. Geraldo thought that it must be a mockingbird. He loved the idea of a mockingbird. A bird that mocked. Was that what he and his comrades were doing? Mocking the establishment? The mockingbird started singing two notes over and over. Geraldo realized they were the first two notes to the Beatles song *Hey Jude*. C to F. But then there was another bird singing a high pitch tone. It was not a bird but a whistle. He ran to the entrance of the music room where the others were gathered. Off in the distance was a bank of lights.

Davy said, "Those are police cars. And there are lots of them."

"Looks like the whole fucking police force of Cypress has been mobilized," Barry said

"God damn fascists!"

"What are we going to do? We are practically surrounded," Sunshine lamented.

Tommy said resoundingly, "I'll make a run towards them to distract them, and then you guys run along the side of the building. And get out!"

"Tommy. You can't do that. We can't let you do that," Geraldo implored.

Tommy said quite soberly, "You can't stop me."

Tommy dropped his stack of papers and ran towards the light. There were tiny bursts of light and crackling sounds. Tommy crumpled to the ground. Sunshine screamed, "Tommy!"

Dave opened his backpack, took out glass bottles with cloth sticking out the top, and said, "I was hoping it wouldn't come to this."

Barry smiled wickedly and said, "Molotov cocktails?"

"Damn right!"

Davy handed the bottles around, took out a lighter, and lit each one. They ran towards the police cars. Barry hurled his Molotov which hit the ground near two cops, sending them falling away. Sunshine flung hers, it landed on top of a police car, causing it to go up in flames. Davy launched his at a cop running towards him, madly firing his pistol; it was a direct hit. The cop was blown away. Geraldo ran with his cocktail. He wanted to get close enough to take out the remaining couple of cops. He was hit in the chest by a bullet. Somehow, he stayed standing. Propelled by inertia, he ran towards the cops and slung his Molotov Cocktail; it blew them away. In what seemed like slow motion, he fell, hitting his head soundly on the asphalt. All sound ceased. Was he dead? He opened his eyes and lifted his head. He was in his bedroom. He put his hand to his chest where the bullet had hit. No blood. He looked at the clock: 12:05. He got up, grabbed his shoes, and rapidly made his way downstairs and out the front door. He joined the others on the football field. "What the hell took you so long?" Barry said.

Chapter Thirty-Seven

The world was largely soporific. Everything had been done. All the great music had been made, all the great causes fought for, and all the great leaders assassinated. It made Geraldo sleepy, and it wasn't always easy for him to get out of bed. But this day was different. Something had happened. Even though he only got two hours of sleep, he woke on time, got dressed, and even had a big breakfast by his standards: two bowls of Kaptain Krunch, an English muffin with butter and peanut butter smeared on top, and a large glass of whole milk. He stood by the curb waiting for Barry's Datsun in great anticipation. When it pulled up, it was already filled with the rest of the group. Geraldo got into the backseat. The feeling was a bit muted. They drove along listening to The Clash Sandinista on the tape deck down low. Finally, Tommy said, "They better not have destroyed our paper." Barry laughed. "Don't be insane. There is no way that they could have gone through every locker and gotten rid of each paper." This sunk in, and there was a collective sigh. "Yes," Sunshine said. "He's right, you know. This is a momentous day. Things are going to be different from now on."

"How do you mean?" Davy asked.

"Even though people can't know for sure it was us. They know for sure it was us."

"Yeah. That's true. But fuck them!"

"Yeah, that's right, Savior, fuck them!" Barry said, and the rest of the group shouted in unison, "Fuck them!"

Barry parked the Datsun in the rear of the parking lot. Even from a distance, Geraldo could sense the commotion occurring on campus. They walked onto campus; the kids had Revolutionary Presses in their hands, scrutinizing the document, looking up to see the gang, realizing it was them and uncertain what to think. It was hard not to admire them, the CCCP, how they walked together like they were a band, like they were rock stars. The Griswold brothers in their trench coats, Davy in his white tracksuit and Mexican leather sandals, Sunshine in her fishnets, red plaid Catholic school girl skirt and leather jacket, Tommy wearing platform shoes, bell bottoms, white sleeveless t-shirt with Rolling Stones logo of the tongue, hair up in a glam pompadour, and Geraldo wearing a forest green houndstooth sports coat that he had found at a Salvation Army, a white t-shirt, beige poplin pants and black wingtips with no socks. He looked like a young Jack Kerouac.

The jocks spotted them, pushed the other kids out of the way, and Duane, in the lead, made a beeline for Barry. He pointed his finger into Barry's chest and said, "You fucking commie. I meant it when I said that you were asking for trouble. You're going to get it. Your life is over. You and all your loser friends. Just look at you. What a bunch of freaks. This one here thinks he is Jesus Christ, and this one here," he said, pointing at Sunshine. "Doesn't get freakier. My friend went to school with her in Newport back when she was a he. I can't believe they even let it attend school that way." Tommy came up and tried to slug Duane, who grabbed his arm and threw him to the ground. Duane laughed and lifted his leg to kick Tommy in the face. Mr. Magg walked up then. Duane lowered his leg and said, "Hello, Mr. Magg."

"Duane. What happened here?"

"The pinko tripped."

Mr. Magg looked down at Tommy, who got a hand up from Davy. Tommy walked over to Sunshine and put his arm around her. Sunshine had no expression. Like somehow, her spirit had vacated her body. She turned and walked away with Tommy. Mr. Magg said to Duane, "Alright. That's enough. For now." Duane and his jock friends cleared out. Mr. Magg came up to Barry and said, seething, "I'll get you for this."

"I don't know what you're talking about."

"Don't play dumb, Barry. You and your commie friends are responsible for spreading this vile Russian propaganda. I may not have the proof right now. But I will get it. You can rest assured. You will be expelled. Or worse."

"First of all, Fuck Russia! I don't consider the Soviet Union an exemplar of a true democratic-socialist government. Which is what I, we, believe in. It's a fucking fascist oligarchy. Second of all. There is no proof. There is no proof. You can't substantiate your allegations. So, if you'll excuse me, I need to get to class. AP history."

Chapter Thirty-Eight

Sitting at a table in the plaza, Geraldo and Davy quietly fondled their sandwiches. Each one waited in anticipation of some kind of harassment, the kind they had endured throughout the day: jeers, curse words, but also flirtatious glances by some girls. Geraldo had a mix of immense anxiety and titillation. Barry came running over, holding papers rolled up in his hand. "Did you see the student newspaper?" Both Davy and Geraldo shrugged. "You'll never believe it. Those idiots. They tried to critique the Revolutionary Press." Barry handed them each a copy. "How could they do it so quickly?" Davy asked incredulously.

"They reviewed the first one. The one they tore down. The one nobody saw."

Geraldo started laughing. Davy said, "What's so funny?"

"Just read it," Barry said.

Davy read it and then started laughing hysterically. "Those idiots!"

"The only thing they criticized was the grammatical mistakes, which we have since corrected! They didn't even dispute the main thesis about U.S. imperialism in Central America."

"Because they couldn't," Geraldo said righteously.

Barry looked around. "Where's Tommy? Where's Sunshine?"

"They left. They left school. Cut class. I saw them walking off campus before the first period." Davy said. "What did that jackass mean about Sunshine being a he and now a she?"

"Don't know," Barry said. "Did you guys get called into Magg's office?"

Davy and Geraldo shook their heads. "Weird," Barry said. "Well, it's coming. But he has no proof. No proof."

After school, Barry went to look for Tommy. Geraldo and Davy walked through the football field to head home. Davy said, "All in all, fairly uneventful. I mean, I got shoved up against the lockers by a few jocks and spat at and called many unchristian things that I could barely mention, but all in all, fairly uneventful."

"Yes, I, too, was randomly punched in the arm by some neanderthal, and another tripped me, but being good at falling, I was able to tuck and roll."

"So, not bad. I wonder what happened to Tommy and Sunshine."

"I don't understand. What was that jerk Duane getting at?"

"I think he was trying to say that Sunshine is a fag or something."

"How could a girl be a fag?"

"That's just it. He was saying that she is not a girl."

"What?"

"Yeah."

"If she is a boy, wouldn't they have her in boys P.E.?"

"She doesn't take P.E."

"How do you know?"

"We've hung out some. I had a crush on her. I admit it. But then she and Tommy got together."

Just then, an arrow whizzed by Geraldo's head, missing it by a few inches. They stopped walking. Looked at each other blankly and then looked around. The football team was doing drills at the far end of the field, but they didn't see anyone with a bow. Geraldo walked a few feet and pulled an arrow out of the ground. It had a sharp steel tip. He showed it to Davy. "I take back what I said about today being uneventful. Someone just tried to kill you or me. That makes today eventful."

Chapter Thirty-Nine

The boys said goodbye on the corner of Moody and Bell. They planned to rehearse the next day. Davy said he would try to get a hold of Sunshine to let her know. Each boy went in their separate directions. Each boy grappling with the question of mortality. Each boy realized that if not for a few inches of empty space, one of them might well be dead. Or brain damaged. Or painfully injured. All because they had put a piece of paper in lockers. A few pieces of paper with words about the crimes of their country. Words on paper could cause the death of another human being. Geraldo was thinking, "Who would be so sick, so homicidal that they would be willing to risk their own freedom by attempting to kill another? Another kid. If it was a kid who fired the arrow? Who knows? It could have been Mr. Magg. But Magg would use a gun, of this Geraldo was certain.

Davy was thinking as he walked on the sidewalk of Moody Street: was this the martyrdom he was toying with? Afterall, he was not surprised by this attempt on his life. Not at all. In fact, he expected it. But in the form of an arrow? How stupidly ironic, considering Davy was one-quarter Cahuilla. His grandmother on his mother's side. Grandma still lived in Palm Springs in a mobile home park. Not a trashy trailer park. A famous mobile home park called Blue Skies Village is nestled at the base of the San Jacinto mountains. Originally founded by Bing Crosby, for whom Davy's grandfather was a friend, having been a set decorator on some of Bing's "Road to…" movies. Bing helped get his grandparents into the exclusive park, circumventing any questions concerning his grandmother's ethnicity. Maybe that's where he got it from. His hatred for white people. Even though he was technically white himself, his grandmother married a white man whom she loved to his dying days in the cancer ward. Lifetime chain smoker that he was.

He walked past his older brother Donnie in the driveway, waxing his blue, silver, spackled Ford Ranchero, blasting Foghat from the eight-track car stereo, a Marlboro dangling between his lips. "Hey, Savior," he said. It had been Donnie who had first laid this moniker on the boy last year when he first got his now-famous facial hair. It was partly because of the nickname that Davy began his identification with Jesus, which was now full-blown. Ever since he saw Jesus Christ Superstar on television last Easter, with its sympathetic depiction of Judas Iscariot, sexy Mary Magdalene, and a truly conflicted Pontius Pilate, he could really see the whole scene as something real. How Jesus, filled with self-righteousness, tweaked the Romans and caused destruction at the market in a flagrant act of anti-capitalist incitement. Jesus did not give a fuck. And Davy did not give a fuck. And then he got a hold of the Jefferson Bible at a Salvation Army; at last, a book that distilled the Jesus message. Now, he could fully understand. He had it right there on his bookshelf, next to the Anarchist Cookbook.

Chapter Forty

Geraldo walked in the door, set down his backpack, and smelled smoke. Charles was sitting on the sofa, staring into space. "Charles, what's the smoke coming from?" Charles pointed to the fireplace. "Remember that manilla envelope Dad left for us? Burnt it." Geraldo went over to inspect. Indeed, it was burning in there only Charles hadn't opened the flue. Geraldo reached up into the chimney, opened it, turned, and faced his brother, slightly exasperated. "What are you doing here?"

"I'm meeting up with April later. It's her birthday. They're having a little party. You and mom can come."

"Oh. That's cool. I have a date."

Geraldo sat down next to Charles. He reeked of cigarettes and some kind of alcohol. And he smelled as if he hadn't bathed for a while.

"You have a date? That's cool. But, you know, make sure you use protection."

"What?"

"Protection. You don't want to catch a venereal disease. I was around your same age when I lost my virginity. I got something else in exchange."

"Well, we don't, we're not."

"Oh, I see. Well. You got to at least try to get to second base, buddy."

"Second base?"

"Cop a feel dummy. Come on, you can't turn sixteen without having touched a girl's tit. It's a rite of passage."

"Oh yeah. Yeah, sure."

"How are the Griswold brothers?"

Geraldo looked around to make sure no one was there and whispered, "We did it."

Charles whispered back, "You did what?

"The Revolutionary Press. We distributed it last night. One in every locker. Three thousand lockers. Took all night. But we did it. You should have seen Mr. Magg this morning."

"Jesus! Kudos kid. You guys have a lot of balls. But. Of course, it's just a matter of time before they catch up with you. And then you'll be fucked."

"There is no proof."

"They don't need proof. But still. I'm, I'm proud of you anyway."

Geraldo felt a cold shiver go down his spine at the words, 'You'll be fucked.'

Carmen walked through the front door, home from work and the market carrying two shopping bags. She saw the boys sitting on the sofa. Engaged in conversation. Not registering her. She was thinking. Who are these kids? Her boys but barely boys. Now, they were awkward young men. God, what a terrible thing. People think women have it bad: the life of a woman, the misogyny, even the cruelty of their physiology, the menstrual cycle, the act of giving birth, all of it constructed with an almost malicious, even sadistic intent. But these boys, what they go through, how they get possessed by hormones and testosterone, it seems another being gets inside their body, mind, and spirit, controls the energy until they are almost incapable of making rational decisions, and yet they are the ones in charge of the machinery. It's no wonder there are so many wars. But still, she loved them. They were her boys. Her boys. She was the one who raised them almost single-handedly.

Geraldo saw his mom and wondered what she was thinking about as she stood in the doorway, not moving, looking at him and Charles.

"Hi, mom."

"Hi, kiddo. Look what the cat dragged in," she said, walking into the room. "Are you coming to April's?"

"Um, I…"

"He has a date."

"Oh well. La di da. Another one. You're doing better than me. Don't stay out too late. It's a school night." She set down the groceries on the dining room table.

"Okay, mom. How was your date? I never asked."

"Mom had a date?" Charles inquired incredulously.

"If you could call it that. It wasn't much to speak of. The guy is kind of a creep. Oh well."

"Beggars can't be choosers," Charles quipped teasingly, though it fell flat.

She sat down next to the boys. "I'm exhausted."

"You still up for going to April's?" Charles asked with an air of desperation in his voice.

"Oh yes. I just need to have a cup of tea and freshen up. I am very much looking forward to meeting her parents. I want to see what a happily married couple looks like."

Chapter Forty-One

Charles sat in the passenger seat of Carmen's Volvo, the car that she got by default when Seymour bought his Porsche. Charles got Carmen's Dodge Dart by default; she had previously received it from her in-laws when they bought the Thunderbird. Carmen drove nice and steady, Charles was thinking. And when on the freeway always the middle lane. Not the way Seymour drove. He was always trying to stay ahead, going in and out of the fast lane. Cursing at the other cars while he puffed away at his cigar and had jazz music blasting from the car radio. It was nerve-racking to drive with him and be exposed to his constant anger and hostility towards the other drivers. But also, kind of exciting. His father was a large man and had a large personality. A bloated id running rampant.

Carmen took an occasional glance from the road to look at Charles. He was so quiet, which was atypical. As a kid, he was given the nickname 'motormouth' by his grandfather for his unceasing monologues. It never got on Carmen's nerves, though it seemed to grate on almost everyone else's. Maybe because he was her son, and she loved him. But she also liked him. Just look at him, Jesus; he looks like Seymour. Same bulbous nose and arrogant eyes. What are arrogant eyes, Carmen? Eyes that are held in a kind of clamped position, scrutinizing everything as being dubious. Yet, everything was pretty dubious. She had found that out. Still, she was worried about him. He seemed to take Seymour leaving harder than anyone, though he was internalizing it. But she could tell that he was suffering.

"How's school?"

"It's okay. Not very stimulating. But. It's okay."

"And. How are you? You seem all right."

"Yeah, I'm all right, mom."

"Have you spoken to your father?"

"Fuck no!"

"Charles!"

"Sorry. Sorry, mom."

"It's ok. I understand. Geraldo was telling me about something the other day. Have you ever heard of primal scream therapy?"

"Oh yeah. His Beatles obsession continues. The martyrdom of John Lennon. On John's first solo album, he sang a song called, 'Mother' and at the end he did some of that primal scream therapy. It's hard to listen to, but I guess it did him and Yoko some good. Why?"

"Oh, nothing. I thought I'd give it a try sometime." Charles looked at his mother and tried to imagine her doing primal scream therapy. He burst out laughing. It was good for her to hear her dour son laugh. She laughed as well. Nevertheless, she was going to give it a try when there was no one else around, and she was going to find that John Lennon album and listen to it, a song called 'Mother' no less. "Why was he doing the primal screaming on a song called Mother?"

"Because she died when he was a boy."

"Oh. That is a pity. How are things with you and April? She's such a nice girl."

"Yeah, she is. Sometimes I wonder what she sees in me."

"Charles. You're a nice boy, too. Under that gruff exterior."

"Nice of you to say."

"Well, I am your mother."

"This is the street mom. Make a left."

Carmen did as she was instructed. It was a nice block near Lexington Park. The houses were newer and bigger than on their block, which, when they first moved there in 1962, were all single-story ranch-style homes. By the middle of the 70's, many of these homes had added a second story, which seemed ironic because later, they became fractured households because of the climbing divorce rate. The block that April and her parents lived on was still shiny and seemed resilient to domestic strife somehow. Sturdy hedges, thorny rose bushes, yucca, jacaranda trees, crape myrtle, mimosas, cacti, and grass. Lush green grass. The street lights were bright, and the road was newly repaved. You could still smell the tar. "Right here, mom."

Carmen pulled into the driveway and parked in front of the garage door. "Don't forget the present in the back seat, Charles." They got out and walked through the courtyard to the front door. After a bit, since Charles hadn't, Carmen pressed the doorbell. The door opened. It was April. She was beaming. Carmen was taken aback a bit. My goodness, this girl loves my Charles. "Hello Mrs. Horowitz. So nice that you could come." They walked in, and April gave Carmen a little hug. "Please call me Carmen." April looked at the gift that Charles held tenuously in his hands. She gave him a pursed smile. "Happy birthday," Charles said drolly. He reached around April, pulled her close, and gave her a kiss. He let go of her. She laughed and said, "Thank you."

They walked into the living room, which was stylishly decorated, with a white shag rug, teak sofa, and coffee table, eggshell white walls, a small Japanese maple tree in an iron pot by the fireplace, Noguchi lamps, and a round wicker chair. It smelled nice to Carmen, steamed vegetables, and teriyaki salmon. April's mom greeted them warmly. She seemed older than Carmen but still had a vibrant energy. "So nice to finally meet you," she said to Carmen. "We just love Charles. Thank you so much for coming." They exchanged a friendly embrace, each one noticing the other's perfume. Each one reacted positively to it. At that moment, Clive entered the room holding a bottle of white wine. Carmen wondered, what in god's name is he doing here? And then she realized.

Chapter Forty-Two

Maria's hands were both soft and hard, soft in the way she held Geraldo's hand, not holding on too tightly but firmly ensconced in his like they had been holding hands for years. They were rough, the texture was rough, and he could feel her *journey* in them as he imagined it. He had thought about what it must have been like for her to make the trip, the migration, on her own, an orphan from Guatemala, only a teenager, and barely that. He hadn't asked her age, but in some ways, she seemed somehow both younger and older than him. Something about her eyes and how they scrutinized the world and the skin around her eyes, smooth and full of color. The thing was, he had never held a girl's hand before and so this was new. Not just any girl, but a girl who was pretty and funny and who symbolized what it was that he and the group were fighting for and against. He couldn't believe his luck, especially since it was obvious that she liked him too.

They walked along a path in El Dorado Park near the golf courses. The sky was cloudless, fluorescent blue; the sun, though nearing the horizon, was strong on their faces, and the air smelled like sulfur, felt thick, that chemical presence that made one's eyes sting a little; after a time, one had come to, if not adjust to, then barely acknowledge the ubiquitous smog. Maria pulled out a pack of Chiclets and held it out to Geraldo. He let go of her hand, took the pack, undid the cellophane, pulled out a piece, and handed it to her then took one for himself. He gave the pack back to her, and she put it in her jeans pocket. It was the first time he had seen her in jeans, and she wore a white cotton blouse with little pink flowers on it.

Maria, without constraint, said, "I have missed you."

"Me too. You." He realized that he meant it. And then wondered what it meant.

"How was your week?" Maria asked, getting more adept at conversing in English by watching American talk shows.

"It was good. It was very good. How about you?"

She did not want to answer too quickly; she wanted to play the question a couple of times in her head. She wanted the boy to know her. She did not want to pretend. "Not too good. My cousin got a letter. They want to send her back to Guatemala."

"Why?"

She stepped over a branch in their pathway and then said, "I don't know. She has papers. They want to see her papers. But she has them. So it will be okay."

"That's good. What about you? Do you have papers?"

"No. I don't have papers."

They stopped walking, and Geraldo turned to her and said, "Can you get them?"

"Yes. I think so. My uncle is working on it. Because his job, they are helping him. So, it should be ok."

"Whew! That's good. I really like you."

Geraldo took hold of her hand again; she smiled at him. Her eyes were bright and exuded strength. It made him feel warm. Gosh, he wondered, does she love me? He thought it was the time to try and kiss her. She took a step, and they started walking again.

"You're very nice, Geraldo. I was thinking about you. You were muy bold. To ask me out. Do you do that a lot?"

"Do what?"

"Ask chicas to go out."

"No. I never have."

"Really?"

"Really."

They came to a bench beneath a Eucalyptus tree. It smelled like mint and oranges. It diminished the toxic smell of the smog. They sat down. They stared into each other's eyes for a time. Geraldo said, "Your eyes are so dark brown and beautiful."

"Oh. Thank you. Your eyes. They are like brown and green."

"They call it hazel. I was told that hazel eyes are kind of rare."

"Oh. Bonita. Um. Dame un besito."

Geraldo was not sure if he had heard right. Is she asking me to kiss her? And if so, how do I go about it? I guess the same way you go about anything. You just do it. "Si. Por favor."

He moved in close to her. They kissed lightly at first. They each giggled a little. Then they kissed again.

Maria pulled away. She took the gum from her mouth. Geraldo took the gum from his mouth and held out his hand. She put her piece in his hand next to his discarded piece of gum. He stood up and walked over to the green trash barrel and dropped the pieces of gum in there. He turned around and looked at her. She wore that blouse, which seemed a little small for her. He could see the outline of her breasts, and he remembered what his brother said. He went back to the bench, sat down next to her, put his arm around her, and pulled her close. They kissed for a while. Geraldo moved his hand and put it on Maria's breast. She gently pushed it away. They kissed some more. Geraldo tried again. This time, she pushed it away more forcefully. He tried one more time.

"Please, no, do that."

"Why? I just want to feel it. It's only natural."

"I don't like."

"Don't be so uptight."

"This is not you. You're a nice boy. I am a nice girl. I don't do that."

They sat quietly. Geraldo felt embarrassed, almost humiliated. She was right; it didn't feel natural for him to do that. He didn't know why he did it. Now, she seemed mad at him. Disappointed in him. She didn't have that same look in her eyes anymore.

"Maybe we better go," he said.

"Que?"

"Let's go. I'll walk you home."

Maria felt tinges of sadness, and then a feeling of anger began to circulate in her blood. She could feel her veins create heat throughout her body. She said, "You don't have to walk me home. I can walk home by myself."

She got up and walked away leaving Geraldo unsure of what just happened.

Chapter Forty-Three

The salmon was delicious. Clive had cooked it in his hibachi, an impressive forest green dome which was made of "rigid blocks of diatomaceous earth" and not your typical cast iron North American grill, as he informed Charles and Carmen during the tour of the house, backyard, and patio. He had cooked the fish perfectly, charred on the outside, tender, and pink in the middle. The white wine went deliciously with the fish and the steamed vegetable medley that had a balsamic vinegar and ginger glaze. They had already polished off two bottles of wine by the time they were halfway through dinner; Carmen played no small part and was close to finishing her third glass. When she asked for her fourth refill, she received a circumspect look from her son and a hand that nervously shook from Clive as he poured it for her. Carmen sighed. Oh, that Clive. Was he nervous? Yes. Did his wife notice? I don't think so. Yes, Clive's wife Samara was one lucky woman to have such a fine cook and such a good-looking man. Those turtlenecks surely did become him. He looked like Sidney Portier. She was a handsome woman in her own right, though a bit matronly, Carmen thought. Poor woman. Poor stupid woman.

April and Charles sat on one side of the patio table, April's older brother Bruce and Carmen on the other side and Samara and Clive at either end. Clive next to Carmen and near the screen door to the house. Charles kept casting a concerned eye in his mother's direction. Memories of Thanksgiving all too fresh, his mother's over consumption of alcohol, and emotionally volatile exuberance. She seemed okay for now. She was automatically engaging in topical conversation. The weather, television, things like that. What no one else could hear was the running commentary going on in her brain. Samara addressed Carmen directly.

"And. How are you doing, Carmen?"

"Me. Oh, I'm doing good. Just fine."

"That's good. I was sorry to hear about, you know…"

"My husband leaving me after over twenty years?"

"Yes. I don't mean to bring it up at such a nice little party, but I also think it's okay to talk about things."

"Mom! Jeez," April said from across the table, but not too severely. "Mom is a Jungian analyst."

Carmen laughed. "You don't say. Jungian, no less. Have you heard of this primal scream therapy?"

"Yes. Of course. My personal or professional opinion is that it is plasticine at best and dangerous at worst. There was a study a few years ago, and the results were not good. Most of the patients ultimately had a negative reaction, and I believe there was even a suicide."

"Really? All just for screaming your guts out. What does a Jungian analyst do?"

"Oh, that's a complicated question, but mostly, we try to help people become their authentic self."

"How do you do that?"

"Helping you tap into your subconscious as a source of wisdom and guidance. I can recommend someone if you'd like."

"Perhaps," Carmen said and then finished off her glass of wine.

Samara, sensing that she had inquired into Carmen's well-being sufficiently, turned to Charles. "Charles, how is school?"

"It's fine."

Bruce, just back from four years at Howard University and feeling avuncular, said, "Freshman year is weird. You'll get into the groove of things."

She hated it when he felt avuncular. April said with the old sibling tension rising. "It's not weird. It's not that different from high school."

Charles said, "That's because all your classes were AP in your last year of high school."

"Yours too."

Bruce laughed and said, "And you still live at home."

"I like it here. Good food, soft bed, Mom, Dad, what more could you ask?"

Carmen looked at Clive, who had been quietly, nervously, eating his food, and sounding a little like Blanch DuBois said, "Is there more wine?"

Samara apologizing for Clive said, "Oh, I'm sorry Carmen. Seems like we need another."

Samara stood up, walked by Clive, put a hand on his shoulder, and went into the house.

Charles said, "Mom, maybe you should, you should…"

"What?"

Samara walked back in with the bottle of wine and a corkscrew. Red this time. She gave it to Clive.

"Here, Clive, you do the honors."

"But of course."

Clive fumbled with getting the cork out. Everyone watched him because he was making such a fuss about it.

"This, god, damn, cork!"

It finally popped out, and he poured wine into Carmen's glass, spilling some on the white table cloth.

"Bloody hell."

"So, Carmen, what do you do?" Samara said, trying to sound casual.

"I work in a hospital. I'm a hematologist."

"What a coincidence. Clive is a ...'"

"Pathologist," Carmen said before taking a sip of the wine.

"Wow, wow, wow," Clive said, suddenly springing to life. "That's right. Wow, what a coincidence. It's rather funny. Wow."

Carmen was enjoying this. She knew it on their date, taking her to San Pedro, for God's sake. This Clive, this charlatan. Yes, she knew he was married, but to her son's girlfriend! Así es la vida! And that they work in the same hospital. Amazing.

Samara was not quite computing this. "But, so, you know each other?"

"Know each other? I mean, do you ever really know someone?" Clive replied weakly. Attempting a guffaw.

"I should think so."

Carmen took a big gulp of wine and said, "Well, the truth of the matter is. Your husband is having an affair with me."

Clive burst out laughing. A contorted sort of laugh. An uncomfortable, weird laugh that convulsed his upper body. "She's funny. She is quite funny."

Samara, unsure of what exactly was happening, said, "You're joking?"

Charles looked at his mom; he knew that she was becoming unhinged. This was a whole side of her he had never seen before. Not until his dad left. He had never seen her drunk; he had never heard her say odd things. He tried to make light of it and said, "Mom has a kind of wicked sense of humor. Sometimes. Don't you, mom?"

Sensing that she was making things uncomfortable and problematic for her son, she said, "I do? Oh yes. I do. No, we are not having an affair. But…"

"But what?" Samara asked, attempting lightness in her tone.

"We do work in the same hospital. Only I am one of the many lab technicians, and your husband is the star pathologist. There he is behind tempered glass, digging into organs while my head is usually buried in a microscope. So, when I saw him tonight, I wasn't sure it was him."

"Oh yes, oh yes. Now I recognize you. Isn't that funny? Wow! Isn't that a funny coincidence?" Clive tried to correct himself.

Samara had from time to time had her doubts about her husband's fidelity. Especially when he was working in Hollywood, afterall, it couldn't be denied that he was a beautiful man, and she was well aware, in regards to the traditional ideas of beauty, she was perhaps not on his same level. Yet he seemed to truly adore her, was always attentive, and they had a great rapport. He was a loving and devoted husband and father. And yet. This was weird. Felt weird. "Yes, it is. A rather funny coincidence," she said after a long and awkward pause.

"It's beyond funny. It is incredible." April said, practically shouting.

"And cool, I guess," Charles said.

Bruce cleared his throat, "But if you guys work in the same lab, it seems that you would have recognized each other."

"Bruce just graduated from law school," April said to the table. "He passed the bar with flying colors."

"Thanks sis. I guess life is full of funny coincidences." Things quieted, and people went back to eating. Bruce said, "What's your major, Charles?"

"Global Affairs," Charles said, with a mouth full of vegetables.

"And what's your take on global affairs?"

He swallowed and said, "You could say that I am a communist sympathizer."

"In other words, a rebel without a cause."

"I have a cause. But this is April's birthday, so I won't bore everyone."

Charles raised his glass, and everyone else did the same. "Here's to April. Truly the kindest, sweetest comrade in arms."

April beamed at Charles. "You know, for all of his rhetoric, he is very romantic and quite suave in his own irascible way." They kissed, and soon, those around the table knew that they were practically nonexistent to the couple.

Samara said philosophically, "Nothing keeps a relationship in shape better than expressions of affection." Clive gave her a sweet, if not forced, smile.

Carmen finished her fourth glass of wine and said, "I'll drink to that."

Chapter Forty-Four

Driving his mother's Volvo was a kind of transferential event for Charles. He had so many memories of his father driving this car he could feel himself embodying his mannerisms at the wheel, but considering his mother's condition, he kept things steady and not too aggressive. The streets were quiet anyhow. She had curtailed her outlandish performance and consumption of alcohol towards the end of the evening and fell into a more dolorous disposition. Still, what the hell was happening to her?

"Mom, what the hell happened to you? You turned into Charles Bukowski."

"Who is Charles Bukowski?"

"He's a poet. He lives in Los Angeles."

"I sounded like a poet tonight? What kind of books does he write?"

"He is a poet and an alcoholic. He writes books with titles like "Play the Piano Drunk Like a Percussion Instrument Until the Fingers Begin to Bleed a Bit."

"I'll have to try that sometime. Sounds cathartic."

"Mom!"

"What!"

"You need to cut out the drinking."

"Why? It brings relief."

"Maybe take Mrs. Gray up on a therapist."

"I don't need a therapist. You're the one who needs a therapist."

"I don't dispute that."

"Well, let's get you one. I'm worried about you."

"I'm fine."

"No, you're not."

"Well, we were talking about your drinking."

"Oh, come on. I don't drink like this very often. And don't bring up Thanksgiving. It's just that tonight was stressful."

"What was so stressful about it? They are very nice."

"Yes. I suppose. On the surface of it."

They drove along. Charles turned on the radio. It was still set on his father's jazz station. He would have thought that his mom didn't want to listen to jazz anymore, that the music would make her feel sad or mad. But then again, she always liked jazz, even before meeting his father. In fact she almost married a jazz musician, as she'd like to remind everyone from time to time.

"What is the name of some of his other books?

"Who?"

"This Charles Bukowski."

Charles smiled and laughed a little. "He's got one called, 'Love is a Dog From Hell'."

"Ooh. I like this, Charles Bukowski. Where can I find his books?"

Charles loved to proselytize people about Bukowski, even his own mother. "Try Acres of Books in Long Beach. You might even bump into him there. It's his favorite bookstore."

Chapter Forty-Five

Love will tear us apart again. Davy kept playing the song over and over. The voice of the singer sounded like Jim Morrison's but with not as much technique, not as much tunefulness, but it had the same Sinatra-esque heft. He sings, "When resentments ride hard, but emotion won't grow, and we're changing our ways, taking different roads, then love, love will tear us apart again." Davy feels something that he has yet to know. Yet he knows it in his bones. The singer, Ian Curtis, committed suicide the year before Davy sat in his room listening to this song. Curtis hung himself with a clothesline. He had been suffering from epilepsy, dealing with seizures that had been growing in severity and frequency. Once, when he was performing, dancing to the music of his band, he had a tonic-clonic seizure. Took a minute for his bandmates to register what was happening.

Because Curtis had been reading Dostoevsky's The Idiot in the days preceding his suicide Davy had since checked it out of the library, now overdue by three weeks. Like Ian Curtis, the protagonist of the story, Prince Myshkin, too, suffered from epilepsy, as did the author of the novel, as did Davy. He wondered if Ian Curtis had available to him the drug Davy had been taking, ethosuximide, since he was twelve. He hadn't had a seizure since.

Prince Myshkin was mistaken for an idiot because he was simple and good-hearted. And the fates had made him suffer, physically and spiritually. He encounters true hatred, but he stays true to his idea of what it is to be Christlike which to him are the ideas of beauty, truth, and brotherhood. He has more in common with atheists and socialists than with the Catholic Church, which he considers God by coercion, God by the sword. Ian Curtis, Prince Myshkin, and Dostoevsky were Christ figures in their own right to Davy.

Davy sat on the floor and had before him the cover of the 12-inch single, which was adorned with a photograph of a sculpture by Onorato Toso taken at Genoa's Monumental Cemetery of Staglieno by the French American photographer Bernard Pierre Wolff. Davy collected fanzines dedicated to the memory of Ian Curtis and the music of Joy Division, which supplied such relevant information. The angel reposed backward on her wings, on a crypt, with one arm stretched out, prone, and the other hand covering her eyes and forehead in despair, resignation, to some uncompromising tragedy. No doubt the inevitability of death. This image, combined with the music, which, though dour, was catchier than any of the band's other songs. The music had Davy transfixed.

All the images and ideas occupying Davy's thoughts seemed to coalesce: Christ, crucifixion, angels, death, revolution, masturbation, beauty, words, camaraderie, and the female form, which, to Davy, was the highest form of beauty. Even the angel, in her sorrow. Through the sheer veneer of her dress, he could see her breasts protruding upwards to the infinite sky, a dark, deep belly button, the flesh of her arms were languorous and lithe, a perfect aquiline chin and supple if not sorrowful lips; Davy stuck his hand down his pajamas. There was a quiet knock on the door. Davy put the cover of the album over his erection and said, "Come in."

Davy's mom entered the room. Madge was in her early forties, tall, with dyed blonde hair which was nestled in a pink satinette sleep cap. She had on a yellow nylon night dress and fuzzy light green slippers. "Davy, it is almost midnight." The song came to an end as if on cue. The needle lifted, and the arm retracted back to its resting position. "Sorry, mom." She came over and sat down on the bed. "Davy, I need to talk to you about something."

"Yeah?" he said, scratching the fuzz on his chin.

"I want you to come to church this Sunday."

"Why this Sunday?"

"Not this Sunday per se, but I just think it might do you some good. What happened at Saint Irene when you were in school there, I know, was hard. But you don't throw the baby out with the bathwater. The church is more than one man; it is a community. It provides comfort. And it would mean a lot to me. And your father. Though, he won't say it. There is a bazaar this Sunday, and I think you would like it. I have friends who have children in the youth group. They say the kids like it, and it is not square."

"Not square, you say. Is it round?"

"Oh, Davy, don't tease me."

"Okay, mom. I'll go."

"Really?"

"Yes. But I don't know about the youth group."

"Oh good." She stood up and walked to the door and turned around. "You know Father Ingels was transferred to another parish. Just wanted to let you know."

"Transferred? He should be defrocked."

"Yes. But thank god he didn't, you know."

"He didn't. Not to me."

Davy's mom left the room; he could smell the lingering aroma of Oil of Olay. He picked up the rotary phone on the floor next to him and dialed Sunshine's phone again. This time, somebody picked up. It was the gruff, agitated voice of a man. "Hello. Simon's residence."

"Hello. May I speak to Sunshine?"

"Sunshine? You mean Sonny. Who is this?"

"This is a friend of hers."

"Which friend?"

"Savior."

"Huh? Well, you can't speak to him right now. He's not here. He won't be back for a while."

"Where did she go?"

"He went away for treatment."

"Treatment for what?"

"Listen, you sound like a nice kid. Maybe you didn't know because he is new to the school this year, but Sonny is a boy."

"She's not. She's a girl. Didn't you know?"

"Admittedly, his mother and I haven't been around as much as we would have wished. We have to work. But now we are doing something about his condition."

"What are you doing to her?"

"He is a he."

"No, she's not."

"Jesus."

"Yes?"

"What?"

"You said my name."

"Your name is Jesus?"

"Yes."

"I thought you said it was Savior. You nut."

"What did you do to Sunshine?"

"He's going to have conversion therapy. He'll be gone for two weeks, and when he is back, she will be back to being a boy. Understand?"

"I understand. And I forgive you."

"You what?"

"I forgive you. You know not of what you do."

"You're out of your mind. I've got to go."

Sunshine's father hung up the phone.

Davy got his headphones out, plugged the quarter-inch jack into his stereo, and put Love Will Tear Us Apart back on. He cranked it up so loud that it made his eyes hurt.

Chapter Forty-Six

The next day when Barry came to pick up Davy, who was usually the first. He got into the car, into the empty front passenger seat. "Where's Tommy?" Davy asked.

"Don't know. He was gone this morning."

"Oh. Might have something to do with Sunshine."

"No shit."

"I talked to her dad last night."

"You did? What did he say?"

"Said they took her to have conversion therapy."

"Conversion therapy?"

"Yes. I assume it is what it sounds like."

"Jesus."

"Yes?"

"Cut the shit. What should we do? Tommy is going to lose his mind."

"What about Sunshine?"

"Yes. Terrible. Why can't they just leave people alone? Everyone has to conform to the norm. Or else they put them into concentration camps. Maybe not literally, but in some cases literally."

"Sucks."

"We've got to break her out."

"Indeed."

"Well, let's find out where this fucking conversion therapy place is. It shouldn't be too hard. How many can there be? Let's go get Geraldo and undertake this mission."

"Amen."

Chapter Forty-Seven

"**T**his is ridiculous," Geraldo said morosely.

"No, it is not. It's the perfect plan."

"That's because you're not wearing a dress and a wig, Barry."

"That's because I am too old to be Davy's younger brother, and Davy has to be your older brother slash guardian because he has the goatee!"

"And you're going to try to enroll me in this conversion therapy?" Geraldo said, practically shouting.

"Yes. Well, no. We don't know where this place is. So, we are going to take you over to that born-again church on Katella, and Davy is going to tell them that his little brother is queer and he needs to get fixed." Barry explained methodically.

"Yeah, and they will tell us where the fucking conversion therapy place is," Davy said.

"And we can free Sunshine."

"And then what?" Geraldo asked. Seeing the logic of their plan, but wondered if it ultimately would do any good.

"I talked to Sunshine's father last night. He didn't sound like a bad guy, just confused. I think he could be reasoned with. But God knows what they do to convert someone. Could be shock therapy or a lobotomy. We've got to stop them. I am serious. This is what they do. This isn't the dark ages. And yet it is. We got to save her!"

"Okay. Fine. Let's do it. What should I say when we get there?"

“Don't say anything. I'll do the talking.” Davy said confidently.

“Are we all square? Because there it is,” Barry said as he pulled his Datsun into the parking lot of the New Life Church of Cypress, California. Davy got out of the passenger seat wearing the three-piece dark brown polyester suit that he usually wore to church. Geraldo was dressed in a cute calico dress that they had bought at a Salvation Army. He looked like Melissa Sue Anderson from Little House on the Prairie. He felt like a fool. Though he had sometimes put on his mother's dresses when he was sure no one would find him. He would look at himself in the full-length mirror in his parent's bedroom and imagine what it would be like to be a woman. A woman, not a girl. That was a while ago, though. When he was nine years old. And, of course, the dresses were ludicrously too big. This was different. Not only was he dressed like a girl, he had to act like it; he had to act like it was the way that he *chose* to dress and what he *wanted* to be. He thought to himself how do I think that way? What would I tell myself to get into that kind of mindset? And then he realized that it wasn't a mindset any more than how he went about his day-to-day life was a mindset. It wasn't a mindset it just was.

Davy and Geraldo walked into the church located on the busy intersection of Katella Ave and Valley View. The building was a single-story structure with a flat roof. Geraldo hadn't been in too many churches before, mostly the ones he'd seen when his family had visited Mexico two years prior. This church, if you could call it that, was different; the ceiling wasn't vaulted, and there were no shrines. There were large photos on the wall of Jesus and his disciples, and a Mary with long blonde feathered hair, she looked like Farah Fawcett. Jesus and his merry men looked like male models, as if their hair had been blown dry with a Clairol Super Zap. At the altar, which was little more than a two-foot lift covered in gray industrial carpet, there was just a podium and a large brass cross on the wall. The pews were simple wood benches with purple cushions. And it smelled funny; it smelled like his chemistry class. Davy tugged Geraldo's arm and pulled him in the direction of a door that had a brass plate that said Office. He knocked.

The Jesus Christ College of Irvine was where the conversions took place, according to Pastor Larry. He gave Davy the address and wished him luck, touching Geraldo ever so sweetly on his shoulder and applauding Davy's devotion to Christ and scripture. "They are doing amazing things over there at the JCCI," Davy asked him what exactly went into the treatments. Pastor Larry, tall, ginger, thin with a 1970's bushy mustache and long hair. He looked like a Hudson Brother. He gesticulated widely with lengthy limbs; the blue veins on his forehead protruded prominently. He explained, never taking his eyes from Geraldo, that depending on the case, the course of treatment varied but certain things were not ruled out, including, as Davy feared, shock therapy. "Things like brain surgery no longer take place," he said, kind of sadly. "They diagnose the patient and then begin a course of treatment, aversion therapy of varying degrees, which is where the shock therapy comes in. I am not trying to frighten you," he said to Geraldo in a gentle voice. "Just letting you know that it works and that there is hope." Davy shook his head and put his hands together, "That's what I pray for." Pastor Larry cleared his throat and said, "The path has not been easy. They even lost two of the founding members."

"They died?" Davy asked.

"Um, no. They succumbed to temptation. But there are more successes in Christ's glory than the other way around.

Hallelujah." Pastor Larry went to his desk and pulled out a few pamphlets and handed them to Davy. One was titled *Health Hazards of Homosexuality*, and another was titled *Conversion: How and Why It Works*. "Can I keep these?" Davy asked.

Barry drove in the carpool lane down I-5 South, knowing that when they got to the Jesus Christ College of Irvine, it might be difficult to infiltrate and locate where they were keeping Sunshine, and as it was already her second day, they might have begun with the shock therapy. They could keep using Geraldo as the clay pigeon, but he felt bad for him, and it was getting late; they had already played hooky from school. Basically, they were asking for more trouble. But there was no choice. Mostly, he was worried about his brother. He knew how Tommy was, happy-go-lucky, but when the wheels came off, boy, did they come off, and he knew they were coming off, if they were not already gone. What started out as a glorious week was turning into war. But that's what they signed up for. It was good that this kind of activity was in his blood.

Out front of the Jesus Christ College of Irvine was a police car, shiny and black, white doors- big gold star, chrome bumpers glinting in the afternoon sun, a red light on top rotating quickly; the rear passenger door was open, and Tommy was being led out of the building in handcuffs. He was screaming, "Fucking fascists! Bloody mother fucking fascists!" One big cop had his hand on the top of Tommy's head and was trying to guide him towards the open door of the cop car. Barry pulled up with a screech, jumped out of the Datsun, and ran towards Tommy. "What the hell are you doing to my brother?"

"This is your brother? He was causing a disturbance."

Tommy screamed, "Sunshine! They've got her in there. They are going to harm her."

A man dressed in a dark blue polyester pinstripe suit, wide red argyle tie and out-of-fashion sideburns walked briskly to where Tommy, Barry, and the cop were standing. "Now listen, son, we don't want to cause harm to anyone."

"Then please have them take those handcuffs off of my brother."

"He was causing a disturbance," the man in the argyle tie said.

"I'm here now. I'll take him home."

"You must understand, we are here to help. We are here for anyone in need."

"Thank you, pastor, I appreciate that," Barry said, trying to mask his condescension.

"I am not a pastor."

"Oh? What are you?"

"Just an administrator, head administrator."

"Barry!" Tommy yelled, struggling in the cop's arms. "They are torturing her."

"I assure you; we are doing nothing of the kind."

"Tommy, settle down. Now sir. I assure you that there will be no further disturbances. Can you have my brother released, please?"

Argyle tie looked at the cop and then to Tommy, who was settling down, and finally to Barry. "Are you sure there will be no further disturbances?"

"I assure you. That right, Tommy?"

Tommy nodded.

"Okay, officer, you can release the boy."

They walked to the car, Davy was sitting on the front hood cross-legged, and Geraldo was leaning against the side of the car. Tommy looked at Geraldo dressed in the Calico dress and said, "Oh nice. I get it. Thanks, Geraldo."

"Sure thing. Comrade."

They got into the car, pulled onto I-5, and headed towards Cypress. Geraldo was thinking that he might not get home before his mom. He could figure out a way to explain the dress, but missing school, she might find out about that. Barry said forging a note was a breeze. Still, he felt the anxiety swell in his chest, so much so that he was tuning out the boys and their voices. So many different things were going through his mind. He was thinking about Sunshine, thinking about the first time he saw her in Mr. Magg's office, how glamorous she seemed to him, so brave, so brazen, and so alluring. And now what? They were going to put electricity into her. They were going to try to shock her into being something she wasn't. She wasn't a boy. Anyone could see that. Jesus. Thinking about it made his chest feel as if *it* was being electro-shocked. And what about Maria? He really messed that up. He liked her so much. Really liked her. She was another brave one. Couldn't get any braver than these two. And so pretty and so smart and so funny. He wished he could see her. He wished he could go back in time and do that whole date over again and not try any funny stuff. And lastly, his mom. He was concerned about her. She seemed odd, oft-kilter; she was laughing a lot to herself. She was less preoccupied with what was going on with him. And yet she needed him to be there, but he didn't want to be there, and he felt really guilty about it. He wanted to be with his friends or with Maria. He had nothing against his mom; he loved her, and he liked her too, but there were things that he was feeling that he had never felt before.

"Geraldo!" Davy said, punching him in the arm.

"What?"

"What do you think?"

"About what?"

"Oh my god. What we've been talking about."

"It's okay, Davy," Barry said. "It's been a long day. We figured we would go over to Sunshine's house and see if we could reason with her parents. Tommy thinks that it would be pretty tough to break Sunshine out. That place is locked down. He cased it thoroughly. I think you are right, Geraldo. Even if we could bust her out, then what? Davy, for some reason, thinks we can reason with the dad, maybe the mom. We should at least try."

"Um, yeah. That seems like a good idea. When?"

"Now," Tommy shouted.

"I need to go home; otherwise, my mom will be worried," Geraldo said.

"Okay," Tommy said, calming down. "And besides, from what Sunshine tells me, her parents are never home until eight at the earliest. They both work in Los Angeles."

Chapter Forty-Eight

Carmen was sitting at the kitchen table, a bottle of Cabernet Sauvignon, poached from Seymour's wine storage in front of her. She found that she was quite handy with the claw part of a hammer. Seymour had left with the keys to the lock of the wine locker, which was ostensibly put on to prevent Charles' pilfering. She never drank much, yet Seymour always kept a bottle of Chablis in the refrigerator for her. She thought he was being thoughtful, but in reality, he'd rather have her drink the white wine from Trader Joe's than touch his good stuff, at least when he wasn't around. Now she wanted something with more body. On the table, next to the wine, was her old Olympic typewriter from college days, and beside that was *Love is a Dog from Hell.* She liked reading Bukowski because he was honest. He was disgusting and abhorrent, but at least he was honest. The only male writer she had ever read who was honest about how men really are. No pretense. No bullshit. And if he could be this honest, then why the hell shouldn't she? But it takes bravery; it takes courage and temerity. That's where the wine came in.

She knew she couldn't drink like Bukowski, and best that she didn't try. But one glass of this thick red will get the juices flowing. She popped the cork and filled up a coffee mug with it. She looked at the blank piece of paper in the typewriter. She picked up the Bukowski and randomly opened a page. She read these lines:

she'll miss me

not my love

but the taste of my blood

Yes, that's it. He, not she. He won't miss my love. He'll miss my blood. We are connected by blood. Nothing will change that. The blood of our sons. Nah. He won't miss any of this. Men are not like that. They move on, and that's it. No regrets. "I'm not happy."- that's all they need to say. That justifies anything. Affairs, infidelity, abandonment, treachery, robbery, lawyers, litigation. I wasn't happy, so I had to leave. I love you, but I'm not happy. What the fuck does that mean. Nobody is happy, so why pretend that you can be happy with another woman? Seymour? You will never be happy. Seymour is always happy. He has never denied himself the things that make him happy. The only child syndrome. Wine, food, cigars, records, vacations, nice cars. Stepping out. God knows how many women before this one. Oh well. Not me. It's not my blood anymore. This wine is so good. I need another cup.

After her second mug of Cabernet Sauvignon, she started typing. It just poured out of her. She filled up ten pages, like Bukowski, with no capital letters. Easier that way; just type, just let the words flow. It wasn't like the poetry she used to write in college. It was mean, and it was funny. And it was bad. She knew it was awful, and that's what she liked most about it. It was like puking, she thought. Puking your guts out. What was this pain that she felt? Was it heartache or humiliation? If it was only humiliation, then that was nothing too much to cry about. It *was* that, and it was heartache. She missed Seymour. There was so much about him that she found annoying, but she really liked that he was passionate about things, just not her. His music, cooking, books, politics, movies. Yet, he was always kind to her. Rarely a harsh word. Almost a reverence. Perhaps that was the problem. How can you be passionate about someone you feel reverent towards? Bukowski wasn't reverent, and she wasn't being reverent in what she was writing. She was writing about sex, she was writing about how stupid men were, and she was writing about blood. That's one thing she knew a lot about- blood. After all, she was a hematologist. Blood was blood. Blood was the metaphor- Christ's blood, the wine is his blood, can't get blood from a stone, bad blood, out for someone's blood, blood, sweat, and tears, period blood, making someone's blood boil. Yes, she knew all about blood, and now she was putting it into her poetry.

The front door opened, and Geraldo came in. He said, "Hi, Mom," and rushed upstairs to his room. Was he wearing a dress? Okay, maybe it is time to stop with the wine and start getting dinner ready.

Chapter Forty-Nine

It felt like she had been sitting in that room for days. In the long mirror on the wall, she could see herself, her face freshly scrubbed of all paint and gloss, her parents ghoulishly illuminated by the fluorescent lighting, a square heavy, dark wood table and four similarly heavy chairs in the middle of a room where they all sat with a Dr. Slowcumb. Her parents looked ruffled. Like someone had disturbed them from their sleep or from a good meal, or something else, they had taken from Sunshine her skirt and put her in a pair of pants that no longer fit, so the top button was undone. She kept shifting in her chair. The parents had to confess that they did not know what had been happening. They knew that Sonny wore feminine clothing on the weekends when they were home. They assumed that it was a form of dress-up and that during the week, Sonny dressed normally, like a boy, for school. The mom smoked Benson and Hedges cigarettes throughout the conference. She feigned tears but Sunshine knew it was forced, and only half-hearted at that. Still, she felt bad for her mom and her dad. She knew that they didn't know how to deal. When asked by Dr Slowcumb if she wanted to upset her parents, she shook her head. When asked if she wanted to please her parents, she nodded. Dr Slowcumb also asked, in a somber voice, if she ever had thoughts of suicide. She nodded. And she had thoughts; she even had a plan.

After the parents signed some papers, they left, and she was alone with Slowcumb. At first, he was sympathetic with how hard it must be to be different from everyone else. But then he started saying what an abomination it was, that the children of today must go without the guidance so necessary; they were rudderless without Jesus Christ to steer their ship. Sunshine asked if he was a doctor or a priest. This seemed to anger Slowcumb, but he smiled. He told her that homosexuality was a sin and that it was a certain ticket to hell. He picked up the bible next to a stack of books and magazines and a pitcher of water. He opened the bible, cleared his throat, and read this passage, "'If a man practices homosexuality, having sex with another man as with a woman, both men have committed a detestable act. They must both be put to death, for they are guilty of a capital offense.' Now, nobody is putting anybody to death. Not in this day and age. But you see, it is a capital offense against God."

"But I am not a homosexual," Sunshine said.

Dr Slowcumb seemed caught off guard. "Then why do you dress the way you do and put all that makeup on your face?"

"Because I am a girl."

He laughed. "Well, Sonny. That's not what your parents tell me. Nor what was evident when you got out of that skirt and panties and into your proper boy's pants."

"How do you know?"

"I know more than you think."

Sunshine looked at the long mirror on the wall, and it registered.

They went over it again and again. Sunshine explained that she was a girl, and she was attracted to boys. She just happened to have a penis. Dr Slowcumb read from the bible, and books on psychology, passages from psychoanalytic quarterlies. He kept at it for hours until he got her to admit that she wanted to change. In a flood of tears, she shouted, "I want to be normal!" Slowcumb nodded approvingly. A meal was brought in consisting of canned spaghetti, white bread and green beans. Sunshine hadn't eaten all day, so she consumed the food. Slowcumb watched her eat, and when she was finished, he said, "Now we need to go to the next step."

"What is that?"

"It is what is called reparative therapy."

He took her to another room, which had a little brown loveseat where Sunshine was told to sit. There was a film projector, some electric contraption which she was attached to by way of a strap around her wrist and a wire running to the machine. There were two i.v's, one which they put into the vein of her left arm, and the other into the vein of her right arm. Dr Slowcumb asked her again if she really wanted to change and if she really wanted to be normal. Overwhelmingly frightened, she nodded. He asked her to take off her pants, and they put a Velcro strap around her penis, which had a wire coming out of it that ran to another machine.

Chapter Fifty

I t was almost 9 o'clock when they got to Sunshine's house. As the little circular clock on the dashboard turned 10, Barry let out a big sigh. "Where the hell are they?" He looked at Tommy, who shrugged. "From what I know, this is kind of normal."

"Maybe they're visiting Sunshine," Geraldo said hopefully.

"It's possible, but I think it's past visiting hours," Davy said realistically.

A car pulled into the driveway. A nice blue Mercedes Benz CL. Both of Sunshine's parents got out of it. The boys waited until Sunshine's parents had gone inside then they got out of the car and walked towards the house. They stood for a minute. "Ring the bell," Davy said to Barry. Barry stuck out his finger like it was a pistol and pushed the doorbell. It played a nice little melody, Beethoven Fur Elise, sounded like church bells. They glanced at each other, facial expressions full of raw nerves and resolve. The door opened. It was Sunshine's father. He looked just as Davy imagined: tall, in expensive clothes, mustache, Italian eyeglasses, thick, wavy, expertly coiffed hair, and a shocked expression on his face like he had opened the door to the Manson Family.

"Hello, Sunshine's dad. We are Sunshine's friends," Barry said matter-of-factly.

"Oh, I see. What can I do for you?"

"It's not what you can do for us," Davy said calmly. "It's what you can do for your daughter."

"I don't have a daughter."

"The hell you don't!" Tommy exclaimed. Barry turned and gave him a look to cool it.

"Listen, sir, we know how confusing it is, but you've got to listen to us. Will you at least do that and perhaps you will learn something about your child, something that will help you through what I am sure is a very difficult time." Davy said, sounding like FM radio. "It won't take long. Just give us fifteen minutes and then you think about what is best. But as the treatment that your child will receive at the place you left her will involve electric shock and other forms of coercion, I think it is best to have this talk now."

"I don't think you are correct about electric shock. But okay, come in, but just for a little while."

Sunshine's father led the kids into the house and into the living room, where Sunshine's mother sat on a sofa by the electric fireplace with legs curled under a long black maxi dress. She held half a glass of red wine. "Oliver. Who are these people?" she said. Her expression was static.

"These are Sunshine, Sonny's friends. I told them we would hear them out. They care for, for our child."

"Well then, I need another drink." She drained her glass and then moved to stand up, but Oliver said, "I'll bring you a fresh one, dear. Go ahead and sit down, kids."

Everyone found a place to sit. Davy sat nearest to Sunshine's mother. They looked at each other somewhat intently. "This one seems familiar," she said. "Did you know we used to be hippies? That's right, bonafide hippies."

"What happened?" Tommy said tartly.

"Yes indeed. What happened? Real life intruded. The harsh reality of idealism's limits and the pragmatism of prosperity."

"How do you go from being part of a liberation movement to incarcerating your own child, your own flesh and blood in a concentration camp," Tommy said, practically shouting.

"Don't you think that is an exaggeration?"

"Tommy, please, let's stay calm," Davy said, trying to bring the tone of the room back down. "But he is right. You have put her in a place where they are actually torturing her, sending electrical currents into her body in order to make her into something that she is not."

"Oliver. Is that right?"

"I don't think so, Madge," Oliver said, coming back into the room and handing the drink to Madge. "It didn't say anything about that in the papers that we signed."

"I guarantee you that what they are attempting to do to your daughter is nothing short of torture; it's called aversion therapy." Davy pulled from his jacket pocket the pamphlets he took from the born-again church and gave a pamphlet to Madge and the other to Oliver. The mom got the one on conversion, how and why it works. "She is your daughter. Don't you know that she only thinks of herself as a girl? That's who she is. You know that." Madge set down the pamphlet. Davy took her hand and looked her in the eyes. "You know who your daughter is." Madge nodded. "So if you know that, then we have to stop this barbarity. Before it is too late."

"But how will she ever fit in; how will she ever find a place in this world being so different?"

"Look at us," Geraldo said, speaking up. "She found a place with us. We think she is great. Do you even know how amazing your daughter is?"

Madge looked up at Oliver who was wiping the tears from his eyes as he let drop from his hand the pamphlet that went into detail about aversion therapy.

Chapter Fifty-One

That Sunday at Saint Irene Church was the big bazaar. Davy did as his mother said and did not wear his white Adidas tracksuit. He wore his three-piece khaki polyester suit, handed down from his older brother. Though he was quite distracted, thinking about Sunshine, he attended mass and listened to the priest, Father Franklin Buckman's homily. He knew this man; he was well known among the boys when he attended Saint Irene Parish School. Yet it wasn't Father Franklin who tried to touch him; it was Father Ruhl who attempted to fondle him one day after school. His breath was hot and acrid on his face, Old Spice venting through his prickly purple pores as he cornered Davy, filling the air between them with the singsong sound of his high Irish brogue, invoking masculine righteousness. He put his arm around Davy's shoulder and, with a quick thrust, drew him nearer. Davy kneed him in the groin and ran out of the room where he was being kept for detention.

He told his mother, and she pulled him from the school and enrolled him in the local public school. Never doubting the veracity of his allegations. Davy's father asked no questions but was relieved at not having to pay the tuition. He was not a believer; he held firm opinions about the Catholic Church, the Vatican, and the Pope that mirrored Roman Castevet, minus Satan worshiping. But he loved his wife and so went along with whatever she thought best. She oversaw the educational aspects of the boys' upbringing. Strictly speaking, she was not a devout Catholic, but she loved its traditions and the pageantry. Davy's allegations of unwanted attention by the priest shook her but did not surprise her. She grew up in the church. They kept the incident from the father. Afterwards she still attended mass and other events at the church, only not as frequently or as fervently.

Madge had seen suffering in her life and always found refuge in the idea of a Jesus Christ, who died for our sins. Her sins. She found the iconography moving and beautiful. The image of the crucifixion, encapsulated in the cross she wore; violent, intense, and sensual. She had sinned, and it was good to know that there was salvation personified by the almost naked man dangling from around her neck. But she identified with both Mary Magdalene and Mary, the mother of Jesus. That was her personal dichotomy. Until *she* became a mother, she took life for granted living day to day. Even after she married. Having children grounded her. She had a strong relationship with both of her boys and tried to imbue them with a sense of righteousness. She knew that they had no inherent kinship to Christianity. At least not like she did. And she didn't force it. Yet she knew they had an innate sense of right and wrong. She attributed that to *her* religious upbringing.

Davy listened to the sermon somberly. When Father Franklin read from Leviticus 19:10, "You shall love your neighbor as yourself," and in the same breath, quotes John 3:16, "For God so loved the world, that he gave his only Son, that whoever believes in him should not perish but have eternal life." Davy thought - Believes *what* in him? And what about the rest? Condemned to burn in the everlasting fires of hell, no doubt. After Mass, Davy's mom took him to the plaza in front of the church where the bazaar was being held, led him past the various tables to where the youth group was. She introduced Davy to some of the kids whom she had become acquainted with in the last few weeks in the hopes of making this introduction. The kids looked at Davy as if he was the second coming of

Christ. It wasn't just the goatee and long hair; there seemed to be an aura that emanated from his presence. Pleased at his friendly reception, Madge walked away to join some of her friends.

"You look like him." One of the kids said.

"Like who?" Davy asked.

The kids snickered. One of the girls asked him if he was in a band. He nodded. She said, "I thought so." Davy looked around at all the people, at the booths where folks were selling t-shirts, coffee mugs, ashtrays, and vases that had Saint Irene logo - *an A-frame facade of the church with four white pillars on either side and below that a Jesus with outstretched arms*. Other booths sold raffle tickets, bibles, crucifixes, and religious artifacts. He started to feel weak. "I think you're foxy," the girl said. "My name is Margot." He looked at her. She was very attractive in her Saint Irene t-shirt a size too small. One of the boys said, "I'm in a band too. I play the drums. We play prog. My name is Bruce." Davy looked at him, smiled, and nodded. "Yes, but what do you think of all of this?" he said.

"All of what?" Magot asked.

"This. This selling of a spiritual message."

"What's the message?" Bruce asked innocently.

"'And when you pray, do not be like the hypocrites, for they love to pray standing in the synagogues and on the street corners to be seen by others. But when you pray, go into your room, close the door, and pray to your Father, who is unseen. And when you pray, do not keep on babbling like pagans, for they think they will be heard because of their many words. Do not be like them.'"

"What's your name?" Margot asked.

"My name is Davy. Though some of my friends call me…"

Father Franklin approached the group. He said, "It seems you know scripture. Margot, who is your friend?"

Margot replied reticently, "I just met him. His name is Davy."

"Hello, Davy. I haven't seen you here before."

"I used to go to the Parish School. But I left."

"That's a shame. We could use more kids who have an interest in scripture."

"Scripture is flawed, easily manipulated by those who want to coerce and spread fear."

"How do you mean Davy?"

"You quoted Leviticus about heaven for the believers, but what about the unbelievers? They go to burn in hell?"

"It's God's law, not mine."

"And what about Leviticus 20:12, 'If a man practices homosexuality, having sex with another man as with a woman, both men have committed a detestable act. They must both be put to death, for they are guilty of a capital offense.' Seems like your bible is homicidal and full of malice."

"I did not write the bible. It is the holy word."

"Well, you should follow it. Do you think that Jesus would approve of your turning his house of prayer into a den of thieves!" Davy screamed.

"Now settle down, son."

"Fuck you. You pederast." Davy spun around and turned over the table where they were selling raffles. He went to the next table, which was full of Bibles, pamphlets, and brass crosses. He turned that one over as well. He went from table to table, either toppling each one or swiping the contents to the ground. Finally, he was restrained by a few men, but he slipped free and ran from the church. He ran until he got to a 7-Eleven. There, he bought a large grape Slurpee. He sucked it hard through the plastic straw but had a terrible brain freeze and dropped the Slurpee to the ground causing a large purple splatter. "What the fuck!" the clerk said. Davy put the palms of his hands on either eye until the pain subsided. He looked at the clerk, who was fuming, and said, "I'm sorry, brother." And walked out of the 7-Eleven into the bright midday sun.

Chapter Fifty-Two

Carmen had a terrible hangover. She loved it. Made her feel alive. Her head felt as if it had been removed from her neck, put in a pot of sangria like an orange slice, and left to soak. She had, in fact, made sangria the night before and had, in fact, drank three, maybe four cups of it. She listened to Brahms' Symphony 1 and 2 and wrote close to twenty poems, half of which she crumpled up and threw in the trash. All in all, a successful evening and a great way to spend a Sunday night. She felt gratified and yet wished she could find somewhere in the lab to take a nap.

She heard a man clearing his throat. She lifted her head from the microscope and turned around to find Clive impeccably adorned in a rust gold turtleneck. But something was off. His great, graceful smile had gone missing. It was then that she realized that she didn't despise Clive. No, not at all. He was an exceptional human, a beautiful man. He had wonderful taste and an authentically gregarious nature. Maybe a tad cloying. But that was ok. She was honored that he would feel so inclined toward her that he would jeopardize his marriage and standing in the community. On the other hand, what the hell was wrong with him?

"Excuse me, Carmen. I just wanted to thank you for coming to our little gathering. I know it must have been a hell of a surprise to see me there, but you handled it with more aplomb than I." He cleared his throat again. "You know."

"I don't know about that, but thank you. Just imagine. My Charles and your April. Incredible." With her hangover, the night was a bit of a foggy memory. She took a few seconds to recall it and place it in the context of everything that was swimming around in her head. "You have a very lovely home." She was going to say a lovely wife to boot. But she stopped herself.

"Thank you," Clive replied gratefully.

She noticed that he had something in his hand. An envelope. Perhaps he was off to mail a letter and was just stopping by to make chit-chat. Indulge his indulgences. The way he stood there, eyes wide and hands at his side, she was fully aware of the sway she had over him. That night, in the front seat of his car, it was evident then. His clumsy movements, and yet he was a pretty good kisser. Seymour wasn't much of a kisser, never was. But he had a large and beautiful penis. Uncircumcised, which was so odd, seeing how he was a Jew and all. Apparently, his father had a revelation on the day of and called off the whole bris and sent the mohel and everyone home. Seymour was always grateful to his father for that, finding out, through various books and magazines, that sex is much more pleasurable for an uncircumcised penis. When it came to his own sons, he acquiesced to the doctors and allowed for their foreskin to be removed in a hospital setting. The doctors said it was common practice and best for the boys hygienically. Carmen wondered if Clive had been circumcised. She wanted to ask him right there.

"So, Clive…"

Clive blurted out, "I just wanted to give this to you, and I'll be on my way." He handed her the envelope and hurried off. Carmen watched him as he retreated to the pathology lab. She looked down at the envelope, there was her name written in the most beautiful calligraphic script. She was curious: what kind of shenanigans was this black Englishman up to, for Christ's sake? It made her laugh, and it made her wish she had a drink. She would like nothing more than to be home, put on a classical music record on Seymour's mighty hi-fi, maybe Chopin or Rachmaninoff, pour herself a coffee mug of red wine, sit down, and read this letter from dear old Clive. Instead, she tore open the envelope and pulled from it a folded piece of paper, and on it, much to her disappointment were the words: *Carmen - I can't help it, but I am in love with you.* She was hoping for a little more meat. A little more of an explanation. The reasons why he was in love with her, something like - from the first time I saw you I knew - yadda yadda… because of your yadda yadda… Some poetry, for Christ's sake! But it was fine. One needs to manage one's expectations. That was her new mantra. She considered numerous ways of responding. Yet, as much as she wanted to torture the man, she wasn't going to let him fuck up his life. And more importantly she didn't want Charles' girlfriend to be unhappy. April was a nice girl. Charles had never had a girlfriend. She didn't want to be the cause of any mishegoss. But how? How to dissuade this impetuous pathologist?

Chapter Fifty-Three

Clive stood in front of the hospital. April was picking him up as his car was in the shop. The ultraviolet rays of the sun were splashing against his Ray Bans, behind which were eyes fixed at approximate nothingness on the horizon. He tried to discern what it was he was feeling at that moment. He felt foolish beyond foolish. And yet, he felt almost proud of his temerity. He wondered if he was getting carried away with himself. How could he be in love with this woman whom he barely knew? Well, that was easy. She was the most beautiful and enchanting woman he had ever seen. She exuded a kind of classical physiognomy, and therefore, he felt like he knew her and had every right to feel the way he felt. Except for the fact that he was married and the father of the girl whom Carmen's son was in a longstanding relationship with. Veritable high school sweethearts. He wished he could just chalk it up to a midlife crisis, which he was certain his wife would spin that way if she knew. She was always letting him off the hook. But it was more than that. Much more than that.

As Carmen walked out of the hospital, she saw Clive standing there like a statue. She thought it a perfect opportunity to try to curtail his advances. She walked up to him and said, "Hello, Clive."

"Oh. Carmen." He had never seen her in the daylight. It took him a second to register. She wore yellow plastic wraparound sunglasses and a lime green dress with daisy prints, which held closely to her body. He usually saw her in a lab coat, and so was caught off guard by her voluptuousness. Her hair was a bit unruly, and he could see the little lines that ran along the side of her face. She looked like an artist standing there with one hand on her hip, staring at him curiously.

"What are you doing standing there?" Carmen asked.

"I'm waiting for my daughter. My Mercedes is in the shop."

"Oh. That's too bad, such a nice car."

"Just a minor repair. Still under warranty."

"That's good. Listen. You've got to stop with this foolishness."

"What foolishness?"

"You're not in love with me. You're just bored."

"I am not bored. I am in love with you."

"No, you're not."

"Yes, I am."

"You're not in love with me, and I can prove it."

"How could you possibly prove it? It is not quantifiable."

"Yes, it is. Listen. You can't be in love with someone who is not in love with you. And I am most definitely not in love with you."

"Even if you're not in love with me, that doesn't mean that I can't be in love with you."

"That's not love. That's infatuation. It's childish."

"How do you even know that you're not in love with me?"

"What?" She burst out laughing. "Because I can barely stand to be around you."

"Oh." He crossed his arms and looked away.

"Oh, Clive. Don't pout. I can barely stand to be around anyone. Not that I wouldn't be tempted. You are an inordinately attractive man and charming and you have impeccable taste. I am honored that, for some reason you chose to direct your attention towards me. It's just what my pride needed. But you've got a nice life. A nice wife and a lovely daughter. Don't be a cliche. You're better than that."

"What if I can prove that not only am I in love with you, but that you are in love with me? What if I can prove it?"

"That is crazy, Clive. Like you said, it is not quantifiable."

"Who knows, maybe it is. Maybe it is."

April pulled into the parking lot and saw her father and Carmen talking. When Carmen burst out laughing at something her father said, she noticed that her father didn't look like someone who had just told a joke. He looked cold, annoyed, lacking any joviality. It was an odd chemistry between the two of them and it caused April to feel that there was something going on. She thought so the night of her birthday party but repressed it. Consciously repressed it.

As she drove nearer, she saw her father was talking so very seriously to Carmen, who had a perplexed expression on her face. April pulled to the curb where they were standing and beeped the horn of her Honda Civic. There was no response from either one of them, so she leaned over, rolled down the passenger window of her car, and said, "Daddy!" He looked at her and then turned to Carmen and smiled cockily. Carmen made her eyes small and wrinkled her nose. Clive got into his daughter's car, and they drove off. Carmen wondered, "Oh my god, was I flirting *with him*?"

*****

April shifted smoothly; her father had taught her well. He had taught her a lot of things. How was it that he still seemed like a stranger to her? Those sunglasses: when did he get those?

He looked neither cool nor slick. Seemed like he was always trying to overcompensate. As a black man from England, he never felt that he truly fit in with his perceived ethnicity, even though he lived in America since he was in his early twenties. Of course, he felt more of an outsider back in London. For all that city's pretenses of liberal cosmopolitanism, one could feel the breath of racial hatred on one's neck, especially after the mass migration of English-speaking Caribbean immigrants in the late 1950s. He couldn't wait to get out of there and finish his degree in the States.

They drove along, not talking. April had the jazz radio station down low. The car smelled a little of cigarettes as Charles had been in it the night before, and she had allowed him to smoke and, in fact, had one for herself. She hoped her father wouldn't notice. He didn't notice. Clive was looking out the window as they drove down Katella Ave, passing plazas and shopping centers and cinder block walls behind which were a plethora of residential housing. One- and two-story ranch, Cape Cod; Pseudo-Spanish revival homes; and condominiums for those unable to swing a house and yard. It was tedious to see the sprawl day after day after day. Sometimes, he missed his former job at the hospital in Hollywood, but then he'd remember the commute. Seemed he spent a substantial portion of his waking life in an automobile. It was better being in Orange County. But also worse. Both. Somehow. He thought, Jesus Christ, Carmen is right; I hadn't thought of it before; it hadn't occurred to me before; it seems like she can peer into me and know things; she is so perceptive, and she is right; I am bored!

"What?" April said.

"What?" Clive replied, snapping out of it.

"You said you were bored. What are you finding so boring?"

"Oh, yes, well, this jazz music. It is so boring. I'm sick of it."

"I thought you loved jazz."

"I do, but not this fusion junk. It is; it is boring." He forced a laugh.

"I'll turn it off."

"No, that's alright. If you like it."

"Actually, I hate it." And they both laughed. April turned off the radio. "So, what were you and Charles' mom talking about?"

"Who?"

"Charles' mom. Carmen."

"Oh yes. Her. Oh, we, she was thanking me for dinner the other night."

"From what he told me, I thought that Charles' father was the weird one, but it turns out Carmen is a bit eccentric herself."

"Now, April, you must make allowances. She is going through a hard time."

"Yes. I guess you're right." She changed the station to a rock station, but it was a never-ending commercial. She turned off the radio. "How about you? How are you doing, Dad?"

"Me. I'm doing fine. Just fine." he said without a trace of emotion.

What could she expect? He wasn't going to open up to her. She wished he would, but he never had and only got annoyed when prodded to do so. But she knew something was not quite right with him, and she wished that he could feel that he *could* talk to her. After all, she was an adult now, and it seemed like he could use someone other than her mother to express himself, too. Yet she knew enough to know that he wouldn't. Not in a million years.

Chapter Fifty-Four

rinking a wine spritzer in the garden, Samara was in a zone when April and Clive arrived. She was relaxing. Attempting to relax. In the process of relaxing. But she was disquieted, and she didn't know why, which she found aggravating. There was a pulsing anxiety in her chest. She ran the checklist: the world, her world, her work, her children, her marriage- none of it could she find to be the source. All of it was fine. More than fine. True, she despised Ronald Reagan but she had become quite apathetic about politics. She loved her home, all the plants, the beautiful furniture, and art, and always delicious meals. Her practice was thriving, and she was pleased with her recent piece for the Psychoanalytic Quarterly on Native American techniques in dream analysis. Her children were thriving. Though she wasn't so sure about this, Charles, April's high school sweetheart, but he was just that, and she'd move on. And as far as her marriage was concerned. It was fine. Clive was a restless spirit. She knew that. But he had his hobbies, his golf, his watercolors, his cooking. And he was always loving towards her. Her marriage was excellent. So what was it?

She could hear them chatting amiably in the kitchen. She could hear the refrigerator door being opened and juice being poured into glasses. She heard, "Where's mom?" And then, "Probably in the garden." Life was predictable. It could be predictable. Or was it a Deja vu? Was she having a Deja vu? Had this exact thing already happened many, many times? She should know. Wasn't the phenomenon of Deja vu just another form of dreaming, and what do the Cherokee say about dreams:

that visions and dreams are gifts from the spirits and that the spirit world and the world of humans are intertwined. Another theory is that Deja vu is memory leaking in from a past life. It didn't matter because here they were.

"Hello, mum!"

"Daughter, Clive."

"Hello, darling." Clive leaned down and kissed Samara's cheek. He and April sat down and put their drinks on the teak table. The garden was dense with majesty palms, ferns, hydrangeas, jacarandas, and assorted flowers. The air felt moist and smelled of gardenias and lilacs.

"How was your day, dear?" Samara asked automatically.

"Fine. Just fine."

"Mom, have you seen Dad's new sunglasses?" April said teasingly.

"Why no. I don't think so."

"He looks like he's in the C.I.A."

"Stop teasing him. I'm sure they are very cool."

Oh my god. Clive thought. What am I, twelve years old? They are so patronizing. This is unbearable. How can I go on? I just want to be with Carmen or just be alone. Carmen understands me. She gets me. I love these two. I love them beyond measure. But I am not satisfied. The Russians could bomb us tomorrow, and I am spending my life in utter torpidity.

"No. I guess they're kind of stupid." Clive said morosely.

"Oh, Daddy. I was just teasing. They are cool. You are the coolest dad in all of Orange County."

"Well, that's not saying much, but I'll take it." He chuckled as if this little bit of self-deprecation could leave this conversation about his fucking sunglasses in the dirt.

"Are you alright, dear?" Samara asked, maintaining a materterine posture.

"Yes. I'm fine. Just tired. I think I'll take a shower."

Clive stood up, looked down at his wife and then his daughter, smiled wanly, and left. April looked at her mom and raised her eyebrows. Samara grimaced in return. "He's so sensitive," April said.

"Yes. He's still adjusting to the new hospital."

April took a sip from her drink and then said, "So, that was some night.".

"Which night was that?"

"My birthday."

"Oh. Did you have fun?"

"Yes. I guess. Charles' mom was so strange. And she drank a lot."

"Divorce is hard."

"I guess so. Seems like you and Daddy are the last of a dying breed."

"Don't say that."

"What?"

"Don't be cynical. It's so fashionable these days, but I think it is boring. Try to think for yourself."

"I do think for myself. I'm just pointing out the obvious. Doesn't seem like I can say anything right these days."

April looked at her mother with quiet scrutiny and thought; it seems like Charles and I are the only couple I can think of that get along. He may be eccentric in his own right, but he is smart and lovable.

Samara said, "Gosh, everyone is so sensitive."

"Well, isn't that why you get paid the big bucks."

"And precocious."

"Don't blame me. That's how you raised me." April stood up. "I'm going to go and study." As she went to leave, she brushed her mother's shoulder with her hand. Samara grabbed it quickly, patted it a few times, and then let her go.

Upstairs in the master bathroom, Clive was taking a long, hot shower. He was thinking of Carmen, he was thinking of him and Carmen, he was imagining that he was making love to her on some tropical island, like the beach scene in From Here to Eternity. He had lathered up his groin and was stroking furiously his moderately sized, circumcised penis, and with almost animal emotion, came in one large splurge against the tempered glass of the shower stall; the water from the shower head washed his load down to the avocado green tiled floor, which then coagulated on the drain before going down with the help of Clive's toes.

Chapter Fifty-Five

Waiting at the curb when the Datsun pulled up, Geraldo was thinking about a phone call he received the night before, and he was thinking how much he hated Mondays. As per usual, Barry was at the wheel, Tommy beside him and Davy in the backseat. Davy pushed the door open. Geraldo got in. KROQ was on the radio. The DJ Rodney Bingenheimer was giving a rundown of some upcoming concerts in his youthful, laconic voice. He didn't sound like any other DJ; he sounded like one of them. He sounded like he was fifteen years old. He spoke with subdued ebullience. Rodney announced the next song, Wreckless Eric - Whole Wide World. Plunking downstrokes of a gritty guitar, and then a snotty voice started singing, "When I was a young boy, my mama said to me, there's only one girl in the world for you, she probably lives in Tahiti," and when the chorus came on the boys began to sing along loudly, "I'd go the whole wide world, I'd go the whole wide world just to find her!"

When the song was over, Tommy reduced the volume, turned in his seat, and caught everyone up on Sunshine. "She called last night, though she didn't talk long, and she sounded very down. But she was grateful to us for getting her parents to have her released from that torture asylum."

"When will she be coming back to school," Geraldo asked.

"I don't know," Tommy said. "Soon, though."

"That's good."

"I got arrested yesterday," Davy said matter of fact.

"What?" All three boys asked in synch.

"Yeah. The Catholics. Saint Irene."

"What the hell?" Barry shouted.

"I kind of went berserk and wrecked their whole festival. I turned over a bunch of tables and stuff."

"What'd you do that for?" Tommy asked. "Playing Jesus and the money changers?"

"Well, my mom wanted me to go, you know. And I thought I would, to make her happy."

"Even after everything you went through?" Barry asked.

"Yeah. Well, it meant a lot to her. But then, all of it just rubbed me the wrong way. Especially after the priest quoted from Leviticus. Such hypocrisy. So, I went berserk. My mom made me go down to the police station because she got a call saying there was a warrant. They were going to press charges, but Mom brought up some things that I am sure they would rather people didn't know about. So, they let me go. I'm not to go back, though."

"That's so insane!" Tommy cried. "Savior, you are the man!"

"Yeah. I guess so."

They drove along listening to the radio, Talking Heads, Psycho Killer.

"I got a death threat on the phone last night," Geraldo said, subdued.

"Your first one?" Barry asked.

"What? Yeah. Said they were going to kill me and burn down my house. I am just glad my mom didn't pick up."

"Comes with the territory, kid," Barry said as if he was Humphrey Bogart.

The Datsun pulled into the school's parking lot; as it was mostly filled, Barry parked in the back. They walked onto campus humming the theme to The Bridge Over the River Kwai. And then they saw it. It surrounded all the lockers with giant silver mesh metal fences. A security wall for the lockers. Mr. Magg walked up to them and said, "You try anything; you try to mess with those fences, then it will be over. Over!" And he walked off.

"What will be over?" Geraldo asked.

"His job," Barry replied.

Chapter Fifty-Six

When Geraldo got home, he made himself a large glass of Ovaltine. He took it to his bedroom, set it down on his nightstand, and then picked up his guitar, the one his father bought him for his last birthday. He asked for an electric. Seymour said no way. He hated rock and roll and didn't want Geraldo "making a racket." Instead, he got the Yamaha acoustic, which he had to restring upside down because he was left-handed. He picked out a Turco Flex-50, his favorite guitar pick, from on top of the nightstand and started strumming a D chord, alternating from a D suspended to the straight triad. He sang, "When I was a little boy, the world seemed so small; now I am a little older, the world…" He stopped strumming. What is a good rhyme for small? Tall, call, crawl, fall. He set down his guitar and reclined on his bed. It was so quiet in the house. Why was that? He recalled a time when there was rarely a quiet moment. When his brother was home and always running off at the mouth or his father blasting jazz music on the stereo. He picked up the copy of Catcher in the Rye, which he had retrieved from the trash bin. After all, it was "essential reading," along with Clockwork Orange and Death on the Installment Plan, according to his brother. He opened it to where a Jerry Remy baseball card served as a bookmark and started reading, but it was no use. He just didn't like the voice; in fact, he hated the voice of Holden Caulfield, and he hated that this was the book that inspired Mark David Chapman to kill John Lennon. Chapman thought that *he* would be the Catcher in the Rye, catching the falling children. What a psychopath. It's not the book's fault but still, he hated it. He skipped to the last page. The last two sentences. *Don't tell anybody anything. If you do, you start missing everybody.* He threw the book across the room; it hit a poster of Jimi Hendrix and fell to the ground.

The phone started ringing. He didn't want to pick up. He didn't want to hear somebody threatening to kill him and burn down the house. But when he heard his mother come home, he didn't want *her* to pick up. He bolted from his bed and ran down the stairs to the phone in the foyer, shouting, "I'll get it!" But it was too late. She had already picked up. "It's for you," she said from across the room. He walked to where she was standing in the living room. He looked at her to see if she had heard anything that upset her. She took off her sunglasses, raised her eyebrows, and then smiled, "It's a girl." She handed him the phone. "I'm going to go lie down." He watched her go up the stairs to her bedroom. He took the phone and sat down on the sofa. "Hello?" he said.

"Hola Geraldo."

"Hi Maria."

"Que pasa?"

"Nothing."

"Oh. You were different. When we go to park."

"What?"

"You were not nice. Is that you?"

"I don't know."

"I like the old you."

"Maria. A lot has happened. Muy malo things."

"Por que? You can tell me."

"I don't think you would understand. No comprende."

"I understand. You no like me anymore."

"It's not that. I just don't have time."

"Oh."

"I've got to go."

"Okay."

Geraldo hung up the phone. He immediately felt like a jerk. Why had he done that? He wanted nothing more than to see Maria and apologize for how he behaved the last time he saw her. She was someone who was nice to him. She understood what he was going through as well as anybody. She had been the victim of real political persecution, and it drove her from her land and cost her the lives of her loved ones. What had it cost him to go around claiming he was a communist and stirring up animosity? Nothing. Nothing really. A little intimidation, that's all. Some creeps bullying him. But they had always bullied him. Nothing much had changed about that since kindergarten when Joe Simpson punched him in the nose for no reason. Or when, in third grade, some kids slashed the tires of his bike. Or all during study hour in fifth grade, in the Mentally Gifted Minors program, when the selected kids were left to their own devices in the library, it became like Lord of the Flies, and Ben Fulton would literally throw him across the room from time to time. He had always been bullied. Because he was small and quiet, and would say things to antagonize the bigger kids. But Maria's family had been killed. And she was so nice and sweet to him. The phone rang. He lunged for it, picked it up quickly, and said, "Hello. Maria?" It was quiet; he heard heavy breathing. "This is not Maria, you commie scum. But this is the person who is going to come to your house one night, slash your throat, and burn down your fucking..." Geraldo slammed down the phone.

*****

Carmen whipped up stir-fried fajitas in the wok that Seymour left behind. They sat at the dining room table, both preoccupied and barely eating. Carmen looked at Geraldo and realized that she was not paying any attention to her son. She noticed his gloom and said, "Don't you like my Chinese Mexican cuisine?"

"I love it, Mom. Just not too hungry."

And he did love her food. He loved all his mother's cooking even though his father was supposed to be the chef in the family. Carmen made great burgers, fried in vegetable oil and crispy around the edges. Seymour's burgers were so fat it was hard to get your mouth around them and too pink in the middle. Carmen made a great tuna salad with bits of carrots and sweet pickles in it, but never tuna casserole, or bologna casserole, for that matter. And never American cheese. Only cheddar or Swiss. She made Beef stroganoff that was creamy, peppery and delicious. And a salad with avocado, red onion and tomato in her own red wine vinaigrette at almost every meal. "You need your roughage," she would say, as if the children were goats.

Geraldo had a bite and then realized that he *was* very hungry. He took a spoonful of guacamole and mixed it in with the sauteed chicken, bell peppers and onions, wrapped it in a flour tortilla, and stuck it in his mouth. He noticed something was missing. Oh yes, the Tapatio hot sauce. He grabbed the bottle and poured some on the food and took another bite. He then finished three wraps in quick succession. Carmen watched, transfixed. She loved to watch her children eat her food. Found it very gratifying. She grew up without a mother; her mother had died of tuberculosis when she was quite young. It was her older sister, Florencia, who made most of the meals when Carmen was home from the Crippled Children's Home. And she was not a very good cook nor a very friendly personality. Florencia didn't care if Carmen or her brothers and sisters liked her food. She just resented that it was she who had been placed in charge of it.

"Are you okay, sweetie?" Carmen said, touching Geraldo's hand.

"Yeah. I guess."

"What's wrong? Girl problems?"

"What? Oh yeah. I guess."

"Do you like her? What's her name?"

"Maria."

"Maria? Is she Mexican?"

"She's from Guatemala."

"Oh, that's funny. Does she speak much English? Because I know your Spanish is not so bueno."

"She speaks a little. We can talk, okay."

"We can talk, okay? Sounds like your English could use a little work, too." Carmen giggled. Geraldo smiled at her and forced a chuckle.

"She's cool. But it seems like we come from different worlds."

"Where did you meet her?"

"She works at the donut shop."

"Maybe undocumented," Carmen said to herself.

"What?"

"She might be a refugee."

"Yeah. She is. Her whole family was killed by the fascists." Geraldo said vehemently.

"The fascists? You sound like your brother. Is she nice?"

"Yeah. Real nice. But."

"But what?"

"But I think she likes me more than I like her."

"Oh. I know that phenomenon."

"But maybe I like her as much as she likes me. I don't know."

"I know that phenomenon, too."

After the meal, Geraldo helped clear the table. Carmen rinsed the dishes and handed them to Geraldo to put into the dishwasher. Didn't take long. After they finished, Carmen said, "Do you want to have ice cream sundaes and watch Charlie's Angels?" Usually, the idea of ice cream sundaes and Charlie's Angels would get him excited. But, somehow, he had trouble mustering much enthusiasm. "I think I'll go practice guitar. I'm trying to write a song."

"That's a great sweetie. How's the band?"

"It's okay. Sunshine, our drummer, has been sick."

"That's too bad."

"Yeah."

Carmen gave Geraldo a hug and watched him slouch off. She pulled a coffee mug from out of the cupboard, poured herself a glass of Merlot, carried it to the den, put on a record of Scriabin piano sonatas as played by Ruth Laredo, sat down at her desk, put a sheet of onion paper in her Olympia typewriter and began to write a poem composed of the first things that came into her head; which was a list of her most primal desires. Clive came up repeatedly.

Chapter Fifty-Seven

Finally, Tommy was able to see Sunshine. She hadn't returned to school, but her parents said she would the following Monday. After a tepid welcome at the door by Sunshine's father, he pointed Tommy in the direction of Sunshine's bedroom. It was 11 a.m. on a Saturday, and she was still in her pajamas, a pink two-piece covered with images from the Archies comics. She was sitting on her bed reading Truman Capote's Other Voices Other Rooms. She smiled with mitigated fatigue upon seeing Tommy. He rushed over to her and put his arms around her. She began to cry, and he kissed her cheeks. He couldn't think of anything to say and so he said, "I love you. I love you so much." She hugged him tightly. "I didn't think I would ever see you again. I thought that I was going to die. I wanted to die."

She explained what had happened to her. She spoke, detached from her words, as if she was describing an event from history for class. She described how they showed a film of homosexual porn and how they had injected her with something that made her throw up. They attached a Velcro strap with wires to her penis, and if she got an erection, she would get a shock there. That only happened once when they showed a man and woman kissing, which appeared at the beginning of the movie. Turns out the woman was a man in drag. After that film, they let her rest for a little while. Then they showed images of men and women together, not porn, just scenes from old romance movies, and injected her with something that made her feel euphoric. But by then, she was so messed up by what she had experienced before; the euphoric feeling was muddied in trauma. When the session was over, they told her that this was just the beginning. That it would get more intense in the next session; and then days of bible study to follow. By the end of the week, she would be cured. But the next day, her parents came for her.

Tommy was filled with stultifying anger, but he tried to contain it so as not to upset Sunshine. "Those barbarians," he said clench mouthed. "I'm just glad it's over," Sunshine said. And it was over, but it wasn't over. She had trouble sleeping, and she felt very lethargic. Her parents were being nice to her, though awkward. She wasn't sure what was affecting them. The expression *shamefaced* came to mind when she spoke to them. But what were they ashamed of? Were they ashamed of their behavior in relinquishing her to such brutality? Or shame that Sunshine was not who they thought she was or what they wanted her to be. Or were they ashamed of their inability to understand? Or, being ex-hippies, were they ashamed of the callous society that we live in that is out to destroy anyone who doesn't conform to the standard? Sunshine wanted to say that she forgave them but there wasn't really anything to forgive. They were who they were. If she wanted them to accept her for who she was, then she had to accept them for who they were. They were doing what they thought best. What they thought could help her fit in. What could cure her from this affliction, that of identifying as a girl. It wasn't their fault. They were confused. So, she wasn't angry with them. She just couldn't let them try to harm her again. She could not let that happen, even if she had to kill herself to prevent it. And she was prepared to do that. She just didn't want to. She had very much enjoyed her life, especially the last few months. She had a group of friends, and she had a boyfriend, a really great boyfriend who loved her for who she was, not what she was expected to be. She didn't want to give that up. But she would if she had to.

Tommy inched closer and moved to kiss Sunshine. She was tentative and so he pulled back. He wanted to show her that his ardor was still as strong as ever in the hope that this would help buoy her spirits. He realized that he was not being sensitive. She needed more time. And he realized that he was afraid that he might go back to his old practice, his old technique in regard to pleasuring himself. It had been weeks now since he stopped. Yet, he felt it was inevitable to slip back to old patterns. At least until Sunshine returned to her former self. They heard the phone ring from another room. And then her father's voice, "Sunny. It's for you." She and her parents agreed that they could still call her that name, only; it was now Sunny, short for Sunshine, her middle name, just not Sonny. "Can you bring the phone in here, Dad?" she said in a raised voice.

Her father opened the door, carrying a yellow banana phone and pulling the extension cord. He set it down on the bed where Sunshine and Tommy were sitting. "Here you go, sweetie," he said. He looked at the two of them, stuck out his lower lip, smiled, and left the room. "Hello?" She turned to Tommy and smiled just a little. "It's Savior." She listened to him speaking. Tommy could hear some of the words. He was telling her about the scene at the church and his whole Jesus and the money changers routine. "No way!" Sunshine said and burst out laughing. Tommy was so happy to hear that sound. He had thought that maybe he would never hear it again. That Savior: he was one hell of a kid.

"I don't know Savior. I'm not that good. It would be embarrassing." Suddenly, her gaiety was gone. She ended the conversation by saying, "Okay, I'll think about it." And hung up. She turned to Tommy, shook her head, and said, "We have a gig. But I don't know." Davy had told her that the band had been invited to play at, of all places, a church dance. The girl, Margot, whom he met at the church bazaar, asked him if his band would play for the youth group dance. It wasn't affiliated with Saint Irene, so there would be no problem there. Davy told her that even though she hadn't heard the band, she said she knew they must be good if he was the band's leader. It would be in a few weeks, so there was time to prepare. "What do you think, Tommy? Do you think I am good enough?" Tommy embraced her and said, "You are the most talented, brave, and incredible person I have ever known." She smiled; this time, it was a real smile. She looked down at his lap, where he had a most prominent erection. She touched it and rubbed it a few times until he came in his pants.

Chapter Fifty-Eight

"Savior, I think I am pregnant," Margot said.

"Why do you say that?"

"Missed my period."

"But it's only been two weeks since we did it."

"Two and a half. And now I am a week and a half late."

"Oh no. What are we going to do?"

"What do you think?"

"Have the baby?"

"No, dummy. Got to get an abortion. My sister had one last year. She can help. I'm so stupid."

"No, you're not. It was my fault."

"It was our fault. But no use crying over spilled milk. I'll go to the clinic to find out for sure and then make an appointment."

"I'll come with you."

"I'd appreciate that. And Savior."

"Yeah?"

"From now on, we've got to be more careful. Much more careful."

Chapter Fifty-Nine

It smelled as if something had died. In fact, something had died. Tommy and Barry's pet rat. Leon Trotsky had passed away the preceding week. They didn't discover him until they smelled his rotting corpse. There was a misunderstanding as to which one was supposed to oversee making sure Leon had food and water. They had since surreptitiously buried the poor rat in Forest Lawn Cemetery, but his death lingered in the air, which was also polluted by the smell of dirty underwear and soiled socks. Sunshine felt as if she was going to throw up, but she was so glad to be out of her parent's house that even the nausea caused by the olfactory assault was mitigated by a sense of liberation.

Davy was less grateful. "It smells like death in here."

"Trotsky died," Barry said coldly.

"You mean your pet rat?" Geraldo asked.

"I'm afraid so," Tommy replied sadly and with a tinge of guilt.

Sunshine turned to Tommy and, with great compassion, said, "Why didn't you tell me?"

"I didn't want to, you know, upset you."

"Oh, darling."

Barry cleared his throat. "Okay. Let's get down to business. There are two big issues on the agenda. One, there are the student body elections coming up, and I think we should run a candidate from the CCCP. And two, volume two of the Revolutionary Press."

"But they put that fence around the lockers," Geraldo said meekly.

"Nothing a pair of wire cutters couldn't handle," Barry replied cinematically.

"Yes. Has to happen," Davy said with supreme conviction. "We make this one a call for revolution,"

"Perhaps Savior," Barry said, turning his eyes to the rest of the room for added comments. "Any other ideas?" Barry loved this role, the role of chief of operations. He couldn't believe it had happened this way, but here it was. He looked at the gang, each one, to him, a superstar in their own right. He couldn't have been prouder to be a part of this micro movement. Sure, he believed in the cause, but this was just good fun. And yes, they made mistakes. Like when they spray painted on the side of the gym, misspelling fascists by writing Fashists! Grammar was not a strong suit. But with Charles, they had an expert copy editor. They humiliated the school into spending thousands of dollars on a fence with the first Revolutionary Press, and they rescued Sunshine from a modern-day concentration camp. No doubt about it, they were a force to be reckoned with.

"Who is going to be our candidate for student body president?" Sunshine asked.

Barry looked at Davy and said, "How about you, Savior?"

"No thanks. I have enough trouble on my hands right now."

"What's going on? Something the CCCP could help with?" Tommy asked with alacrity.

Davy thought about it. But no, there was nothing his comrades could do. This was something he and Margot would have to handle alone. It was amazing how it all came to pass. He lost his virginity and got a girl pregnant at the same moment. It happened on the day of the church incident. After dropping the Slurpee, he walked home. Margot was riding her yellow banana seat bike down Moody Street passed right by Davy. It turned out she lived on Moody Street as well. Miracle of miracles. She stopped and turned around, realizing she had passed *him*. For some reason, he was not at all surprised to see her. Like fate had meant for this moment to happen. She told him how impressed she was by his tenacity, bravery, and righteousness. She told him that she was worried that he was going to be arrested; the way people were talking at the church, and she invited him to the treehouse in her backyard to hide out. The same treehouse where her older sister got into trouble.

It was a proper treehouse; a ladder led up to the opening at about twenty feet off the ground. It had a floor and walls and even a window. Inside was a rug, throw pillows, board games, dolls that looked like they hadn't been touched for a while, and books, many books. They sat up there for a long while, just talking. They pretty much saw eye to eye on all spiritual matters. They both thought that Jesus was cool and that he was the original hippie and punk rocker all rolled into one. They didn't believe any of that son of god business; they thought he was just a man and that his girlfriend, Mary Magdalene, was super cool in her own right. And they knew the church for what they thought it to be: a home for pedophiles and hypocrites. But a lot of Margot's friends went to the church, and she liked the youth group and all the activities they did, like camping trips, dances, and just hanging out.

They sat cross-legged facing each other. Davy listened to Margot tell him of the wild things that had happened to different members of the church youth group. After a while, he stopped hearing the specific words; he was so transfixed by her lips, how they moved with subtle and graceful motion; her eyes round and filled with emotion, and the sound of her voice like the trickling water from a mountain spring. He leaned over and kissed her. She put her tongue in his mouth. This was a revelation of sensation. Something cleared in his head as if he had discovered one of the prime posteriori justifications for existence, and in it, he had clarity. All the misery and corruption, the beauty and ugliness, the good and the bad alike, it all coalesced into a transcendental wholeness. The next thing he knew, they were naked. No, there was nothing the CCCP could do to help.

"What about you, Geraldo?" Barry said, pointing at the boy. Geraldo shook his head adamantly.

"What about Tommy?" Sunshine proclaimed. "He gets better grades than any of us, plus he is charismatic and a great speaker."

"I don't know," Barry said, feeling resistant to the idea. He loved and admired his brother, but he knew that he could be erratic. Could they count on him? As if he was reading his brother's mind, Tommy said, "You can count on me."

"You're not afraid of public speaking?"

"Not anymore."

"Let's put it to a vote. All in favor of Tommy being the candidate for student body president for the Cypress Centurion Communist Party raise their hand." Everyone raised their hand. "It's unanimous! Now, let's go to the beach!"

Chapter Sixty

They dropped off Sunshine before heading to Seal Beach Pier. She was tired and she didn't want to worry her parents, especially since they were being so nice to her. Her mom had formed a begrudging affection towards Tommy; he had stayed over for dinner consecutive nights. She found it remarkable how Tommy and his group of friends were so devoted to her daughter. Her child, her daughter. She had always wanted a daughter and now she had one. She just had to practice acceptance, and with the help of her psychoanalyst, she was already making good progress.

In conversations with Tommy both of Sunshine's parents were impressed by his intellect and knowledge of history. He knew explicitly about the Japanese internment camps during World War Two and had, in fact, written a paper on the subject for his A.P. U.S. History class. Madge's parents had spent a year and a half in one. When Tommy found out how Oliver's grandparents had perished in the Holocaust, he understood why Sunshine's parents behaved in such a desperate way upon finding out about Sunshine's gender identification. They had a subconscious fear of her being persecuted for being an outsider.

Tommy walked Sunshine to her doorstep. They embraced. "You get some rest, okay," Tommy said after kissing her softly on the lips.

She nodded, sighed, and said, "You have fun. And watch out for the cops."

Tommy got back into the car, and Barry handed him a Coors. "God, can't we get a better beer than Coors?"

"I called Charles; he said he would bring a bottle of Jack Daniels."

"You called my brother?" Geraldo said from the backseat. "Isn't he in San Diego?"

"I called him about the election, thought he might have some advice. And if he would copy-edit the next Revolutionary Press. He said that he and April would meet us at the beach."

*****

April told Charles on the phone that she had to see him, even though it had only been a couple days since they last saw each other. Charles suspected, by the flatness in her voice, that there was something going on and felt anxious. He feared that she was going to break up with him. April drove down I-5 South in her Honda Civic, blasting a Bowie mixtape Charles had made for her. The first thing she saw upon entering his dorm room was a giant flag of the Soviet Union that covered an entire wall. This made her burst out laughing. Charles loved that about April. He knew that she knew what that giant red Soviet flag really stood for. From time to time, April felt guilty about dating a white boy. But here was a white boy who was vehemently critical of his racist country. A white boy who had read Malcolm X, not because it was assigned to him but because he had a thirst for knowledge and a true quest to understand the plight of exploited peoples. It was Charles who gave her books such as Pedagogy of the Oppressed, and she, in turn, made him read John Stuart Mill's Principles of Political Economy. They weren't on the same page on many issues, but they shared the same sense of having their eyes open.

April didn't break up with Charles and, in fact, was more affectionate and passionate than ever. It was a good thing that Charles' dorm mate had gone to a San Diego Padres baseball game. Still, Charles was pleasantly confused. She had never come to his dorm room before, and he knew she was missing classes. He also knew she had something she wanted to tell him, but she was not forthcoming. He wouldn't press it. She would eventually open up. They laid in his standard stock freshman single bed, sharing a Chesterfield. He was on the outer edge and had his right arm around her, holding her tightly, partly for a post-coital display of affection and partly to keep from falling off the side of the bed. The skin on her upper arm was cool and soft; he thought - if I could just be like this indefinitely, I would be that elusive thing always: happy. The phone rang. It was on the floor directly beneath him. All he had to do was reach out and get it, which he did. "Oh, hi Barry… Yeah sure. I'd be happy to… What time? …Yeah. Me and April will come by… so long, comrade." He hung up the phone. "We'll come by where?" April asked. "To the beach. They're having a little party out there."

******

The bonfire was roaring. They had made it roar that way by combining cardboard, paper bags, wood from busted-up milk crates and lots of charcoal lighter fluid. Barry had brought the last of the Coors and found a bottle of white wine buried in the back of his mom's closet. His mother, Tina, bought in bulk at Tesco's on the first of every month. Liters of soda, pasta, canned everything, frozen meat, ice cream, dry goods, beer, which she didn't drink a lot herself but didn't mind her sons having a few cans every now and then. They were old enough. She was a sweet yet dispassionate woman, and her boys were quite affectionate towards her. Losing her husband the way she did took a toll on her. She also lost her figure. She didn't lose it but consciously gave it up. A trade of sorts. For losing her husband. She indulged in food and lethargy as a way of compensating herself. Yet, she was a dutiful mom, and she did her best to encourage her boys to develop their minds and intellect. Without a father, she knew she would have to be the one to give them the support they needed. She didn't have a lot of money, but she would buy them any book they wanted if it wasn't carried at the local public library, and even if it was a book that was needed for their own library.

Everyone sat around the fire, drinking beer and passing around the wine bottle. Barry started singing the International; the others joined in:

> *So come brothers and sisters*
>
> *For the struggle carries on*
>
> *The International*
>
> *Unites the world in song*
>
> *So, comrades, come rally*
>
> *For this is the time and place!*
>
> *The International*
>
> *Unites the human race*

Geraldo had finished two cans of beer in short order and was starting to feel very giddy. He was transfixed by the fire; it was beautiful the way it glowed and sparkled. And his group of friends were hilarious. This whole communist thing was the best thing that had ever happened to him. Before meeting the Griswold brothers, his life was boring. Now he was doing stuff, really doing stuff. He imagined that John Lennon would be very proud of him and his comrades. If he was alive. It would be such a shame what happened to him, but that is what they were fighting for, for justice and against hatred and violence and *injustice*. Geraldo started singing the Beatles song Revolution, "You say you want a revolution, well you know, WE ALL WANT TO CHANGE THE WORLD!"

"I'm going swimming!" Tommy shouted. He stood, took off his clothes, and ran towards the water.

"Me too," Davy sang out. He discarded his clothing, and followed suit.

"The water is too cold for me," Barry shouted at the backs of the boys in motion.

"Well, I don't mind some cold water." Geraldo ran after the other two, shedding his clothing along the way.

"Hey, Barry," Charles said as he and April walked up to the bonfire. Barry turned and smiled so largely that he thought his face was going to break in two. He admired, almost idolized, Geraldo's brother, and here he was. The O.G. communist of Cypress High School. "This is my girlfriend, April."

"Hi," Barry said shyly.

"Where is my brother and the others?"

"They went skinny dipping."

"Oh my," April said. "That water is cold."

"I know! I don't imagine they're feeling it, though," Barry said, laughing.

"Speaking of which, I brought the Jack. Though there is not a lot left, it turns out."

Charles twisted off the cap, took a swig, and handed it to April, who shook her head; he handed the bottle to Barry, who took a long pull. "So, you guys are going to run for student body president. Which one of you?" Charles asked.

"Tommy. But we are all going to work on his speech and the platform."

"You guys are way more serious about it than I ever was. At least back then."

"Yeah, because you had fun with it," April said. "And the funny thing is he actually won."

"Incredible!" Barry shouted. "But, but..."

"Yeah, they wouldn't let him. Came up with some excuse and handed it to the jock who ran against him."

"Yes. It's true. The difference between me and you guys is that I was popular, at least with half of my class. But the school and a lot of other kids hated me. When I flipped off Magg because of the election swindle I got suspended for a week. They changed it to a one-day suspension when Dad lost his shit."

"Amazing!" Barry said, star-struck.

"And you all are doing another issue of the Revolutionary Press. You better let me copy-edit. You guys are practically illiterate."

"I would appreciate that."

"What is this one going to cover?" April asked.

"Not sure. Davy thought it should be a rallying cry for revolution."

Charles laughed. "That might be premature. Though, I have a strong feeling that there is going to be a complete economic collapse. Worse than the Great Depression. You should go on record calling it."

"You really think so?"

"It's possible," April said. "In fact, economic indicators point to the likelihood of super stagflation, high inflation, high unemployment, and a stagnant economy for years to come."

"And then what?" Barry asked.

"Then you might have conditions ripe for rampant unrest," Charles said seriously.

"Will you help us write it? Both of you?"

"I'm no communist," April said. "I'm a free market socialist."

Chapter Sixty-One

Tommy was a bit drunker than the others, having polished off a small bottle of peppermint schnapps that he had nicked from Sunshine's parents. He put his arm around Geraldo. "Listen, Geraldo. I have something to tell you. I got to tell someone."

"What is it?" Geraldo said, laughing inexplicably.

"I can suck my own dick!"

"OOOH, No way!"

"YES way!"

"But, but, but how?"

"Yoga. You just got to know yoga. But since I met Sunshine, I don't want to do it anymore. But I slipped. God damn it, man, I slipped."

A naked Barry came running up. "Hey! I'm going to go skinny dipping. Where's Savior?"

"He's over there. He's trying to walk on the water."

They watched Davy take a running start, only to fall into the break of the waves.

******

April and Charles sat on the sand, staring into the waning bonfire. April asked for the Jack Daniels. Charles, pleased, handed the nearly empty bottle to her. She took a sip and then another and passed it back to Charles who finished it off. "Another dead soldier," he said and flung it with a flourish. He looked at April. She was lost, lost somewhere. Her countenance appeared vexed. Her eyes looked tired. Charles, his demeanor altered because of the whiskey, felt as if he was another person, or a different version of himself, a more mature, caring, and considerate person. He realized that he wanted to be the kind of person that April could turn to for comfort. "April. It feels like something is bothering you."

She let out a big breath and said, "Yes. There is."

"What is it? You can tell me."

"I think my father is having an affair."

"No! He doesn't seem like the type. But what would I know?"

"And the thing is, the very strange thing is, I think he is having an affair with Carmen."

"With who?"

"With Carmen. With your mother!"

"What?! That's crazy. Because of what she said at the party? She was just drunk. She's been drinking a lot since my dad left, but she was just messing around. She's not herself. I mean, she's reading Bukowski and writing poetry these days."

"Maybe she is herself. Maybe this is who she really is."

"Excuse me? I've known her for a while now, so I think I would know who my own mother *really is*."

"You thought you knew who your father really was."

"Oh dang. That's true. But my mom and your dad. That's too far-fetched. What are the chances? Impossible."

"Oh yeah. Well then, who is that walking along the shore?"

Charles looked to where April was pointing, and there was his mother and Clive walking hand in hand.

Chapter Sixty-Two

"Clive, you need to get real. You can't wreck your marriage. I won't be a part of it."

"But I love you. More than I have loved anyone in my life."

"Don't say that."

"Why not."

"Because you don't know what you are talking about."

Clive laughed. "I know myself. I know of myself. 'I celebrate myself and sing myself, and what I assume you shall assume, for every atom belonging to me as good belongs to you.'"

"Okay, nice, quoting Walt Whitman, but can't we just be friends?"

"How can we be just friends if I want to kiss you? All the time."

Carmen didn't mind hearing that. And would also not mind doing that especially after they had those martinis at the Beachcomber. But she would be strong. She would be the one to be strong. Charles would never forgive her if she messed around with his girlfriend's dad.

"Why did you agree to go out with me?" Clive remonstrated her, starting to get frustrated.

"You said you wanted to hear my poems."

"I did. They're brilliant. You are a great poetess. Another reason that I love you."

"Thank you." She reached out and grabbed hold of his hand. "But Clive, it's never going to happen. I just can't be complicit." They stood motionless as the waves crashed against the shore. The full moon shone brightly on their static figures, making moon shadows on the sand. They were caught in each other's eyes. Carmen felt herself getting weak. Clive sensed this and was about to lean in to kiss her when April came running up.

"What the hell, Dad!"

Charles added, "What the hell, Mom!" coming a few steps behind April.

"April, but how did you know we were here? Were you spying on me?"

"No! We just happened to be here. I knew it. I knew you were messing around. Oh, Daddy, how could you?"

"I didn't do anything."

Carmen spoke up, "It's true. Nothing has happened. I was just showing Clive some of my poems."

"Then why were you holding hands?!"

Carmen stammered, "Because, because…"

"Because I told her that I loved her!"

Charles shouted, "This is getting crazy! Mom, what the hell is going on?"

"It's true. About the poetry," she responded coyly.

"Since when have you been writing poetry?"

"Since I started reading Bukowski. He's disgusting, but he opened that door for me. Thanks to you, Charles."

"Jesus Christ!"

Down the beach they heard the voice of someone shouting, "Somebody help!" It was Barry.

Charles and Clive went running in the direction of Barry's voice. When they got there, Barry told them that Davy was being carried out to sea. He pointed to a flailing figure off on the horizon. "It's a riptide," Clive said. He expeditiously removed his clothing and jumped into the water. He was an expert swimmer and had won many meets in college. He reached Davy and quickly grabbed hold of him just as he was going under; he swam with Davy in tow, dragging him laterally and then to the shore.

When they got to the shore, everyone was gathered: Barry, Tommy, and Geraldo unsteady, naked and drunk. Clive was also naked as he pulled the unconscious Davy from the water. Carmen couldn't help herself but observe Clive's circumcised penis, thus answering the question she had posed to herself weeks before. And she couldn't help but be impressed by his heroic performance. Charles helped Clive pull Davy to the sand. Clive turned him around and did cpr. Davy coughed, expelled water from his lungs, and started breathing hard. Davy lay motionless. He opened his eyes and said, "Why look at that moon!" Carmen looked at the group of naked boys and noticed that Geraldo was swaying. She went over to her son and put her hands on his arms to steady him. She smelled the alcohol. "Geraldo, were you drinking?" He shook his head and then fell to his knees and threw up.

Chapter Sixty-Three

After he helped Barry and Tommy load a semi-conscious Davy into the Datsun, April told Charles to go with his mother; they would talk later, but first, she needed to confront her father. Charles begrudgingly abided by her wishes. He was uncomfortable with the idea of sitting in a car with his mom after all that had transpired; April was right; he didn't know her. With Geraldo passed out in the backseat, Carmen spoke plainly as she drove. She didn't love Clive and she wasn't having an affair with him. He had a crush on her, and that is all. Perhaps it didn't show the best judgment to meet with him, but god damn it, she was lonely. And she wanted someone to read her poems. But the kids were right; it didn't look good, and she would put a stop to it.

But she didn't want to put a stop to it. And Clive didn't want her to put a stop to it. Clive, if he had his druthers, would move out, into an apartment by the beach and rent an art studio to work on his watercolors or maybe even try oil painting. Recently he wanted to give a stab at abstract expressionist painting, ever since seeing a William De Kooning exhibition at LACMA a couple of months back. And Carmen and her poetry inspired him. If he could be as honest in his art and his life as she was in her poetry then he just might be happy, or if not happy, at least have peace of mind.

******

Clive watched as his daughter wretched. He was helpless to do anything except keep his hand on her back as she threw up into the sand. This was after she screamed at him for a full five minutes, a full five minutes of uninterrupted rage and indictment. All the wrongs and slights of her childhood. She repeatedly used the word narcissist. Fucking narcissist. She didn't mention in the least that she suspected her father of adultery with her boyfriend's mother. If someone had been eavesdropping on this altercation, they would never have known the pretext for her unbridled onslaught of resentment. Clive was not hurt. None of it came as any surprise. He had learned a long time ago that he was incapable of providing the kind of attention and affection his daughter demanded. He did his best, but he knew that it might be insufficient. He had faith that, in time, she would recognize the unlimited depth of love he had for her. But after all, no matter what, he was English, and the English are not always the most expressive when it comes to these things.

Clive drove April's Honda as she was in no shape to. It was like driving a go-cart. He couldn't wait to get his Benz back. It had been in the shop now for almost two weeks. "I'm sorry, Daddy." He looked at his abstruse and crying daughter. "I don't particularly think that whiskey agrees with you." He stopped at a light, reached over, and patted her knee. The light turned green, and he made the gears grind going into second by not stepping completely down on the clutch pedal. "I do that all the time," April said, though it never happened to her. "Daddy, are you going to leave mom?"

"I don't know. I'm not happy. It is not her fault. She is a wonderful woman."

"Should I believe what Carmen said?"

"Of course you should. She is a very honest person. And, it appears she doesn't share the same feeling that I have for her."

"Maybe that's for the best, Dad."

Clive realized that *he* was getting teary himself and tried to cover up by laughing. "Isn't life funny?"

"I suppose. It can be."

They pulled into the driveway. Clive turned off the engine. Each wanted to ask the other the same question; April went first, "What are you going to tell Mom?"

"I don't know. Maybe I won't tell her anything for now. Maybe there is nothing to tell."

"Okay. I won't if you I won't." And they shook on it.

Chapter Sixty-Four

Davy lay in bed recollecting what had transpired; he had almost drowned. Maybe he did drown. Maybe he died and was resurrected. What did this mean? Surely, it was a sign. A man, a black man came to his rescue, brought him back to life, and for what purpose? For the purpose of spreading the good news, for spreading the gospel, the gospel according to Davy. He may not know everything, he may not be as smart as, let's say, Tommy or as gentle as Geraldo, but he was the one who had been chosen. Chosen not by god but by fate. If someone asked him, he couldn't say for certain if there was a god or even that he was a Christian per se. He was a pantheist, but he dug the myth of Jesus with all its legend, permutations, and iconography. It was a model that he could utilize for the purpose of trying to make the world a better place, which was truly and sincerely his ambition. His mission. But first, he would have to do the right thing by Margot. He needed to get the money to pay for her abortion. Two hundred dollars. He had given it a lot of thought, and there were only two possibilities. He could ask his mother, but that poor woman had been through enough already. Or he could break into the church and go to where they stashed the collections. After all, in an indirect way, the church was the cause of their predicament.

****

"Where did you get the money?"

"I'll tell you later."

"Well, thank you. Who knows, maybe one day we could, you know."

“I know. And we will.”

******

It was a cloudy Saturday morning. A destitute fog had descended on Orange County. Margot was hoping that she would be well enough to go to school on Monday. They rode the OCTD bus from Cypress to Santa Ana to the same clinic where Margot's sister had her abortion. Davy held Margot's hand most of the way. She told him that he was very brave. He laughed and said it was her; she was the brave one. As they sat side by side in the quiet of a practically vacant bus, their gazes traipsed from the window to the hands that were locked steadfastly, and then to each other's faces filled with expressions of consolation. Margot couldn't help but think how attractive Davy was, how he seemed so much older than sixteen. At first, she had thought he was a senior like herself, as if that would have made a difference. She should have known not to let him come in her. She should have told him to pull out. But there was something inevitable about their coming together. Or at least it felt that way. It didn't matter. It was done now, and there was no way to undo it. She just didn't know how painful it was going to be. Her sister was very vague on the matter.

They got off at 17th Street and walked a couple blocks to the clinic. As they approached, they saw a smattering of people holding placards saying things like *Abortion is Murder. Fetuses are Human Beings, too*. “Oh Jesus,” Margot said. Davy put his arm around her and ushered her through the front door. When they got into the reception area, Margot said, “I think I saw Gary Lawson from the church.”

“Who?”

“Gary and his son were the main ones pushing the priest to ‘hunt you down’ and have you arrested.”

229

"Don't worry about that. Just relax. Everything is going to be alright."

Margot was given a clipboard to fill out, which she did using her sister's name. Davy went and paid for the procedure. When he was done, he sat down next to her while she wrote down the requested information. They could hear the people chanting out front, "Abortion kills children!" Margot bowed her head and prayed. Prayed for comfort. Prayed for forgiveness. She couldn't help but feel shame and anger at herself. She couldn't help but feel deep sorrow for taking this life away from a child created out of the passion and attraction that Davy and Margot felt for each other. And now that Davy has shown himself to be an honorable and brave person it was all the more a shame. Yet, it had to be done. It was the only smart thing to do to undo a truly stupid mistake. Davy sat down next to Margot and took her hand. When someone shouted, "Stupid fucking Jesus freaks!" from a passing car, Margot and Davy looked at each other and couldn't help but laugh. That's when her name was called.

A nurse-led them to a room; inside was a table very similar to the one in her gynecologist's office. Margot was very glad and relieved that they let Davy accompany her. She was given a gown, which she put on. Davy glanced away and then glanced back at her. "You're so beautiful. I have never seen anything more beautiful." She started to cry, and he comforted her as best he could. He had a hard time finding the right words, so he just held her. Then she got on the table. After a short while a nurse came in, or they thought she was a nurse. She told Margot to sit back and put her feet into the stirrups. She gave Margot a local anesthesia near her cervix. Davy was surprised that they didn't put her under. After all, they put him under when he had his wisdom teeth removed, and this was much more serious than that. Davy stood by her side and held her hand. They heard a machine turning on; it sounded like an air conditioner, Margot thought. Or a vacuum cleaner. The nurse inserted a tube into Margot's vagina. Margot felt otherworldly as if she was disconnected from what was going on. She felt a huge sense of relief and a more subtle sense of loss. Aside from that, she didn't feel anything.

After it was done, she was given some ibuprofen and was told that if she felt right, then she could go to school on Monday. But if she felt any discomfort then wait. And if she began to bleed profusely, don't hesitate to go to the emergency room. They left the clinic and hurried along by the vehemence of the protesters, one of whom shouted, "Anti-Christ!" That made Davy think of the Sex Pistols song, Anarchy in the UK. He played the song in his head as they walked to the bus stop. It was difficult for Margot to walk too fast. But she wanted to get the hell out there, so she pushed herself.

When they got on the bus and sat down, Margot said, "Did Gary Junior just call you the Anti-Christ?"

"I believe so. Do you know the song by the Sex Pistols, Anarchy in the UK?"

"I don't think so. Sounds fun."

"It is. How do you feel?"

"Not too good. I'll be happy to get home."

Margot fell asleep on the bus. Davy had to wake her when they got to the stop. They walked to her house. This time, they took their time. The fog had lifted, but the sun was still obscured by clouds. On the doorstep, she put her arms around his neck and then started to laugh. "What's so funny," Davy asked, wanting in on the joke. "Oh, well, it's funny how he called you the Anti-Christ when you are the most Christ-like person I have ever known."

"Life is full of irony."

"Don't I know it."

They kissed gently, and then Margot went inside her house.

Chapter Sixty-Five

The second Revolutionary Press came quickly. Charles practically wrote it himself. Barry had some input, but the rest of the crew virtually had nothing to do with the writing of it. Nevertheless, everyone was impressed by the dense economic hypothesizing. It read like a one-page summary of Das Kapital. Davy was gratified that it closed with a call for revolution when the collapse of Capitalism came, which, going by R.P. Vol 2, might happen any day. Even April was pleased with it, especially as it contained, verbatim, her theory on the possibility of super-stagflation that would cripple the economy. When Barry took it to the printer, the printer refused to work on it, crumpling it up and throwing it in his face. Barry had to drive all the way to San Diego to a bookstore run by anarchists that Charles told him about. They not only had a professional Xerox machine, but they liked it so much that they made copies for the store to give away. Barry thought the anarchists were quite silly, but he kept that to himself.

This was to be a stealth operation. Instead of Barry doing pickup with the Datsun, everyone came on foot to the school, again at midnight. Barry had bought a pair of Standard Craftsman wire cutters at Sears. They were sturdy and felt hefty in his gloved hand. Each kid was given surgical gloves before operations began to ensure no fingerprints were left. They stood by as Barry began to cut a nice square hole for them to climb through. It took longer than Barry thought it would and Tommy told him just to make a flap of it, but Barry wanted that square hole, something symbolic about a hole more so than a flap. After an anxious interval, it was done, and Barry, Tommy, and Davy went through to the lockers and began disseminating the Revolutionary Press Volume Two. Geraldo was a bit squeamish this time and took on the role of lookout. He was given a police whistle. Since they were short, both his hands and Sunshine's, it took almost until dawn to get the job done.

Geraldo listened to Sandinista in its entirety on his Walkman. He had put it all on a one-hundred-and-twenty-minute cassette tape plus the extended play Black Market Clash, and when it was over, he listened to it again. He needed something to keep him awake, to keep him lively. He did jumping jacks, he did running in place, he did shadow boxing. Joe Strummer was singing Bank robber Dub for the second time when his voice started to go slower and lower until the music stopped completely. Geraldo took off his headphones and put his Walkman into his backpack. He felt a great fatigue wash over him, and the usual anxiety started to envelop his chest. He sat down on the ground, leaned against the fence, and thought of the darkness beneath us all, the limitless expanse of nothingness that awaits us, the black hole of death. This was his usual remedy for anxiety. To fixate on the inevitable made everything else seem small including that unsettled feeling. How when one's life comes to an end, most likely there is just oblivion, endless oblivion. But if it is endless oblivion, oblivion is not emptiness; one is conscious of it, even if one is unconscious, which is a form of consciousness. Or maybe when you die, you enter a dream state where all constraints of time no longer pertain, and you exist in a multiverse populated by not just your personal experiences and memories but those of every person who is part of your DNA, going back to prehistoric times. His job was to be lookout, not to digress on these existential thoughts and ideas. He sat and looked out, just sitting and looking, until he became the thing he looked at. Then he saw Mr. Magg in the distance, holding a large flashlight and a Doberman pinscher on a leash, walking steadily with Duane and a few jocks by his side. Geraldo reached for his whistle, brought it to his lips, and blew. Nothing came out, no sounds. He tried and tried but to no avail. Mr. Magg took the Doberman off its leash, and it came running towards Geraldo. If he couldn't warn the others, then he would have to save himself. He got up to run away, but then he thought that he couldn't sacrifice his comrades like that. And so he started to sing the International loudly. The fellas would hear and make a run for it.

> *So come brothers and sisters*
> *For the struggle carries on*
> *The International*
> *Unites the world in song*
> *So, comrades, come rally*
> *For this is the time and place!*
> *The International*
> *Unites the human race*

The dog jumped on Geraldo and went for his throat. Geraldo screamed out in agony.

Walking back through the football field, Tommy was snickering; Barry had to elbow him. He couldn't help it. He knew Geraldo felt bad for falling asleep, but it was pretty hilarious to hear him singing the International in his sleep. His mirth was infectious, Davy too began to chuckle and finally, Barry as well. Geraldo, on the other hand, did not find it amusing that he had fallen asleep on the job, and now it was almost dawn; his mother might very well be awake when he got home.

Chapter Sixty-Six

Not only was his mother awake when he got home, but she was sitting at the dining room table with his father. Geraldo entered the house quietly and saw that they were ensconced in some intense topic of conversation; he clandestinely snuck to the stairs and up to his bedroom. When he got to his bedroom, he flopped on his bed, rolled over, and thought, what is my father doing here? Are they planning a reconciliation? Geraldo realized that this would be his worst nightmare. Things were so much freer without his father and brother around, he had room to have his own thoughts, quietness to breathe, to come and go as he pleased. And his mother seemed to be coming into her own as well. Seymour was not trustworthy, was a cheater, and a narcissist to the umpteenth degree. Not to say that he didn't love his father. He did. And he had fond memories of him. Baseball games, camping, holidays, trips abroad, or just sitting around the living room watching a football game and farting. But he was older now and valued his independence.

He heard high-pitched screaming downstairs. Was his mother losing it? No, the voice was that of Charles. After deciding whether he was curious enough to find out the source of the disturbance or to stay in bed, he finally got up, went down the stairs, and sat down on the landing to observe matters from a distance. Charles was standing between his mother and father, pointing at his mother and shouting, "You're having an affair with April's dad!"

"I told you, Charles, that I am not. He is just a good friend."

"People your age don't have good friends who are married men."

"That is absurd."

"So, is this true?" Seymour asked, sounding sanctimonious.

"How dare you ask me about what is true or not. Furthermore, what the hell are you doing here?"

"I told you."

"It is completely out of the question."

"Then I will take this house."

"What?"

"That's right, as matrimonial property, it is an asset and must be evenly divided as such. As an asset."

"Fuck you, Seymour."

"Who are you? I've never heard you use such language."

"Mom. What are you doing with your life!?" Charles sat down between his mother and father, putting his head on his folded arms.

"April broke up with him," Seymour explained. "That's why he came to me. We had some wine and got to talking, and I realized, or I have been coming to realize, that I belong here with you and the boys."

"Or else you're taking the house?"

"Something like that."

Carmen sat quietly, fuming. Yet, she calmed herself. She thought about her life with Seymour, how, for the most part, it was a loving marriage, and how she truly enjoyed Seymour's company most of the time. She thought about how in love he was with her when they first met and how he continued to show affection throughout their time together, even up to the days before he moved out. Even though he was not too tall and a bit portly, she found him quite handsome. She thought about the boys and how much Charles idolized his father. And Geraldo and what it was like, how it was, living there, just the two of them. "Very well"

"Very well?" Seymour asked eagerly.

"Yes. Take the fucking house."

"Carmen!"

"I mean it, Seymour. We can sell the house, but not until Geraldo is out of high school."

"Jesus Christ."

"And what the hell happened between April and Charles?"

Charles lifted his head. "She said that I need to get into therapy if we were to continue seeing each other."

"That's what I've been saying."

Seymour looked at Carmen, thinking if he implored her with his eyes, she might change her mind. And completely against his will, he began to cry. Carmen stood, put her hands on her hips, and said, "Perhaps you can use some therapy yourself, Seymour. Now I'm going to make some coffee. I have to get to work soon." She saw Geraldo, who smiled at her. She smiled back and then went into the kitchen to make coffee.

Chapter Sixty-Seven

The cops were all over the school. There was a forensic team working at the hole in the fence, dusting it for fingerprints, and detectives questioning students. Mr. Magg was talking to the towering figure of Principal Smithson near the first bank of lockers, who, with a pointed finger leveled at Mr. Magg's center chest, was in the act of verbally berating him. Geraldo felt so nervous that he thought that he might throw up. They had no idea that their latest dissemination of the Revolutionary Press would cause this level of tumult. They saw school kids reading the paper, looking confused as if they were reading Sanskrit, so technical was the language of Marxist economic theory. This reaction gratified Barry. "Come on, let's go register Tommy as a candidate for president," he said to the others with gleefulness. Davy and Geraldo left for their lockers; Tommy and Barry walked across campus to the office, followed by Mr. Magg. When they got there, they went to the front desk, Magg right behind them who said, "Have you come to turn yourself in?" Barry turned and feigned a confused look. "What?"

"I've come to register to make myself a candidate for student body president," Tommy said proudly.

Incredulous, Magg said, "You're kidding?"

Tommy puffed himself up. "I kid you not."

"How are you going to run for president when most of the student body hates you and your group of reds? Not only that, but you'll also be lucky if someone doesn't kill you. Not only that, how are you going to run for student body president from behind bars?"

"What are you talking about, Vice Principal Magg?" Barry said calmly.

"Breaking and entering. Destruction of school property and, and, other charges."

Two detectives entered the office, came close to Mr. Magg, said a few words to him in hushed tones, and then went into his office. The receptionist, Mrs. Bloom, a cheery woman in her sixties, who knew Barry quite well on account of the fact that he had spent an inordinate amount of time visiting Mr. Magg, had taken quite a liking to him since he was the rare kid who willingly made conversation with her. She told the Griswold boys that they had come just in time, as this was the last day to register for the election. The debates, which were to take place on Wednesday, were only two days away.

"Debates?" Tommy asked.

"Well, they are not really debates as such, but each period, kids come to the auditorium, and then each candidate says what they would do if they were student body president. Not really a debate." Mrs. Bloom explained.

Mrs. Bloom handed Tommy a clipboard where he signed his name to a small list of other kids who had decided to run.

"Not too many running this year. You might stand a chance," Mrs. Bloom said gaily.

Tommy looked at the names, one of whom was the jock who slapped Davy across the face and punched Barry in the stomach.

*****

Walking through campus Tommy sensed a begrudging admiration coming from his schoolmates; for himself and his

240

comrades and their subversive activities. He had no delusion that he could actually win the presidency, but maybe it wasn't as far-fetched as they had thought. Were girls making eyes at him? And none of the jocks attempted to harass him. That will most likely change when his name is posted alongside Duane and the others running. But for now, he felt superior, so much so that he had actually forgotten that he hadn't spoken with Sunshine the night before. It was the first time that they hadn't spoken or seen each other since she was released from the clinic. He felt guilty, and he was worried about her, especially since she hadn't returned to school that day as planned. Judging from how she was when last he saw her, he didn't think she was going to be ready anyhow, so it wasn't surprising that she didn't attend school. He told her to take more time; he felt that she was far too fragile to be able to endure any callous comments.

None of the boys had been called into Mr. Magg's office. Since there were no fingerprints and there was no evidence linking anyone to the break-in or to the document, at least for now. Magg was powerless, and he did not want to face the insolent faces of a bunch of pinko kids who, if he had his way, would wring their necks. Yet Magg was assured by the detectives that they would keep working on it. In the meantime, they told him he might consider hiring a night watchman. Mr. Magg knew that he had exhausted and exceeded all the funds allocated for security by calling for and having the fence installed. That it hadn't prevented another incident was the cause of great consternation for principal Smithson and the school board, who had signed off on the fence, but it was Mr. Magg who would take the blame.

****

They met at the courtyard at the end of the school day, each one ready to drop after not having gotten any sleep the night before. The sky was gray, covered in dense, aggrieved clouds. Davy and Geraldo split off to go to Davy's to meet up with Margot's friend, Bruce, the kid from the church youth group who played the drums. Davy, in particular, felt guilty at having to replace Sunshine on the drums, but they had a gig, their first performance coming up, and not only did it seem that Sunshine was out of commission for the time being, he felt that she never really cared that much about playing drums, and truth be told, she wasn't very good at it. Tommy and Barry walked to the parking lot. From the anonymous mass of kids, Barry heard his first "Fucking commie" of the day. And with it came a sense of recognition. A sense of pride.

Parked in front of the school in the fire zone was an orange Corvette and standing next to it was Sunshine's father. He signaled Tommy with a wave of the hand. Tommy told Barry to go on, and he walked over. Mr. Simon told Tommy that Sunshine was in the hospital; she had taken an overdose of sleeping pills.

"Did she try to kill herself?" Tommy asked desperately.

"It appears so. She is better today and has implored me to ask you to visit her. I should tell you that we have decided to move back east to New York City. She will, I think, have a better chance there for a fresh start. To be herself. I know you mean so much to her, and I respect that, so I hope that you can help us, help us to let her know that we want to support her."

"God damn it, you should have thought of that before turning her over to the fucking born-again Gestapo!"

"It was a mistake. A terrible mistake. If I could undo it, I would. But now we must do something to save her. So please, please, will you help us?"

Tommy felt his head might explode. His eyes were incensed and turbulent. His legs were unsteady as if all energy might leave them. He thought he might collapse and so he imagined his feet were stakes planted in the ground. He looked up at the sky, at a bank of clouds that resembled an elephant. This calmed him. He looked at Sunshine's father smoking a cigarette as if it were a mini respirator. He wanted to hate this man, but he could see Sunshine in his face. And he seemed sincere and not only filled with remorse but scared. Very scared. He obviously loved his daughter. Loved her enough to refer to her with the proper pronoun. He knew that not many parents would be able to make that adjustment. Tommy loved her, too. He wanted to be with Sunshine, always wanted to be with Sunshine. He didn't want to lose her. But she would die in Orange County; there was no question about that.

"Of course, Mr. Simon. I'll help."

Tommy got into the orange Corvette with Sunshine's father, and they drove to Los Alamitos Hospital.

Chapter Sixty-Eight

In the staff parking lot at Los Alamitos Hospital, Carmen sat in Clive's Mercedes, just back from the repair shop, and was being kissed fervently. She quite enjoyed it, the delicate complexity of sensations, all the while taking inventory of the rationale for going against what she had sworn to Clive and herself she would not allow. But ultimately it came down to both Clive's persistence and her willingness; no, her desire. Much to her reluctance to admit it, Clive was irresistible. It didn't matter that he confided to her that he wanted to leave his wife and planned to move out in June. He would do it sooner, but he didn't want to throw April off her studies in this important freshman year. Though April already seemed as discombobulated as he had ever seen her. Carmen wasn't thinking that they had a future; she was in the moment. Yet she didn't want to be the one responsible for the breakup of Clive's marriage. On the other hand, she took at face value that he was not happy in the marriage. That was plain to see. He was not fulfilled, and he was looking for fulfillment. If this was a mid-life crisis, then so be it. Mid-life crisis or existential crisis; *who wasn't* having an existential crisis? She knew that she was. And she knew that both of her sons were. Maybe crisis was not the right word, more like an existential life event of which there were to be many in the course of one's life. These existential life events caused one to reconfigure the way one views the world. How could that be a bad thing?

Poor Seymour. He had had an existential life event and had left his wife and family, and now he wanted them back, but it was too late. Don't look back, Seymour. Keep moving on your path. Your new life, your new soon-to-be wife. Sometimes the existential life event will fuck with you to such an extent that you second guess it. No time for second-guessing. First thought, best thought, as Jack Kerouac said. All of this went through Carmen's mind as she French kissed Clive for a good fifteen minutes.

Chapter Sixty-Nine

Margot made it to school and then to Davy's garage to hear the band rehearse. She didn't feel terrible; it was like a semi-bad period. Probably because they had caught it so early in the pregnancy, she felt lighter in many ways. Like she had gone backward and regained a certain innocence, this was counterintuitive. She thought that she was going to feel as if she had passed to a new phase of life, into a more adult and corrupted sense of self. But it was just the opposite. She felt that she had somehow restored herself. She wouldn't be so careless in the future, and that meant a more mature thought process and yet now she was looking at things in an entirely new way. The world seemed more vibrant, more exciting, as if possibilities were endless.

And the band sounded amazing. Davy and Geraldo were ebullient. Each felt like they were in a real rock band. Bruce made the difference. He kept a steady beat but made these technically outstanding flourishes. He was like a cross between Ringo Starr and Keith Moon. They were playing Geraldo's new song, a song called Little Boy. When he taught Davy the song for him to sing, Davy was so impressed that he told him, with complete seriousness and sincerity, that he was a great songwriter. These words resonated in Geraldo's head. It was like, for the first time, he felt validated that he had found the thing that he was meant to do.

After the band had been practicing for over an hour, Davy's mom opened the door that led to the kitchen and motioned to Davy by running her hand across her throat. Davy was in the middle of a guitar solo and abruptly stopped playing.

Geraldo and Bruce continued with their heads down not noticing that the guitar had stopped, so deep into the groove were they. After putting the equipment away, they went out to the backyard and sat around the dilapidated patio table. The air was balmy, and the ground was wet from the rain. But now the sky was clear. Davy's mom came out with a pitcher of Minute Maid lemonade and cardboard cups on a tray. "Sorry to shut you down, but nine is curfew. But you sounded very good tonight. Sounded like music."

"Thanks, Mom."

After taking the tray from his mom, Davy handed the cardboard cups around and poured for Margot and then himself and then handed the pitcher to Bruce who in turn turned it over to Geraldo. Madge looked at Margot and smiled. Margot smiled self-consciously and nodded her head. It finally occurred to Madge that she had seen both Margot and Bruce at church; they were in the church youth group. She was glad that the whole incident at the church had yielded some new friends for Davy. And she comprehended that these kids admired her son for what he did. So much so that they wanted to be friends, she got it. "I've seen you two at church. You are in the youth group."

"Oh yeah, sorry, Mom. This is Bruce; he plays drums and Margot."

"Hello." Looking at Margot, she said, "Are you in the band too?"

"No, I'm just listening."

"Well, you should have her in the band, Davy. It's nice for the audience to have a pretty girl to look at."

"I don't play anything, Mrs. Jones."

"I bet you sing, and I bet you could play a tambourine."

"That's a good idea, Mom."

"Just my two cents. Nice to meet you and nice to see you, Geraldo."

After she went back inside, Davy said to Margot, "She is right."

"She is?" Margot replied.

"I bet you sing. I bet you sing really nice."

"Maybe," Margot said, laughing.

Davy thought to himself, is this what it means to be in love? This feeling. It's going all through me. I feel it in my arms and in my legs and in my belly and in my chest but mostly in my head. Just look at her. So, god damn beautiful. A real Mary Magdalene. And it hit him. The sense of loss. A sense of lost opportunity. What might a child conceive from a pure intention of love have looked like, grown like, or been like? He could imagine the melding of bodies and personalities and souls, that of his and Margot's and knew that the result would have been something divine.

On the other hand, he had just turned sixteen years old. He hadn't yet gotten his driver's license. And though neither of them was of legal age, they had wielded the ultimate power, that of removing the possibility from a potential human being. He didn't second guess their decision.

"Do you want to smoke a doobie?" Bruce said, pulling out a Marlboro cigarette pack from his shirt pocket, tilting it downwards, and shaking it until it produced a joint. He stuck it between his lips and then pointed to the corner of the yard. "What's that?" Everyone looked to where Bruce was pointing.

"That's my cross," Davy said. There stood a cross of more substantial proportions than the one he brought to school for Halloween.

Chapter Seventy

Sunshine looked like she was dead. Her skin tone pallid, and her eyes shut solemnly. Tommy realized that he had never seen her not in motion. He felt as if he were in a movie. It was all new to him. This realization that something very important was happening, something with life and death implications. And he could make a difference. He had the power to make a difference. Because Sunshine trusted him, he knew this. She trusted him implicitly. He had earned this trust. But she had given *him* something even more valuable: a sense of self. Before he met her, he had an opaque idea of himself; he hadn't even a self, he felt more like an organism, something only in the shadow of his father and his older brother. Now, he was more assured of himself and of the physiological manifestation of himself. He was running for goddamn class president, for Christ's sake. He would never have been able to do that without having met and fallen in love with Sunshine. And felt her love. Felt her love so completely.

She opened her eyes and saw Tommy sitting in a chair next to her, tears streaming down his face. "Tommy? Is that you?"

"Yes," he said, wiping his face with his shirt sleeve.

She began to cry. "Oh. I'm sorry. I'm so sorry. You just don't know."

"Don't be sorry."

"I never want to make you sad."

"It's okay. But, listen. You don't have to do that again," he said pleadingly.

"Yes. I know."

"Everything is going to be okay."

She laughed. "Depends on what you mean by okay."

"I mean good. They're going to be good. You are the most incredible person I have ever met. You're going to make a difference. You have already made a difference in my life."

"Really?"

"Oh god, yes."

"That's good."

He leaned over her and kissed her eyes and then her lips. He put his hand on her arm and pulled himself close, almost getting into bed with her. A nurse came in. She looked at them, then quickly looked away. She checked the clipboard at the foot of the bed and left. Tommy sat back down in the chair.

"Guess what?" Tommy said.

"What?"

"I am officially running for class president."

"That's the best news ever."

"And we circulated the Revolutionary Press. You should have seen it. There were cops everywhere."

"Oh, Tommy. You won't get into trouble?"

"Nope."

"You're my hero."

"You're mine."

They looked at each other. Sunshine was taking deep breaths. "I'm so tired," she said.

"Yes, I know. You should rest."

"Okay. You'll be here when I wake up?"

"Yes. Of course."

Sunshine closed her eyes and went back to sleep. She had a strange and vivid dream. She dreamed she was flying high above Cypress, like the Flying Nun in the T.V. show, and all the people below were not people but ants. Ants were going in and out of buildings and houses. Ants rushing to and fro. Then she dreamt she was on the beach, dressed like Zsa Zsa Gabor and she was drinking a martini. Tommy came out of the water to where she was standing. The seawater was dripping off of him unceasingly; it was actually coming out of him, out of his pores, and out of his eyes. She was dreaming that she was in the shower, and her penis dropped off, turned into a snake, and slithered down the drain. A beautiful golden monarch butterfly landed right where her penis had been. Tommy was on the toilet reading the Los Angeles Times. The headline said Atomic Bomb Dropped on Orange County and there was a large color photo of a mushroom cloud. She looked down at her butterfly vagina and giggled. Tommy asked, "What's so funny?" The butterfly flew away, and there was just a hole where it had been. Her mother walked into the bathroom as Sunshine was getting out of the shower and looked down at her hole and said, "I've always wanted a daughter. Just didn't think I'd get one this way." Tommy folded up the newspaper, stood, flushed the toilet, and said, "Beggars can't be choosers." Sunshine's mom laughed extravagantly and spoke. "I'm no beggar. I'm a very rich woman." She became a mushroom cloud and dissipated. Sunshine was dancing with her father. She was wearing a white bridal gown in a grand ballroom where there was an old-fashioned jazz orchestra on stage playing an easy-listening version of the David Bowie song, Rebel, Rebel. Tommy was wearing a tuxedo, standing on the edge of the dance floor with the rest of the CCCP. A bunch of jocks from school burst in with machine guns and killed everyone except Sunshine. Duane walked up to her, holding a machete, and stabbed her repeatedly in the stomach. Her white bridal gown turned red with blood. But she kept standing. "It's like I'm having my period," she said. "Why aren't you dead?" Duane cried in astonishment. "It's not my time," she replied. "It's not my fucking time." She grabbed his machete and chopped off his head.

She woke up with a start. Tommy was asleep in the chair. His head was resting on her hospital bed. His face was pointed at her; his righteous young outline was as familiar to her as her own thoughts. She reached down and ran her fingers through his long hair. He raised his head and looked up at her. She smiled and said, "Everything is going to be alright." Tommy nodded. He sat up, stretched his arms, and yawned. "Your father told me that you guys were going to move to New York City."

She felt the vibration of faint surprise. "He told you."

"Yeah. I don't want you to go. But I think it's good. I just wish I could go. Get out of fucking Orange County."

"Why do you think they are doing that? What has happened to them?"

"People can change. I mean, people don't really change. But maybe they lose sight of who they really are. Anyway, I think they love you and want to do right by you."

She felt as if that was a foregone conclusion. "I would die here. I really would"

"I know."

She pointed at him accusingly, "And you better be careful, too. These people here are brutal. They are out for blood, and we are just asking for it. You know?"

"That's for sure. I'll come to New York City too. Just as soon as I am able. Maybe I'll go to college there."

She felt herself getting tired again. "You know, Tommy, it's very possible that we will never see each other again."

"I disagree. That's not a possibility."

"You think?"

"I know."

Chapter Seventy-One

The boys were loaded in the Datsun-like bullets in the chamber of a gun. Ready to instigate tumult and controversy for the day's election activities. They spent the night before working on Tommy's speech. As Mrs. Bloom told them, it was not so much a debate as a forum; each candidate was given time to speak and share their platform as to what they would want to accomplish as student body president. The group had narrowed the CCCP platform to four points. Student-led study groups to learn about the history of racism, genocide, and imperialism in U.S. history. Student-chosen repertoire for the school band. The disbanding of the student council is to be replaced by a dictatorship of the proletariat (students). And the need for a safe space for gay, glam, punk, and bullied kids. Each kid had chosen a point on the platform. Geraldo made his about students choosing which songs to perform for the school band. He wasn't in the school band, but that was because of the lame songs that were chosen to be performed. He didn't need to hear the theme of Star Wars ever again. Barry inserted the part about the study groups. Davy called for the disbanding of the student council in lieu of the dictatorship of the proletariat. Even though they were unclear as to what that meant. And Tommy called for the inclusion of the point about a safe space for bullied kids. It was Barry who suggested this, but he did so to pull Tommy out of the depression that had taken hold of him after visiting Sunshine. It seemed for a while that Tommy wasn't going to be able to follow through with his candidacy, so sad was he. But when everyone showed up, it buoyed his spirits and he realized, as Davy told him, Sunshine wouldn't want him to give up.

The Datsun pulled into the parking lot of Winchell's Donuts. "What are we doing here?" Geraldo asked. "We need to get fortified," Barry said. "It's going to be a long day." Everyone got out of the car, each wearing a trench coat. Geraldo did not move. Through the windshield of the car, he watched the boys enter Winchell's, with Davy stopping short, turning around, and motioning for Geraldo to come. He slowly got out of the car and walked towards Davy, who held the door open for him. "What's the matter with you?" Davy said. They went to the counter. Maria wasn't anywhere to be seen. After everyone ordered Geraldo ordered a chocolate glazed donut from the same woman who was there the first time he saw Maria. He took his donut and sat down with the rest of them. "Where's your girlfriend?" Barry asked. Geraldo shrugged.

They strategized for the day. The way it worked was that each English class attended the student forum in the assembly hall to hear the candidates. But since Davy, Barry, and Geraldo wanted to attend for each period, they would just skip their classes that day. Tommy needed them there for moral support, and security. It was important that Tommy stay on script and not get distracted by any taunts. Since Duane was one of the candidates, he was sure to try to intimidate him, especially when Tommy brought up the part about a safe zone for gay kids. "Are you going to include those stats from the Kinsey Report?" Davy asked. Tommy said, "Maybe. We'll see." Barry let out a big whoop. "This is going to be one hell of a day."

As the boys got up to leave, Maria came out from the back carrying a tray of assorted glazed donuts. She set them in the display case, looked up, and her eyes caught Geraldo's. The boys saw what was going on and left Geraldo to communicate with his girl. Geraldo gathered up his courage, walked to her, and said, "Hello Maria." Maria stood still. She was not prepared for this. She knew she would see Geraldo again, and she knew it would be like this, with him coming into the donut shop, and he was even more cute than she had remembered. Younger somehow. She straightened her posture, made her eyes steady, and tried to make them cold, but it was no use; she could not suppress her joy at seeing him. She smiled widely. Geraldo smiled at her in turn. "It's good to see you," he said. "Si. It is good to see you, too." Geraldo pointed to a chocolate-glazed donut and said, "I had one of those today." Maria pointed to her lip. Geraldo was confused. Did she want him to kiss her? She reached over the display case, pulled out a napkin from the dispenser, and handed it to Geraldo. "Chocolate. On your lip." Geraldo took the napkin from her and wiped his lip. "Gracias," he said. "Maria, I wanted to say that I'm sorry. I'm sorry for, you know, not being respectful." She smiled and said, "It's okay. Maybe we can go again. To the park." The horn of the Datsun started beeping. Geraldo heard Barry call his name. "I've got to go. But I'll come back later. After school. Okay?" Maria smiled and nodded.

In the assembly hall, on the stage was a microphone and a chair for each candidate. There was Duane at the far end stage left. Next to him was Debbie Heinz, a cheerleader, maybe as popular as Duane. They were rumored to have been going steady but broke up because each was vying for student body president. On the other side of the microphone was Mikey Traub, surfer, stoner kid, and then Tommy at the far end. For the first-period forum, the hall was about a quarter filled. Barry, Davy, and Geraldo sat a few rows back from the stage. Mr Magg stood by the side of the stage, keeping vigilance. Principal Smithson walked onto the stage, passed Duane, stopped, and shook his hand. He smiled at Debbie, walked to the microphone, and turned to look at Tommy and Mikey. He shook his head in dismay. "Alright, students. Welcome to the forum for the election of your student body president. Please listen respectfully to each candidate and then make an informed and thoughtful decision as to who you wish to be your leader."

Duane went first and spoke about how important it was to support the football team and all the school's sports programs and how it should be almost mandatory for kids to attend the games. After all, a school is like a country, and one needs to show the same kind of patriotism to one's school as one showed to one's country. His speech got to Debbie, and she had to wave her written speech in front of her face as she grew flush. Walking to the podium, passing Duane, she whispered, "Great speech." Debbie's speech reiterated many of the same points Duane made only emphasizing more the role that cheerleaders played in not only motivating the crowds at the games but also by exemplifying the idea of school spirit. She ended her speech by chanting loudly, "We've got razzamatazz! Pep, punch, and pizzazz! To the other team you've been had. The Cypress Centurions have razzamatazz!" Mikey Traub went to the microphone, obviously stoned. His speech consisted of him tittering and mumbling about his main platform, that to outlaw homework. This got a loud round of applause. Finally, Tommy went to the microphone. He said, "Hello everyone. I am Tommy Griswold, and I am running for president as a member of the Cypress Centurion Communist Party." A few kids booed. Duane turned to Debbie and said something to make her laugh. "I have a four-point plan." When Tommy got to the last of the four points, the part about the safe space for gay and bullied kids, Duane muttered loudly, "Fucking faggot." Mr. Magg turned to him and said, "Keep it to yourself, Duane."

The assembly hall got more crowded with each period as word spread about the "fag commie kid". And each time he went into the part about the safe space, the crowd would yell insults at him. Tommy decided to augment his speech to include information he read in a copy of the Kinsey Report that he had picked up in a used bookstore. "According to the Kinsey Report, at least ten percent of the population in America is gay. If there are a combined three hundred members of the freshmen, sophomore, and senior sports teams, that means there are at least thirty gay players. Maybe more. And out of the three thousand students, that means at least three hundred are gay. We should make them feel that they can come out without being harassed. Vote for me for a safer and more inclusive campus." The crowd erupted in loud jeers and boos and shouts of profane insults. Mr. Magg had to take to the microphone to quiet the crowd since Principal Smithson left after the first-period forum.

By the time of the final period, the hall was packed with kids. And the entire football team. They cheered loudly for Duane and then some more for Debbie. They even gave encouraging squeals of laughter for the stoner surfer boy. But when Tommy went up to speak, their shouts were deafening, completely drowning him out. They started to sing God Bless America. Barry could see that his brother was on the verge of losing it. Davy turned to Geraldo and said, "This has the potential to get very ugly very quickly." Geraldo looked at the twisted, angry faces of the kids in the crowd. "It already looks pretty ugly as far as I can see." Tommy kept trying to read his speech, but he couldn't be heard from the football team's garish singing. Finally, Tommy grabbed the microphone, pulled it from the clip, and shouted at the top of his lungs. "Shut up!" It was so loud, and holding the mic that way made it feedback. This silenced the crowd. He put the mic back in the holder and said,

"You all claim to believe in democracy. Well, you are all a bunch of fucking hypocrites!"

The room was still. The football team and everyone else in the room stood stunned. One of the jocks said, "Did the faggot just call us a bunch of fucking hypochondriacs?" The football players rushed to the stage. Barry, Davy, and Geraldo got up and headed for the exit, sensing that they were in a great deal of danger, as did Tommy, who fled from the stage. They got to the door of the assembly hall, but it was blocked by jocks. Duane jumped down from the stage, spun Tommy around, and slugged him in the face. Barry grabbed hold of a handful of Duane's hair and yanked it, pulling out multiple strands. Duane screamed like a wounded dog.

Davy ran up on the stage, followed by Barry and Tommy. Geraldo was slammed to the front of the stage by a jock who then was about to slug him in the face when the microphone that Tommy had used to call out the crowd, hurled by Davy, hit the jock in the head. Geraldo ran up on the stage, followed by an angry mob of jocks. The boys escaped through the rear door of the stage, which led to the music room. Mr. Magg was there. He stood in front of the door, stopping the marauding athletes from entering. "That's enough fellas. After all, this isn't Watts. Go to football practice."

Chapter Seventy-Two

It took a while for the commotion to calm down outside the band room. Meanwhile, Tommy lay on the floor staring up at the fluorescent lights. Barry sat next to him cross-legged. Davy, who was behind the drum set, said, "I can't believe that just happened?" and he played a rim shot. Geraldo was sitting at the piano, resting his head on the keys. He lifted his head and said, "We were almost killed. We were literally almost killed." The looks on the faces of the angry mob were indelibly marked on their psyche. Printed crisply, cleanly in each one of their recollections. Barry thought: nothing is more powerful or as sinister as an angry, unbridled crowd sensing in their unmitigated power the capacity to wreak terror. It was frightening not just because of the proximity to physical harm but also the sheer surging power of it. Like the way, a huge ocean wave can knock you down and drag you along the ocean floor. That kind of brute power. Yet, they had escaped all but unharmed, except for the punch to Tommy's face, which hurt less than he thought it would, as if Duane was pulling his punch. As if the show of force was only just for show. On the other hand, Barry's extraction of Duane's hair follicles amounted to some real agony.

Geraldo hit the middle c note on the piano and then the a below that. He realized those were the first two notes to Hey Jude. One of the only songs he knew on the piano. He played an f chord, and then he sang, "*Hey Jude, don't make it bad. Take a sad song and make it better. Remember to let it under your skin. Then you begin to make it better.*" Davy played a drum fill and came in with a beat as Geraldo sang the next verse playing the chords to the song. When it came to the bridge, the other three sang along. *"And any time you feel the pain, hey Jude, refrain, don't carry the world upon your shoulders. For well, you know that it's a fool, who plays it cool by making his world a little colder. Nah, nah, nah, nah, nah."*

It happened to be time for choir rehearsal. Twelve girls and three boys filed into the band room from the other door. They realized who it was that was singing the Beatles song. It was the boy who caused the football players to go insane. They crowded around him like he was a movie star. Most of the kids in the choir appreciated what he said about the need for a safe space. And now here he was with his friends playing the great Beatles song. When it came time for the big sendoff of nah nah nah's, the choir joined in singing. Tommy started vamping as if he were Paul McCartney. Barry began to dance with some of the members of the choir. To Davy, who continued to keep the beat, it sounded like a choir of angels. He felt as if he had transcended to a nearby level of heaven. And just as things were reaching a crescendo, Mr. Magg burst into the room and screamed, "All right, you commies, get the hell out of here while you still can without being killed!"

Chapter Seventy-Three

arry called to tell Geraldo that he and Tommy had been suspended for the rest of the week. Tommy for saying the F-word and Barry for assaulting Duane. So, he wouldn't be picking him up in the Datsun for the next few days. Barry found it most amusing that Tommy was suspended for saying fuck when the entire football team was calling him a fucking faggot. Nobody else was suspended. But there was a silver lining: Duane lost. Debbie was elected student body president.

Geraldo decided to ride his bike to school, something he hadn't done in a long while, but first to Winchell's; he felt terrible that he didn't go by after school as he promised Maria he would. He imagined explaining to Maria what had happened and how, even in the U.S., you can get killed for saying that you are a communist. Of course, no one was killed. And to even make a comparison to what happens in Guatemala was insensitive. Nevertheless, it was scary, and he did get death threats. And even though there was a certain excitement to the events of the preceding day, he felt in his heart that he was done with it. He was done provoking the brutes and bullies of Cypress High School. From now on, he would turn his focus to music. After all, whoever got assaulted for playing music? It was music where his passion was. It was music that he was good at. Or at least pretty good at it, and he would get better. Davy said that he was a great songwriter. Songs had changed the world for the better as much as any political movement. Look at Bob Dylan, The Clash, John Lennon. Oh yeah, look at John Lennon.

He parked his bike outside of the donut shop, locked it to the handicap ramp, and went in. He didn't see Maria; he figured she was in the back. He ordered a chocolate-covered glaze, sat down, pulled out a paperback copy of Slaughterhouse-Five, and started to read, peering up every now and then to look for Maria. Fifteen minutes passed. He went to the counter. The woman he had seen before was staring out the window, her face placid, she was somewhere else. Geraldo cleared his throat. There was no acknowledgement from her. He said, "Excuse me." Still no response. Rather than disturb her, he decided to go to school and come back after. Maria was sure to be there.

For A.P. History Mr. Calder was teaching about World War Two and the ascension of fascism in Europe. He spoke about the rise of Adolf Hitler and the Nazis. He drew a parallel between what happened the day before and the tactics of the S.S., drawing a specific correlation to Kristallnacht.

"On November 9th, 1938, the S.S., the Hitler Youth, and mobs of civilians ransacked Jewish neighborhoods throughout Germany, destroying businesses and murdering men and women. What happened yesterday is what that kind of mob violence looks like. It was an attempt to stifle freedom of speech and prevent the democratic process from taking place. Just because you don't like the way someone looks or the opinions someone holds does not give you the right to attack that person or that group of people. But a mob does not have a brain; it is literally like The Blob in the movie, it just moves forward to cause destruction. It cannot discern from logic or compassion; its intent is only to instigate violence."

Okay, Geraldo thought, Calder's mixed metaphors are touching. The football players were like Hitler Youth and The Blob. That sounds about right. Or right enough. Did we earn his begrudging respect somehow? Not only that, but nobody yelled any insults at me or tried to pick a fight so far today, maybe because I left my trench coat at home. Either way, done with it. Completely done with it.

Chapter Seventy-Four

Davy skipped school to get his driver's license. His brother let him borrow his Ford Ranchero so that he could pick up Margot from school. Davy leaned against the Ranchero in front of the school. He wished he had a cigarette. He thought he would look so cool if he had a cigarette. The kids came flooding out, and many of them stopped to check out Davy and his brother's car. Margot was walking with a few of her girlfriends. She stopped, opened her mouth, and then walked coolly towards Davy. "Nice wheels, Savior." She leaned into him, and they kissed. "Thanks. It's my brother's. Got my license today. He said I can use it to haul equipment and stuff for the concert on Saturday." Gary Junior walked up. "What the hell are you doing here, you satanic freak." Margot shoved Davy in the car and then got in herself. "You don't need any more trouble."

They drove down Lincoln Ave and made a left on Moody Street. "You want to go to the pier?" Davy asked. Margot said, "Sure. I could surely use an ice cream cone about now." At the stop light, he put his arm around her and pulled her close. They kissed until the car behind them honked. Margot thought how much like an old movie this all was. And that it was a little stupid. She thought that Davy was acting a part, and she wondered if he really was authentic. If this, like his Christ thing, was just a performance. And if there was one thing that she hated in this world was fakeness. On the other hand, it was nice to ride in a car. She would enjoy it now, but later on, she would bring it up and let Davy know that this whole thing, this whole James Dean thing, was passe'. At best. And misogynist at root.

Davy noticed Magot looked pale, but her eyes were bright. Margot saw his demeanor change. His face became loose and she could tell that he realized that he was being selfish in that he hadn't asked her how she was feeling. She knew him well enough to know that when he apologized for being self-involved and not checking in on her, he was truly sincere. Though she did feel reassured, she didn't want to tell him that she had bled a lot the night before. It wasn't so bad in the morning, but still, she felt kind of weak, and it was difficult to get through the day. Still, this was nice and unexpected. The car. Davy looked very handsome and mature behind the wheel, even if it was a bit old hat. Yet, she had a bad feeling about Gary Junior. She knew that he wasn't going to let them have peace without him causing trouble. All he had to do was to tell the priest that he saw her coming out of the clinic. But there was no way they could know for certain that she went in for an abortion. She could have gone into the for-birth control pills, or for a pelvic exam, or any number of things. Still, there was such hatred in his eyes, and it was primarily directed at Davy.

Chapter Seventy-Five

After school, Maria was not at the donut shop. This time, Geraldo asked the woman at the counter if she knew what had happened to her. She looked at Geraldo. Her eyes fixed searingly on him. She was older than Maria by maybe ten years. She had brown skin and dark features. Her body was heavy and thick but not fat; it filled out too snugly the polyester brown and mustard Winchell's uniform. Geraldo had seen her before but had never *seen* her because he was preoccupied with Maria. But now he recognized the sadness and anger in her because he related to it. She looked at Geraldo and knew who he was. He was sure that Maria had told her about him by the way she looked at him. Yet, the front of admonition wilted. "They took her."

"Who took her?"

"Immigration. You know, operation wetback."

"That's terrible."

"She was a nice girl. But it's rough out here. I got my papers straight. I told her that she should go back and then apply for asylum before she got caught. But now, she won't be able to come back legally. I spotted them in the parking lot and told Maria to beat it. But she didn't move. Like she gave up without a fight. They came in and asked for her papers, and she just told them to fuck themselves. It was so unlike Maria to use language such as that. They were not nice. They handled her roughly. Loaded her into the blue van and hauled her away like she was a criminal."

Geraldo immediately thought if he had come back when he said he would then maybe she wouldn't have given up so easily. She could have gotten away. Maybe she just didn't care. She was mad, mad at him and mad at the world. She was not just telling the immigration police to fuck off, but she was telling him and the whole world to fuck off. And she would be going back to war-torn Guatemala. He would never see her again. It was so unfair. The world was a brutal place where those with power and money treated the people whom they used as workers as slaves; they treated them with cold and ruthless tactics. And there was nothing you could do about it. If you try to speak up, then that same brute force will be turned on you. But you had to try. One mustn't be silenced. You just need to be smart about it. And you need to be pragmatic if you are to make an impact on the hegemony. Barry had used that word. And that's what it was. The fucking hegemony.

The power structure was what it was. He didn't usually think about it. He didn't know about it. But now it was in his bones. Now, it was part of who he was, this recognition of the hegemony, of the hierarchy of class and gender. The fucking patriarchy. For so long he lived under it, feeling it oppressing him, without really knowing about it. Either his father or his brother controlling him with their didactic rhetoric and their verbal abuse. Making him feel that he wasn't as smart as they were or that his tastes in music and film were not refined enough. Just because he didn't listen to jazz or punk rock. Always inferring that he wasn't as smart as they were. Just because his opinions were not written in stone, they were not galvanized because he left the door open to the idea of some kind of spiritual content that pervaded our bodies and our minds. Left the door open to the idea that there was a soul that lived within us. For this, he was called an idiot and ridiculed.

But even worse was how the system oppressed his mother, and he felt bad because he hadn't recognized it; he was part of the problem! She worked at her job full time and then came home and took care of all of the housework, made all of the meals, and did all of the shopping. She was a brown person who was made to slave for the patriarchy, for him and his brother and his father. And now another brown woman who he loved was taken away. A young woman who fled one oppressive state for another in search of a safe haven, in search of somewhere where she would not be persecuted for her thoughts and ideas, for the color of her skin, and she was swooped up like fish in a net and thrown back to the hellish nightmare that she had escaped from. And what had Geraldo done to help her? Nothing. He tried to grope her, and when he wasn't allowed to cop a feel, he abandoned her. He was no better than the system. He was no better than his father.

Chapter Seventy-Six

Samara sat in her study, wondering if she could perform therapy on herself. If she could open herself up and find what it was inside her that caused such mental turbulence. Whenever she began to feel that the cause for her anxiety was a result of her husband's or her daughter's neurosis, she told herself that she couldn't take responsibility for other people's mental and spiritual travails. She was only responsible for her own. And yet they were commingled, and so it was more than rote that she went this way. Something was empty; the thing that brought pleasure and a sense of well-being was not actuating. That was not another person's fault. That was because of herself and the work that she wasn't doing. But she was tired of herself, tired of trying to reach some sort of spiritual or emotional plateau. She just wanted to be loved. She just wanted to be held and taken care of.

She shook herself from her dour reverie and left her study. She went into the living room, to the liquor cabinet and made herself a highball. She took it to the ottoman next to the Japanese maple. She had a sip. It was auburn and bitter, and it ran through her blood like medicine. She was almost dizzy with exhilaration and release. She started flipping through the latest New Yorker. Her newest patient, after seeing her for only two weeks, announced that she was moving to New York City, a decision she thanked Samara for. This new patient's case was quite extraordinary. Her child was transsexual. And the woman, the mother, felt that somehow, she was responsible that her son was identifying as a girl. Samara thought that it might be easy to make the inference that the hypertrophy of her feminine side had caused an intensification of all female instincts in her child. And it was true; this is a woman who presented her femininity in an almost masculine way. She was overcompensating for a lack of love from her father, who himself was traumatized by being interned during World War Two in the American concentration camps for Japanese Americans. As Jung wrote in the Four Archetypes, in the chapter on the mother complex of the daughter, that in a case like this the Eros develops exclusively as a maternal relationship while remaining unconscious as a personal one. An unconscious Eros always expresses itself as a will to power. It doesn't mean that the complex induced in a daughter by such a mother must necessarily result in hypertrophy of the maternal instinct. Quite the contrary, this instinct might be wiped out altogether. In this case, Jung was of no help. Nobody really knew why we are directed the way we are. It could be - it just is.

Frankly, she was sick of Jung, and that was a problem for a Jungian analyst. His writings on sexuality seemed to fall short, even if they were a step up from Freud, which is why Samara cut the crap and simply advised the woman to love her child and to put aside everything else for the welfare of her child, especially because the child had attempted to take her own life. In other words, love herself enough to make whatever sacrifice was necessary for her child. And then she blurted out. Move to New York City. There, a person can be who they want to be. Samara thought, perhaps I should move to New York City too. Maybe I'm just telling this woman what I think I should do for myself. And perhaps there is nothing wrong with that.

When Clive came home Samara observed him from the ottoman, watched him and his boyish gait as he crossed the floor to the liquor cabinet to make his own highball. She watched him as if she were watching a movie, or a play, a Noel Coward play, or Lorraine Hansbury. He sat down on the sofa across from her. He looked down at his drink and shook it a little; the ice made a clinking sound against the glass. He took a sip. And then another, a bigger one. He put the glass to rest on the arm of the sofa. He looked across the room and saw Samara. She looked at him, raised her eyebrows, shook her head, and laughed. "How long have you been there for?" Clive asked, chuckling. "I've been here all along."

"All along?"

"I was here when you came home. You didn't see me."

"No. I didn't."

"Lost in thoughts."

"No," Clive said defensively. But then he realized there was nothing to be defensive about. "Yes. I guess so."

"What were you thinking about?"

"Oh, I don't know. This and that."

"This and that. Coyly vague and insulting at the same time."

"God damn it, Samara, give me a fucking break!"

"And rude on top of it."

"Well, can't a man just have a moment? A private moment."

"All you have are private moments. Even when I am in the same room as you, you are having a private moment."

"I'm sorry. I am sorry."

"For what?"

"That I am not who you want me to be."

"I don't want you to be anything but yourself."

"That's a laugh." Clive took a drink from his glass, emptying it. He stood to make himself another. If there was one thing that he wanted more than anything else at that moment was another highball.

"Clive?"

"What is it now?"

"Could you please make me another one as well?"

"Oh. Yes. Of course."

He walked over to her and took her glass from her hand, avoiding eye contact. He made two more highballs, purposely making them a bit weaker than usual. He didn't think that it was a good idea for either one of them to get too loaded at that moment. He walked back and handed her drink. He sat down at the other end of the sofa, nearer to her. It wasn't in his nature nor his intention to be rude to his wife. Or to be unloving. He loved her. He liked and adored her. He respected her and was fond of her. He just wasn't *in* love with her and hadn't been for a long time.

"I'm worried about April," Samara said, attempting to change the subject for everybody's sake.

"She's okay."

"She is despondent."

"She just broke up with her boyfriend. Her high school sweetheart. The only boyfriend she has ever had. It's a passage of life. It's good for her."

"What do you mean?"

"I mean that she is always presenting happy. She is always trying to please everyone, and she never really looks out for herself. I'm proud of her. Especially as she really likes Charles. You see them together. They are affectionate with each other, and they make each other laugh, but it is true Charles has some growing up to do. They both do. And that is never easy."

"What is never easy?"

"Standing up for yourself. Sacrificing comfort for something more important."

"What is that?"

"A sense of well-being."

"And how do you achieve this vaulted sense of well-being?" Samara said, not meaning to sound hostile.

"Don't patronize me, Samara."

Taking a breath and looking him square in the eye, she said, "I'm not. I really want to know."

He sensed that she was in earnest. In fact, she looked quite desperate, and he didn't really have a formulated answer. So, he said the first thing that came into his head. "It's simple. Just be true to yourself.

Chapter Seventy-Seven

avy showed up at the community center in his brother's Ranchero. In the cargo bed were his guitar amp, Geraldo's bass amp, their instruments, and a very large cross painted black and adorned with neon lights that said Rock and Roll. He had rescued the neon lights from the dumpster in the back of a bar that had recently closed. Margot, Bruce, and Geraldo were waiting for him as he pulled in front. "Oh, Jesus," Bruce said when seeing the cross. "Savior, that thing is awesome!" Geraldo didn't know what to think, except that he had a bad feeling. "Come on," Davy said. "Help me with the equipment."

They loaded the music gear on the stage. Davy played his new Fender Jaguar through a Hi-Watt amplifier that went through a cabinet with two twelve-inch speakers. This was the same amp The Who and The Kinks used. And it was loud. Davy had recently purchased them with money left over from the abortion fund. Geraldo played an upside-down Danelectro Longhorn bass through a Fender Bassman amp. This was equipment bequeathed to Geraldo from Davy's older brother Donald, as he had "Given up music." Donald was pretty much the band's benefactor with the bass setup and the use of the Ranchero. Donald appreciated his younger brother's youthful spirit and eccentric ways. He himself had decided to get a straight job and join the civilized world. He was spending his nights studying for the bar.

Bruce had come early and had already set up his drums. He helped Davy with his amp. "Where are you going to put the cross?" he asked. "I guess on the side of the stage," Davy said nonchalantly. "You do know that this dance is for a Christian youth group?" Bruce said. Davy nodded. Geraldo finished setting up his gear on the opposite side of the stage. He put on his bass, plugged it into the amplifier, and started playing the opening riff to Day Tripper. He looked out into the empty space in front of the stage and felt a sense of exhilaration. It was hard to believe that he would be performing for an audience for the first time. Margot set a microphone and stood in front of him. "What's this for?" Geraldo asked, surprised. "It's for you, dummy. You should sing your own song tonight." Margot smiled benignly at him. She set up two other mics for both her and Davy. When everyone was plugged in, they did a sound check. The sound was completely different from in the garage. It was loud and booming. Geraldo could feel the power of the bass rumbling beneath him. Davy felt like Pete Townsend, and Bruce felt completely untethered. He was grateful to Davy for having him in the band because he liked his songs way more than the prog band he was in before. There was more freedom to express himself and no quirky time changes. When people started coming in, they stopped playing. Davy took off his guitar and said, "Oh, I forgot something." He went over and plugged in the cross. It was resplendent.

Davy enjoyed seeing the reaction of the kids to the cross after he had plugged it in. It was just what he had hoped for: expressions of pure delight. Nobody took offense. The color of the neon was blood red, and the words were written in cursive-*ROCK AND ROLL*. It shone so brightly that Davy was afraid that it might blow a fuse. But it was worth the risk. It was the thing that made the stage look special. Not just the stage but the stage for the coolest band in Cypress, California, The Doubting Thomases. Barry and Tommy showed up and came to the front of the stage. They enthusiastically told their friends how cool they looked. And they did look cool. Davy wore blue jeans, his Mexican sandals, and a plain white t-shirt. Margot had on a paisley mini skirt, a yellow chiffon top, converse sneakers and had her hair in ponytails. Geraldo wore white bell bottoms, Oxfords, and a red terry cloth button-down shirt. Bruce wore purple shorts, a tank top, and flip-flops, which he took off when he played the drums. He liked playing barefoot; he said he could feel the beat better that way.

They took the stage with all eyes on them. Bruce clicked four hits of his drumsticks, and they launched into a raucous version of The Who's song *The Kids Are Alright*. Everyone began to dance. To Geraldo, it looked like The Peanuts cartoon when Schroder began to play piano, and all the kids danced in their own style. They ended the song, and the place erupted in applause. The next song was one Davy had written for Margot to sing. It was called *I Believe. "I don't believe in myths of madness, I don't believe in totems of sadness, but I believe in love."* It went on about all the things that the singer of the song didn't believe, but what she did believe in was love because she had experienced it truly. And then it was time for Geraldo's song. Bruce counted it off, and Davy played the riff of the d chord going back and forth from a suspended chord. Geraldo started singing, *"When I was a little boy, the world seemed so small, now I am all grown, don't seem that way at all. Because we all must take a stand, take a stand, take a stand. Yes, we all must take a stand."* Davy broke into a blistering guitar solo; Bruce played furiously with Geraldo locked into the groove as Margot slapped the tambourine against her thigh. The doors to the hall burst open, and in came a bunch of boys in Halloween masks, werewolves, Frankenstein, and Darth Vader; they threw smoke bombs and Cherry bombs, which exploded, making loud, frightening sounds. They shoved kids to the ground and ran up on the stage. Bruce dropped his drumsticks and fled; Geraldo got punched in the face and was knocked out cold. Margot got thrown from the stage and landed like a rag doll.

When Geraldo came to, he saw Margot rising from the dance floor. "Where's Savior? Where's Davy?" she screamed. Geraldo rubbed his eyes, which were stinging from the smoke bombs. He didn't see Davy, and the cross was gone. The neon rock and roll sign was in pieces on the ground. Barry and Tommy came running to the stage. Tommy cried, "They took Davy. First, they beat the hell out of him, and they took him and his cross." Bruce came back into the hall, ran up on the stage, and got behind his drum set. After he was satisfied that his drums were intact, he told the group that he saw them load Davy and the cross into the back of a pickup truck and drove away, burning rubber.

"Which way did they go?" Barry shouted.

"They made a left out of the parking lot. They made a left on Moody Street."

"Come on, let's go!"

After a brief discussion as to whether to call the police or not, with everyone concurring to wait before doing that, they got into the Datsun and went in search of their comrade. First, they drove to Margot's house. She told them that Gary Junior knew where she lived and, for some reason, might go there to dump Davy's injured body. There was no sign of Davy when they got there. Then they went to Davy's house, which was just up the street, and there was no sign of him there as well. Tommy said. "I hate to say it, but if they took Davy, and the cross, perhaps they would have taken him to the church. Maybe they would try to make him repent or something worse."

They drove to Saint Irene Church. There were no lights on in the parking lot. The darkness added to the brooding feeling that something utterly terrible was happening. Barry drove slowly. He pulled up to the front of the church. Everyone got out. Barry tried the door to the church which was closed and locked. They spread out, some looking on the side of the church others combing the parking lot. There was no sign of anything. Finally, it was decided that they had no choice but to go to the police station.

Chapter Seventy-Eight

At the police station, the kids had to wait for an hour before being able to talk to anyone. Then they were met with first dismissiveness and then suspicion. The desk officer asked Margot, who was tasked to be their point person, as she was the most diplomatic of the group. Margot explained, "The band had just begun playing when a bunch of boys wearing Halloween masks burst into the hall, throwing cherry bombs and smoke bombs and beating up a bunch of kids, including myself, and when the smoke cleared, our friend, my boyfriend, the guitarist of the band was gone."

"How do you know that he didn't just run away?"

"Because I saw them take him and his cross," Bruce said, his voice cracking.

"His what?"

"His cross," everyone said in unison.

"What do you mean, 'his cross'?"

"It was a prop that we used on the stage," Margot explained as reasonably sounding as possible.

"Okay, okay. Can you describe the vehicle?"

Bruce stammered, "It was a white Chevy pickup truck."

"I think it belonged to Gary Lawson," Margot said.

"Reverend Gary?" The officer asked in astonishment.

"No, Gary Junior."

While Margot filled out the paperwork, an officer took Bruce aside to question him further. He told Bruce that he thought he smelled marijuana on him. They took him to a separate room and told him to take off all his clothing. As his high was wearing off, the reality of the situation hit him. But with a less hazy mind, he was able to calm himself. He knew he had no weed on him. He left what he had in the bass drum of his kit. As the cops were looking up his rectum with a flashlight, he tried with all of his might to fart. But he stopped himself; he knew if he were to push any harder, he would shit in the cop's face. And that wouldn't be good. It wasn't the first time he had been strip-searched, and he was pretty sure it wouldn't be the last time; he was philosophical about the whole thing.

By the time they left the police station, it was past midnight. It felt like they had been there all night, and it didn't seem like the cops would be rushing out to look for Davy. The streets were very quiet for a Saturday night. Barry drove with the radio down low. They passed Cypress High School. Tommy said, "We haven't looked there." Barry made a U-turn and pulled into the parking lot. They walked through campus, through the plaza, and around the fenced-in lockers. "Let's go check the football field," Geraldo said in an exhausted voice. "Might as well," Barry responded.

It was quite dark, with no moon and very few stars that were not covered by the massing clouds, but Geraldo saw something at the fifty-yard line. He pointed, "What's that?" They started walking briskly and then running. They found Davy hanging from his cross.

The boys pulled the cross from the ground and set it down gently on the grass. Margot fell upon him. She put her ear to his chest while the boys untied his hands and feet. "Thank god they didn't nail him, the bastards," Barry spat. It was no coincidence that Davy had done a study on crucifixion and what exactly causes death as a result. He found that aside from hemorrhaging from wounds, the primary cause was suffocation. The weight of the body pulls down on the arms, which makes breathing extremely difficult. He had a conversation with Margot about this very same topic. They set him on the grass. She wasted no time; Margot put her mouth on Davy's and started giving him mouth-to-mouth resuscitation.

Chapter Seventy-Nine

At first, white light poured into the room as if a floodlight had been set up outside the window. Then, the room darkened in waves. It was almost tortuous, the acute sensitivity of her senses; every detail of the room, the gradient shades of blue and gray and black on the wall, on the ruffled pale bed sheets, on her hand which she held up in front of her eyes just to make sure she was alive. She could still smell the last vestiges of perfume on the clothing she went to sleep in. She heard the almost inaudible humming of the bedside clock radio, then the tick as it pushed over the number 12 on the little half placard written in Helvetica script. She turned her head so that she could hear more clearly the wind pushing through an open window, making the line from the shade rattle. It was, in a way, glorious that everything was so heightened, especially seeing how her head was splitting. Then, the muted light yielded again to a spree of incandescent illumination.

Carmen sat up, took inventory of the preceding night, and knew that she had lived it exactly as she wished. She reached down to the foot of her bed and gathered the papers that lay sprawled out there. She leafed through them as she had done before she passed out. Yes, it was good work. It was solid, pure, and honest. It was full of pertinent details, and each poem ended. Each poem had a beginning, middle, and resolution. Each an arc. The poems were either self-deprecating or full of hubris. The only thing that she didn't like about the poems was that she could still smell Bukowski in them. But that was okay, they were still in her voice; he was just a filter she was using at the present time until she could fully develop her own style.

She got up, took off her clothing, and went into the bathroom to shower. She lathered herself all up. She put her hand on her belly. It was smaller than before, smaller than when Seymour and Charles still lived there. She was making and eating less meat and less fatty foods in general. Preparing each meal just for herself and Geraldo, she could be more precise about portions. And so, therefore, she looked good. She knew she looked good. She knew she was attractive to men. Even though she had narrow hips, she had a fulsome figure. And she was getting ample attention as of late and not just from Clive. Oh, Clive. Kind of like Eeyore in Winnie the Pooh. Though he wasn't entirely anhedonic, and when tickled, he could be downright uproarious. What was she going to do with Clive? Well, nothing at the moment.

She got out of the shower, dried off, and wrapped herself in a pink terry cloth robe. She opened slightly the door that led to Geraldo's room to peek in on him. He was still asleep and sleeping in the clothes he wore the day before. It must have been a good night. She was tempted to go to the community center and hear the band, but she didn't want to make him feel any more nervous than she knew he did. She was proud of him. She had heard him practicing and thought he sounded pretty good. He wasn't the best singer in the world, but that was less important in today's music than in the music she listened to when she was growing up. It was a big night for him, and she couldn't wait to hear all about it. She put on a brown velvet jumpsuit and went downstairs to make breakfast or lunch, depending on what was there. But first, a pot of coffee.

She was on her second cup of Sanka when Geraldo appeared. He had changed into shorts and a Hang Ten t-shirt. Had yet to bathe. He sat down on the sofa next to his mom and then laid down halfway. "Big night. How did it go?" Geraldo lifted himself and wanted to tell her everything. Everything. But the words couldn't or wouldn't come out and so he reverted to his usual elliptic response. "Great."

"That's good. So, people liked the music?"

"Yes. They seemed to like it a lot."

"That's great, honey. What's the name of the band?"

"What? Oh yeah. The Doubting Thomases."

"Ha-ha. That's funny. Great." She began to laugh, and Geraldo laughed too. But then he began to cry. "Oh, G.G., what's wrong? Did something happen?"

Did something happen? What exactly happened? Something happened. What happened was that Davy died. Again. Davy was crucified. Properly crucified. And then was brought back to life by Margot. His girlfriend Margot. What happened was that another mob of lunatics attacked Geraldo and his friends for the second time in one week. What happened was Geraldo was punched in the head and knocked unconscious. What happened was the girl he liked a lot was deported, maybe because of him. What happened was Tommy told the entire student body that they were a bunch of fucking hypocrites, and then there was a riot. What happened was they distributed another issue of the Revolutionary Press predicting the economic collapse of capitalism in America and calling for revolution. What happened was that their comrade tried to commit suicide. What happened was that Geraldo realized that playing music was what he wanted to do more than anything else in the world and that he just might be very good at it.

Wiping his eyes and nose with the back of his hand, Geraldo said, "No. Nothing happened, Mom. I'm just tired."

"Yeah, I know what you mean. Let's just order a pizza and take it easy today. Sound good?"

"Yeah. That sounds great."

Chapter Eighty

The Datsun pulled up and in it was Barry at the wheel, Tommy by his side and Davy in the back seat. Geraldo got in. He looked at Davy, who seemed alright. "How are you doing, Savior?" Geraldo asked.

"I'm doing okay. Thanks. But maybe don't call me Savior anymore. I'm kind of over that."

"Gotcha."

Barry turned on the radio, KROQ; Rodney Bingenheimer came on and sounded like he had just woken up. "Happy Monday. I am going to play the new single from the triple record set from the Clash, a great song called The Magnificent Seven. This is for all the magnificent kids out there, not afraid to stir things up. And this is Rodney On the ROQ." Topper Head-on played a drum fill on the snare, matched by and in sync with bass notes played by Paul Simonon. The band kicked in. Mick Jones played a slashing rhythm; his guitar being run through a phase shifter. And then Joe Strummer announced, *"The Magnificent Seven! Ring, ring, it's seven a.m., move yourself to go again. Cold water in the face brings you back to this awful place. Knuckle merchants and you bankers, too, must get up and learn those rules..."*

And when it came to the chorus, everyone in the car sang along. *"You lot! What? Don't stop! Give it all you got. You lot! What? Don't stop. Yeah!"*

That song was followed by The Jam, *That's Entertainment*, The Buzzcocks, *What Do I Get?* X, *Los Angeles*, Elvis Costello, *No Action*, The Pretenders, *Brass in Pocket*, The Specials, *Message To*

You Rudy, and then the Datsun pulled into the parking lot of Cypress High School. The front of the lot was filled with fire engines. The boys got out of the car and saw that the school was burning. Not the science building but the main building this time. They walked closer, and Geraldo tapped Barry on the shoulder; he turned around and said, "It wasn't me. I swear!" They walked as close as they could before a group of cops stopped them from going any further. They could feel the heat from the fire on their faces and the smell of burning plaster, burning wire, burning paper, burning asbestos. Then, they saw Mr. Magg being led out in handcuffs. They overheard one of the cops telling the other.

"They found him passed out in the courtyard, a whiskey bottle next to him and an empty can of gasoline. Guess he lost it after they fired him because of those communist kids."

"Too bad. It's a tough job. Could you imagine? Vice principal to a bunch of brats," The other cop said.

Barry turned to the group, "Well, I guess school is canceled for today."

"Looks that way," Tommy replied.

"Let's go to the Copper Penny," Geraldo said.

"Apple ala mode!" Davy shouted.

They walked to the Datsun, and behind them, the school burned, the flames reaching out to the sky, touching and merging with the clouds.

Epilogue

Davy's brother Donald passed the bar on the first try. The firm he landed his first job with also handled Davy's lawsuit. They sued the hell out of Gary Lawson Junior and his father, whose white Chevy pickup truck they used to abduct Davy. Aside from the monetary punishment Gary and a few of the thugs ended up serving some time. After graduating from high school, Davy, Margot, and Geraldo moved to San Francisco. Davy used the crucifixion money to open a coffee shop slash folk music venue right off the panhandle in the Haight. They called it Sacred Grounds. Margot got pregnant and had twins.

Geraldo got a job at a used record store called Recycled Records and saved up enough money to buy a left-handed Martin guitar from a fellow named Duggal Sterner, who made illustrations for Audubon magazine and collected left-handed Martins. Geraldo bought his most inexpensive guitar, but it was still a Martin. With that guitar and a harmonica rack that hung around his neck, and his curly hair and his original protest songs, which targeted things like the Moral Majority and Iran Contra affair, he got a lot of gigs opening for punk bands at places like The Mabuhay Gardens and the I-Beam as a kind of young Bob Dylan clone. Between those gigs and busking on the street, he was making money as a working musician. It wasn't exactly how he imagined his life would go back in high school, but that's what he liked about it. It was his life to make. When his father Seymour told him that if he went to college, he would help support him. If he didn't, he was completely on his own. Geraldo chose the latter.

It didn't come as much of a surprise when Geraldo's mother phoned him to announce the news that she was getting married to Clive. He liked Clive and it was plain to see that he was in love with his mom. Clive's divorce went smoothly, and Samara moved to Brooklyn, where her family owned a brownstone. There were no hard feelings. Or at least not a lot. Geraldo had spoken to his brother to see if he would be going to the wedding. At first, Charles made disparaging comments about the whole institution of marriage but said that he would be there. He was back in touch with April, and even though they hadn't exactly gotten back together, he had hopes. Though, now with his mom marrying April's father, that would technically make them brother and sister.

Geraldo took the Greyhound down and was picked up by Barry in the old Datsun at the bus depot at Terminal Island. Barry had come back from Las Vegas, where he had a job installing air conditioners. Now, he was enrolled in Long Beach State, where he was getting a degree in business management. The irony was lost on no one. Geraldo couldn't believe Barry still had the Datsun. "Only has two hundred thousand miles on it!" Barry said proudly.

"So, how's Tommy?" Geraldo asked.

"He's good. Both he and Sunshine are going to RISDY."

"RISDY?"

"Yeah, Rhode Island School of Design."

"That's cool."

"And how about you? I see you have your guitar. How's the music going?"

"It's going."

"Speaking of going, do you want to go to a party?"

"I guess. What party?"

"You remember Debbie?"

"Debbie. Wasn't there like one hundred Debbie's?"

"Debbie Hessman."

"The cheerleader and class president?"

"The very one."

"Oh my god. Are you friends with her?"

"Maybe a little more than friends."

"Jesus Fucking Christ. You've got to be kidding."

"I kid you not."

"Crazy. It's a crazy world."

"She's pretty cool. She goes to Long Beach State, too. English major. She's actually a pretty good writer. Her stuff is hilarious."

"Well, if you say so. Amazing."

They got to the house, which was not too far from Geraldo's old house. Just around the block. After Geraldo graduated high school, his parents sold the house and Carmen moved to Long Beach, by the water, to a bungalow next to Clive. She was planning on keeping her place after the wedding, as she needed her own space to write. Her stuff was being published by Black Sparrow Press and her books of poetry sold well, well enough that she quit her job at the hospital. She was writing a novel about her time in San Francisco as a single woman in the late fifties.

The party was filled with young adults. There was a kegger, and much to Geraldo's dismay, Supertramp was blasting from the stereo. Barry looked at him, slapped him on the back, and said, "Even Gen Xers can be sentimental." They went over to the keg and Barry drew two beers for him and Geraldo. Out of nowhere, Debbie came, wrapped her arms around Barry, and they kissed passionately. After they separated, Barry looked at Geraldo, smiled, and shrugged his shoulders. "Debbie, do you remember Geraldo? Geraldo Horowitz?" She looked at him quizzically. "Oh yeah. You were one of the CCCPs. The quiet one. So many girls had a crush on you. Did you know?" Geraldo was taking a drink of beer and it almost came out his nose. He laughed and said, "I wish someone would have told me." Somebody put on a record by Styx. Geraldo had reached his limit. He excused himself, went to the record player, sorted through the records in front of the stereo, and found The Beatles The White Album. He took off the Styx record and put on the Beatles. *Back in the USSR* came on.

He stood up and looked around at the party. There were quite a few pretty girls. It couldn't be denied. He never thought that blonde surfer girls were his type but then he realized that he didn't have a type. He was open. Open to experience. And yet, he knew he did have a type. Maria. She was definitely his type. She was his type because he was still always looking for her. Or someone like her. He often wondered what happened to her. He hadn't lost a feeling of guilt. Yet, it was Maria who told him, "People come into your life, and then they go." He shook his head to get out of it. He took a long drink from his red solo cup. Then he saw *him* from across the room. He looked different. He looked harder, but the arrogance was gone, replaced by a kind of stoned sadness. Geraldo could still remember being frightened by the specter of this boy. Who was now a young man? The old anxiety started welling up in his chest. He remembered the threat of violence; of the violence he experienced by this kid and kids like him. Duane spotted Geraldo and started walking in his direction. Geraldo looked around, but there was no egress. Kids were blocking him at every turn, so much so Duane had to crawl over the sofa to reach him.

"It's you," Duane said in astonishment.

"Yes. It is me," Geraldo said, no longer scared. If Duane was going to hit him, he probably would have coldcocked him.

"I've been thinking about you. You and your friends."

"Oh yeah?"

"Isn't it funny how things turned out?"

"How do you mean?"

"Well, Debbie won the election. And now she is with Barry. And you, what are you doing?"

"I live in San Francisco."

"What do you do there?" Duane said with an underlying tone of resentment. Geraldo was pretty sure that he was going to call him a fag.

"I work in a record store and play music."

"You're kidding. That's so cool. That's really cool. I work in a factory." Duane grabbed a cup of beer that was sitting on a stereo speaker and downed it. He put his hand on Geraldo's shoulder. It felt heavy to Geraldo as if Duane needed a place to rest it, as if the weight of his hand was too much for him to take any longer. "Listen. I need to tell you something."

"What's that Duane?"

"You guys were right. You were really, right?"

"We were?"

"Yeah."

"What? Are you gay?"

Duane looked at him and got very serious. Geraldo thought maybe he had pushed it too far again. What? Did he want to get punched in the face? What was it, that thing that made him put himself in harm's way repeatedly in high school, and did that thing crop up again? He knew if he had asked

Duane if he was gay in high school, he would for sure have been punched in the face. Either way, Geraldo steeled himself for whatever was to come. Instead, Duane laughed. "Gay? Am I gay? I don't think so."

"Then what? What were we right about?"

"Your whole thing. The thing you put in your Revolutionary Press, which I still have."

"And what was that?"

"You were right about working. Working sucks."

Geraldo didn't want to explain to Duane that that was not what they were trying to put across in the Revolutionary Presses; that working sucked. Exploitation of workers sucked. Inequality sucked. Wealth disparity sucked. Monopoly capitalism sucked. Imperialism sucked. Racism sucked. Sexism sucked. Homophobia sucked. But he wasn't going to get into all of that with Duane. Instead, he said, "Well, Duane, I'm glad you finally came around."

About the Author

JC Hopkins is an American author, poet, screenwriter and songwriter. He is the author of the novels The Perfect Fourth, Man's Story, and multiple books of poetry. He is the screenwriter for the feature film Poets Are the Destroyers, winner in the best feature film category for the QueerX Film Festival and in the best comedy category for the New York Women's Film Festival. He has been twice nominated by the Grammys, for his song Dreams Come True, written for Norah Jones and Willie Nelson, and for his production of a children's album for actor John Lithgow. He also leads a jazz big band, the world-renowned JC Hopkins Biggish Band.